Please Remember Me

By

Florence Keeling

Cover by
Deborah Bradseth

Edited by
Crimson Cloak Publishing

©Florence Keeling 2016 All Rights Reserved

*To Linda
with love
Florence Keeling
x*

This book is a work of fiction. names, characters, events or locations are fictitious or used fictitiously. Any resemblance to actual persons or events, living or dead, is entirely coincidental. This book is licensed for private, individual entertainment only. The book contained herein constitutes a copyrighted work and may not be reproduced, stored in or introduced into an information retrieval system or transmitted in any form by ANY means (electrical, mechanical, photographic, audio recording or otherwise) for any reason (excepting the uses permitted by the licensee by copyright law under terms of fair use) without the specific written permission of the author.

For Dad

And for Mum and Gary who share this journey of grief with me.

Chapter 1
July 2002

The girls were all silent as they walked slowly along the pavement. Their dresses rustled and their heels clicked noisily with every step that they took. They were huddled together, holding each other's hands for comfort and strength. It was after midnight and the one streetlight in the vicinity was flickering on and off in annoyingly slow intervals, so the only light came from the nearly full moon that shone high above in the clear night sky. A sudden shriek brought them to a standstill.

"What was that?" Laura whispered, her eyes wide open, staring into the shadows.

"I have no idea," Beth replied, clasping her friends' hands even tighter.

"Sounded like a bird," Lucy suggested.

"A bird?" Beth raised her voice to immediate shushes from the other two. "At night?" Her voice was quiet again.

"Let's just keep going. We're nearly there." Laura started walking again, almost dragging Beth and Lucy with her.

"Whose idea was this anyway?" Beth stopped again.

"Yours!" Laura and Lucy hissed in unison. "Now get moving."

The trio didn't speak again but their walking slowed almost to a shuffle as they found themselves in front of a tall, rusty black gate surrounded by unkempt hedges. Peering through, Laura could see the house and its garden in the moonlight.

It was an old, abandoned farmhouse, the fields long since sold and used to build other houses. Tiles were missing from its roof, windows were cracked, and the once pristine paintwork had peeled off many years ago. The garden was overgrown with weeds and brambles but somehow there still seemed to be a freshly cut pathway leading to the door.

"Are you sure no one lives here?" Lucy asked as they pushed open the gate. It squeaked loudly and they looked around nervously.

"Of course they don't," Laura answered. "No one has lived here for years."

"Then why is there a freshly cut path through the garden?" Lucy's mind was working overtime.

"Just stop being silly." Beth took charge. "We always said that if ever there came a time when we wouldn't be together anymore then we'd come and see if this place really was haunted, and on our last night together we'd find out for ourselves. Okay, I didn't expect we'd be in our prom dresses." The other two girls murmured their agreement at this statement. "But Laura leaves in the morning for London and who knows when we'll see each other again. All these years we've walked past here on our way to school, and we've wondered and wondered about all the stories and rumours, never brave enough to go in. Well now we get to see if any of them are actually true."

The girls had reached the front door without even realising it. A crunching sound under their feet revealed a broken sign but the words were illegible. Still holding hands, they lined up with Beth in the front, Lucy in the middle and Laura at the back.

"Here we go." Beth pushed hard on the door, but it opened easier than she had imagined, and the girls found themselves lying in a heap on the floor. Laughing as they picked themselves up and dusted themselves down, they began to look around.

"It's so cold." Laura rubbed her arms shivering a little despite the warm summer night outside.

They were in the hallway with a long wooden floor and tattered pieces of wallpaper hanging from the wall. They peered into each room as they walked but they were all the same. No furniture, no curtains: just years and years of dust and cobwebs. Even the kitchen was empty except for the once white Belfast sink that sat in the far corner of the room.

"Imagine how this was in its heyday!" Laura could see a house full of life and laughter. Children running in from the garden as their mum laid out the dinner.

A creak from upstairs brought Laura back to the present.

"Did you hear that?" Lucy grabbed Beth and Laura's hands instantly. "There's someone up there."

"Don't be daft," Laura reassured them. "All houses make noises, especially old ones. I'm going to check out the bedrooms."

"I'm not." Lucy shook her head frantically. "You two go. I'll wait outside. If there is a ghost, I don't want to see it." Beth and Laura tentatively crept up the wooden stairs, each one creaking loudly under their feet as Lucy went back through the front door.

It felt warmer upstairs as they peeped into each bedroom. Again, these rooms were the same as the empty rooms downstairs. They only knew the bathroom was the bathroom because of the pipes coming up through the floorboards.

"What the hell is that?" Beth hid behind Laura as she pointed into a corner. Laura followed the direction of her finger and saw two bright yellow eyes staring at her.

"It looks like a cat." Laura reassured her and the cat meowed as if to agree. "I should imagine lots of animals have found their way in here." She walked towards it, but it ran off and Laura wasn't about to chase after it in the dark.

They were at the front of the house now, just one room left which they assumed would be the master bedroom. All the doors on all the rooms were either open or non-existent but this room was different, the door to this room was shut.

"I don't think I want to go in." Beth backed away as Laura tried the metal handle. It turned with a little squeak and Laura opened the door just a fraction.

"There's something in there." Laura opened the door wider and stepped in. "It's got a sheet over it."

"Laura?" Beth edged further away. "Come back. I don't like it." But Laura wasn't listening, she wanted to know what was under the sheet. She wanted to know why all the other rooms were empty except for this one.

She was right in front of it now. Its outline was slightly taller than her and about a foot wide.

"I think it's a mirror," she called back to Beth as she pulled the sheet slowly down, but Beth didn't answer, she'd already gone to wait with Lucy.

The sheet slid off to prove Laura right, it was a mirror with a beautifully carved frame surrounding the almost perfect glass. Laura let her hands move over the frame feeling the intricate design.

"You always loved that mirror." A man's quiet voice from behind her froze Laura to the spot. She looked in the mirror and jumped at the sight. A very frail looking old man stood in the reflection. He had neatly combed white hair, was dressed smartly in a full suit and tie, and leaned heavily on a cane. He was holding what appeared to be a piece of paper in his hand. "You look so beautiful. Just how I pictured you would." He held out the paper for her. She turned slowly and stepped a little way towards him. She wanted to speak but found her voice had failed her. She felt terrified yet strangely intrigued.

Tentatively she took the paper from his hand and instinctively moved away from him towards the door. The moon was shining into the room from a window on the landing and Laura could see a faded old photograph of a girl standing in a pretty ball gown, yet the photograph was in colour. Recognition suddenly dawned on her and she dropped the photo as if it was a piece of hot coal.

"That's me!" she squeaked. "But how …"

"I knew you'd be here tonight, Laura." It was the use of her name that scared her the most and without a backward glance she turned on her heel and ran down the stairs, out of the door, past the other two startled girls and didn't stop running until she was out of breath.

"What happened?" Beth and Lucy had finally caught up with her.

"There was a man there," Laura explained through gasps. "He had an old photo of me." Another gasp. "He knew my name."

"We need to ring the police." Beth pulled her new mobile phone out the top of her corset. Her parents had just brought her one for finishing her exams and she couldn't wait to use it for the first time.

"No!" Laura grabbed the phone. "I don't think he wanted to hurt me."

"But you said he had a photo of you and knew your name," Lucy piped in. "What if he's a stalker?" She looked over her shoulder fearfully.

"He was old." Laura's breathing was almost back to normal. "Very old. And the photo he had was of me, like this." She outstretched her hands.

"I don't understand." Beth was confused. "You said the photo was old?"

"It was old." Laura was as confused as they were. "It was faded and tatty around the edges like it had been carried in a pocket or a wallet but…" It sounded ludicrous even to her. "But it was one of the photos we had taken earlier at prom."

"But …" Lucy couldn't think. "All those photos are back at my house. We put them in my room when Dad took us home."

"Are you sure you don't want me to call the police?" Beth took her phone back. "You look all shaken up." She linked her arm through Laura's and started walking, Lucy doing the same the other side.

"No, let's just get back to Lucy's and enjoy our last night together." She hugged her friends close. "I just want to forget about it. I'm moving away tomorrow anyway and like Beth said, who knows when we'll be together again?" But Laura knew that this night would remain with her for a very long time.

Chapter 2
March 2016

"**H**appy birthday to you …" As the last word rang out, Laura pulled back her hair and blew out the candles on her cake. Everyone cheered and clapped with hugs and kisses all round. It was the night before her thirtieth birthday and she was out celebrating with her friends as she was spending the weekend at her mum and dad's house.

Jenny, one of her friends from university, was there as were a few of her fellow teachers from the local primary school. After cutting the cake into various haphazard slices Laura sat down and began opening her cards and presents.

"So sorry I'm late." The tall man sat down beside her, kissing her on the cheek. "Traffic was a nightmare."

"Jack! You're here." Laura threw her arms round his neck excitedly, then smiled as he handed her a small wrapped purple parcel complete with a neatly tied ribbon and bow. Pulling the ribbon, she eagerly unwrapped the present and opened the box to reveal an old antique blue cameo on a thick gold chain. "It's the one from the antique market." Laura recognised it instantly; she couldn't believe he had kept it for her.

Two months ago, she had admired the very same cameo on a stall at the local antique market. It was locked away in a glass display case. Jack and his brother Peter ran the stall every Sunday as well as owning a small antique shop in Islington. The price was way out of her league, so she had declined his offer to have a closer look, opting instead to buy a small brooch as a present for her mum. They had chatted and flirted a little until another customer came along to claim his attention and she had walked rather reluctantly away.

It wasn't until she got home later that she realised Jack had presumptuously written his name and number on the five pound note he had given her in her change. She'd waited a few days, nearly a week in fact before she phoned him and they had arranged to meet up with friends in a club that Saturday night. From then on they had seen each other every weekend and sometimes during the week as well when their work allowed.

"I took it out of the case as soon as I could." He fastened it around her neck for her. "Told my brother I sold it." He winked cheekily. "I don't think he believed me, especially when he counted up that day's takings."

"I absolutely love it." She stared at it again marvelling at its near perfect condition. "The blue ones are so unusual. They're normally on an orange background."

"That was the first day it went on sale as well." Jack recalled its history. "Bit of a strange story actually. It was from a house clearance we'd done up in Birmingham. We never normally go anywhere near that far but this lady …" He paused as he tried to remember her name. "Mrs. Carmichael, I think it was. She'd left specific instructions that we were to come and clear the house after she'd moved into a retirement apartment with her husband. Well, me and Pete couldn't work out any connection with her but never look a gift horse in the mouth, as they say."

"Didn't she have any children?" Laura felt a little sad to think of someone not having family and leaving it to complete strangers to sort out your worldly possessions.

"That's where it gets even stranger." His London accent was thick as he lost himself in the story telling. "We closed the shop for the day, took the big van rather than one of the cars and drove up there. When we get there, we pull up to this massive house and there's me and Pete seeing pound signs." One of Laura's friends placed a glass of wine and a pint of lager on the table in front of them. "Cheers mate." Jack picked up the pint and took a long gulp before placing it back down and looking around the bar.

"And?" Laura couldn't believe he had already lost track of the story.

"This real posh bird is standing there, mid-forties I'd say, introduces herself as Mrs. Carmichael's daughter and hands us a small box. Apparently, there'd been a mix up and the lady only wanted us to have that cameo. You could see she was fuming, obviously wanted it for herself but didn't want to go against her mother's wishes." He took another gulp of lager. "We were pissed off to say the least, all that way for one piece of jewellery but when Pete looked at it he knew it was worth a few quid so we were sorted but needed to sell it as quickly as we could."

"That just makes it all the more interesting." She kissed him again. "I honestly love it."

"So, what time are we leaving in the morning?" He placed his arm around her, pulling her in for a cuddle.

"What do you mean we?" She pushed herself round to look at him. "You said you couldn't get the weekend off?"

"That was just a teeny tiny white lie to throw you off the scent." He screwed up his face as he spoke. "I've got a little surprise for you, so what time do you want me to pick you up?"

"I was going to leave about ten." She looked enquiringly up at him.

"That's fine by me. I shall be outside, all packed and ready to go at ten o'clock." The upbeat tone in his voice changed as he spoke the next words. "To meet your parents."

"Oi!" She slapped him softly in the chest.

"I'm only joking."

It was quite late when Laura got home that night. She'd fallen out of the taxi as Jack had pulled her too quickly as he tried to help her out, he'd seen her to the door and after a long kiss goodbye had got back in the taxi to finish his journey home. Grabbing a large glass of water from the kitchen she made her way into the bedroom, stumbled over the mountain of shoes she'd changed her mind on earlier, threw off her clothes, pulled on her pyjamas and got into bed.

She switched on the lamp and picked up her Kindle, as it turned on and loaded, she looked again at the cameo around her neck. It was so beautiful. Turning it over she squinted at the back. Was that something written there? Chucking the Kindle to one side, she reached up to turn the big light on. There was something there. Neatly etched onto the back of the cameo were the words *Please Remember Me* and a date *5th July 02*. So that made the cameo over a hundred years old at least.

She switched the bright light off and snuggled down under her covers. The cameo was obviously a gift between lovers back in 1902, maybe even 1802. How she wished she could find out more about it. Maybe she'd quiz Jack tomorrow, see if he could remember anything else. Maybe a bit of googling would shed some light on the matter. But now she had to get to sleep. The room was beginning to spin a little as she closed her eyes, her mind whirling with hundreds of different scenarios about the original owner of the cameo.

A loud insistent horn beeping the next morning woke Laura from a deep sleep. Reaching over to her phone to check the time she found it dead as a dodo. Cursing loudly, she stumbled over to the window and drew back the curtain to see a black Bentley waiting with a smartly dressed Jack standing next to it holding an enormous bunch of red roses.

"Five minutes," she shouted, flinging open the window and shutting it again before Jack had chance to answer.

Luckily she had already packed her overnight bag, so it was just a case of having a quick shower and brushing her teeth before getting dressed and rushing out the door to a still smiling Jack.

"Your chariot awaits, my lady." He swept a deep bow and ushered her into the open door before running round to get in the other side.

"I'm so sorry I wasn't ready. My phone died in the night so my alarm didn't go off," she apologised, giving him a quick kiss. "And this is amazing." She ran her hands down the leather seats, marvelling at the space they had in the back. In the front was a black suited and capped chauffeur who smoothly drove off from Laura's little back street.

"You are forgiven." He kissed her lightly on the nose. "But only as it's your birthday."

"Oh, you'll never guess what I found." She showed him the back of the cameo. "I wish I knew more about its history."

"I hadn't even noticed that." He lifted up the arm rest from the middle of the seat to reveal a chilled bottle of champagne and two glasses. "Champagne, my dear?" He asked, opening the bottle with a large pop.

"Jack, this is so lovely." She settled back into the seat, glass in hand as he poured the fizzy champagne and she stared out of the window watching London whizz by as they drove towards her parent's house.

Her mum and dad lived in an old Victorian house in Kingston upon Thames, the house that Laura had moved to after leaving High School. Laura loved coming home; it was so quiet compared to her day-to-day life. Her mum and dad came running out as the Bentley drew up on the drive. Laura rushed out of the car before it had even stopped completely and threw herself into their arms.

"Happy birthday sweetheart," they both said, hugging her tightly. A small cough behind brought their attention back to the present.

"Mum, Dad, this is Jack." Laura introduced him.

"Pleased to meet you Mr. and Mrs. Reynolds." He shook hands with Laura's dad.

"Janice and Steve please." Laura's mum smiled at Jack's infectious grin.

"Janice and Steve it is." He nodded agreement before getting his and Laura's bags from the boot of the car and handing some notes to the chauffeur. As the car drove off, he followed Laura and her parents into the house.

"Are you ready?" Laura asked, knocking on the door before opening it. Jack stood just inside the small bedroom hanging up a pair of jeans in the wardrobe. "Sorry about this." Laura was hoping her mum and dad wouldn't insist on separate rooms but deep down she knew they would.

"It's fine." He came towards her and took her hand. "I'm sure I'll be the same if ever I have a daughter." They linked arms and walked down the staircase and into the lounge. Pink and purple balloons adorned the corners of the ceiling, birthday banners were hung over the fireplace and doors, and a large cake and several cards and presents sat on the small table in the middle of the room next to a tray with a flowery teapot and matching cups, sugar bowl, and jug on. They sat down in the soft floral chairs and Janice poured tea for them all.

"You must open this one first." Steve handed her an ordinary looking brown A4 envelope with her name and parents' address neatly written. "Your mother has been driving me crazy since it came yesterday, she doesn't recognise the writing, you see," he explained to Jack. "Janice prides herself on knowing the senders of all birthday and Christmas cards we get."

"Don't be silly." Janice tapped her husband playfully on the arm but didn't correct him.

Laura peeled open the envelope carefully to reveal a slightly smaller envelope and also what appeared to be a card. The other envelope was again written to her but with no address on, and the card simply had *Laura* on it in elegant script. There was anticipation in the air; everyone seemed to be on the edge of their seats as they watched Laura open the larger envelope.

There was no card or present inside, just what seemed to be a rather legal looking document.

"*Deed of ownership*," Laura read out aloud then went silent as she continued down the paper. "It says here that I own Hampton Cottage, Coventry. Have you bought me a house?" She squealed in delight and hugged her parents.

"Erm …" Steve spoke first. "We haven't bought you a house, sweetheart."

"Then who?" Laura scanned the document but there was nothing about a previous owner only the document naming her as the present owner and dated with today's date. "Where is Hampton Cottage anyway?"

"I don't know," Janice exclaimed. "I don't remember a Hampton Cottage when we lived there."

"Apparently Hampton Cottage is the name of a house on Hampton Court Road." Jack read from his phone then carried on typing. "This is it. It's on Street View." He turned the phone round so everyone could see it, but Laura knew instinctively what it would show.

"It's the old farmhouse, isn't it?" It was a statement rather than a question and Laura's face fell as the picture on Jack's phone confirmed her worst fears.

Chapter 3

"**A**m I missing something?" Jack looked at the three suddenly solemn faces. "You've been given a house!" He couldn't understand why no one else was excited about this. "Okay, it's run down and needs a lot of work, but I can help with that. It'll be worth a pretty penny when it's finished."

"But I don't understand." Laura looked to her parents. "I don't even know the people that owned it. I wasn't even alive when the place was left empty."

"Can someone tell me what I'm missing?" Jack looked from one face to the other waiting for someone to fill him in on the obvious secret.

"We used to live in Coventry, as you know," Laura began. "Beth, Lucy, and I always walked past this house on our way to school. All the kids used to scare each other by saying it was haunted, someone was killed there, you know what kids are like. Well, we always said that one day we'd go and check it out. We were moving to London and it was our last night, the three of us, so when we got back from prom we thought it would be a laugh."

"Wait," Jack interrupted. "You went in your prom dresses?" He suppressed a laugh.

"Okay, I admit, not the best idea." She shot him a look. "Anyway, we look round the house, it's completely empty but then we hear a noise upstairs. Lucy gets scared and goes outside and Beth and I go upstairs. Nothing up there until we get to the last room. Beth won't go in and leaves me on my own." She shivered as she recalled that night. "Right at the end of the room by the window is something covered by a sheet. When I pull off the sheet underneath is this beautiful mirror. It was so gorgeous I couldn't help touching the frame. Then I heard a man's voice behind me, he said, *'you always loved that mirror'*." Laura took a sip of tea before continuing. "When I turned round this man was standing there with a photo in his hand."

"Didn't you scream?" Jack looked at Janice and Steve. "I think I'd have screamed."

"I couldn't. I was sort of mesmerised." Laura had tried to forget that night but found herself able to recall every little detail. "There was moonlight shining in from the window on the landing. The man was dressed in a suit, but he was old, and I mean really old. He still had hair, although it was white as snow and he leaned heavily on a cane. He didn't move, just handed me this old photo he had in his hand."

"And who was in the photo?" Jack was intrigued.

"Me," Laura said simply. "But it was an old photo."

"When you say old do you mean old as in you were little or old as in old?" Jack didn't really know how else to say it.

"It was a photo of me in my prom dress, taken that night but looked like it had been taken decades ago. It was worn and tatty around the edges. But it was what he said next that scared me the most." She paused and looked at her mum who gave her a nod of encouragement. "*I knew you'd be here tonight Laura.*"

"Well, that's not creepy in the slightest is it?" Jack sat back in the chair; he hadn't realised he had literally been on the edge of his seat. "Then what happened?"

"I just dropped the photo and ran as fast as I could." Laura let out a long breath. "I told my mum and dad about it the next morning and they rang the police. They searched the house and he was still there, but he'd died. The policewoman said the mirror had been covered over and he was sitting up against the wall as if he was looking at it. They couldn't find the photo I'd mentioned and he had no ID on him so they shut the house up and took his body away for a postmortem."

"The results came back confirming he had just died of old age, but to this day, no one knows who he was or what he was doing there." Steve carried on the story. "We did a little digging on the house but couldn't find anything really, only that it was owned by the Matthews family. The last known occupants were Walter Matthews and his daughter Lauren in the 1980s but after that nothing."

"The card!" Janice hadn't meant to screech but the highness of her voice caught the others attention.

"Yes, the card." Jack picked it up off the table and handed it to Laura. "I have to say I wasn't expecting to be solving a mystery this weekend." He gave Laura's hand a reassuring squeeze. "It's okay."

The envelope was yellowed with age and the stickiness of the glue virtually non-existent, so it opened with ease. It wasn't a card inside, but a folded piece of paper, again yellow with age and dated December 1986. The writing was flawless and in blue fountain pen.

My Dearest Laura. How long I have waited to write this letter to you. I am getting to be an old man now but I know I still have many years to go until we will be together again. The only thing that keeps me going is knowing that I will see you one last time before I die. I wish I could tell you more but alas time does not allow. I cannot even sign my name at the end of this in case I give too much away. Just know this my love, not a day goes by that I do not think of you. One of my favourite memories is you in a white dress as we watched the sunset. Look after the house, make it a home again. I know how much you love it. Until we meet again. xxx

No one spoke for a few moments as they tried to digest the words, Laura gave the letter to her dad.

"Do you think it's a different Laura?" Janice quizzed. "I mean, absolutely nothing in that letter makes any sense at all. How can he see you one last time? Surely he's already dead if he's left you the house."

"Wait a minute." Her dad was holding the letter up to the light from the window. "There's something written here but it's been erased." He put the letter down and walked out into the kitchen.

"How can it be me?" Laura had to agree with her mum. "I was only a baby when this was written." Steve had come back in with a pencil and was busy scribbling over the bottom part of the letter.

"I have to say I quite like him." Jack was trying to lighten the mood. "I mean, apart from the obvious stalker type issues, he seems a decent chap. Leaving you a house and all that."

"*P.S. Watch out for Jack.*" Steve read from the letter not even realising what the words actually meant till a few seconds after.

"I've changed my mind," Jack said huffily.

"It doesn't say that Dad." Laura snatched the letter out of his hand. "You're making it up." But she knew her dad wouldn't do such a thing and there in plain sight, revealed by the pencil rubbing were those exact words. "I feel sick." She clasped a hand to her mouth and ran upstairs to the bathroom.

Locking the door behind her, she leaned up against the tiles and slid to the floor, hugging her knees to comfort her as she had as a child. Who was he? How did someone in 1986 know she would be alive today, let alone seeing someone called Jack? When were they to meet? Like her mum said, surely he was dead? Maybe he wasn't, but the date of the letter was nearly thirty years ago and he said he was getting old. But why leave your house to a complete stranger?

"You okay sweetheart?" Her mum knocked gently on the door. "We're all ever so worried about you." Laura opened the door and fell into her mum's arms. "It's okay, sweetheart. Your dad and I will get to the bottom of it, don't you worry. He's already on the phone to his old boss."

Laura's dad had been a solicitor with a local firm called McNally, Chicken, & Co. Laura had always giggled at the name of Chicken especially when he had come to the house one day. They hadn't been in London long and her dad's new boss had come round to make sure they were settling into their new home. When her dad had introduced him as Mr. Chicken, Laura had laughed uncontrollably and despite warning looks and elbow digs from her mum she had been unable to stop and immediately sent to her room. She could hear her dad apologising profusely as she walked up the stairs but Mr. Chicken seemed to take it all in his stride, saying it happened all the time and imagine the stick he had gotten at school with such a name. Laura liked Mr. Chicken from then on, even if she did laugh every time she heard his name.

"Mike's told me to take everything in for his son on Monday and he'll do some digging around." Steve met Laura and Janice as they came down the stairs. Jack was standing by the lounge door, leaning on the door frame, his face a mixture of concern and bewilderment.

"I'll be at work," Laura stated. "I can't just get the day off like that."

"I've already thought of that," Steve explained. "I told Mike you wouldn't be able to come and he said as you didn't know any more than we did it didn't really matter. All he wants to see is the letter and the deeds." They went back into the lounge, all sign of the deeds and letter already out of sight.

"I'll make us another pot of tea and then you can open the rest of your cards and presents." Janice hurried off into the kitchen with the teapot, Steve hot on her heels.

"You alright?" Jack put his arm round her and kissed the top of her head. "All a bit shocking really, isn't it? I can't even begin to make head nor tail of it all."

"How does he know me?" This was the one question that kept whirling round and round her head.

"I haven't the foggiest my dear." He hugged her tight. "But I think we need to try and forget about it for now as your mum is really upset. Let's just talk about it when we get back and see what your dad's solicitor friend comes up with."

"I can't just pretend everything's okay you know." Laura felt a little angry at this suggestion. "I feel like someone's been watching me my entire life." She shuddered at the thought.

"I'm not suggesting that for a minute." Jack looked her in the eyes. "But there is absolutely nothing we can do now. Next weekend we'll drive up to Coventry and take a look at this house. See if we can find anything out for ourselves."

"I suppose you're right." Laura shrugged her shoulders. But the day was tainted now and as much as she smiled and laughed for the rest of her birthday, inside she felt like a deer caught in headlights.

Chapter 4

Laura was glad to get back home on Sunday evening. She was tired and emotionally drained. She hadn't slept Saturday night, she just kept going over and over everything that had happened. Her dad had hidden the letter away but it didn't matter, she'd only read it the once but she knew it word for word. *My dearest Laura,* well that intimated that he held some affection for her. *I know that I will see you one last time before I die;* had that meeting already happened? Or was it still to come? And the part about Jack? That was the weirdest bit. She'd only known Jack for two months so how could this man have known about him thirty years ago. Her head ached from the constant thinking. Her mum and dad had looked worried when Jack's brother had picked them up and drove them away, even though they tried very carefully to hide it.

They hadn't spoken about it in the car journey home, not wanting to have to explain it all to Pete. Jack had offered to stay the night but she just wanted to take a long hot bath and watch some meaningless rubbish on the TV.

As the water filled up the tub, Laura made a cup of tea, lit some candles, and turned on her iPod. Lowering herself under the bubbles she sighed as the heat seemed to relax every muscle in her body. She hadn't realised she'd been that tense. She just lay there, enjoying the soothing water, fragrant candles, and her favourite music.

Taylor Swift's album *1989* was playing, one of Laura's favourite songs *Wildest Dreams* came on. She found herself singing along, almost forgetting the past day's events, to the part about being remembered in a nice dress, staring at a sunset. She sat bolt upright in the bath, spilling water over the sides. How apt were those words?

The water felt chilly all of a sudden so she hastily washed her hair and stepped out of the bath, wrapping her thick towelling robe around her. She walked into her bedroom and began drying her hair, unable to get those words out of head. It was just a coincidence, she knew that, but what a coincidence!

The next morning, she awoke feeling more refreshed. She'd slept, which was a bonus, must have been the bath and lavender candles she'd used. Her nan swore by lavender for relaxing and aiding sleep. In fact, one year, Nan had given her lavender scented candles, dried lavender pillows for her drawers, and lavender bubble bath for Christmas. It was the year she was taking her final exams at university so her nan must have thought she needed help relaxing.

There was a missed call from Jack on her phone so once she was dressed, fed, and on her way to work she rang him back. It was just a quick call as he was on his way to open up the shop. It was a strange conversation, small talk didn't seem to come as easily as it normally did but after what had happened at the weekend and the part of the letter about Jack, Laura could understand why he might have seemed a little off.

Work thankfully brought a much-needed diversion. Her class of seven- and eight-year-olds were their normal delightful and equally awful selves. Rebecca had written a beautiful poem about unicorns and Stephen had been sick all over it. Mason and Graham had got into a fight about who liked Chelsea the most, much to the disgust of Chelsea who proclaimed she liked Christopher in year five as he was much more mature.

Satisfyingly tired at the end of the day, Laura declined the offer of a few drinks with Mrs. West and Miss Cox and headed home, eager to speak to her parents about their meeting with Mr. Chicken Junior. This thought alone brought on an immediate giggle.

She had only just walked in the door when the phone rang. It was her mum. Unfortunately, they hadn't found anything new just yet. Only that the house had been empty since the mid-eighties when Walter Matthews had left it to go and live with his daughter Lauren. Initial searches could find no record of a future sale but her mum said they were hopeful about uncovering something.

"But he says that the house is definitely yours." Her mum stated. "The document is genuine and the house passed into your possession on Saturday. But this is even more intriguing." Her mum paused a little. "Guess what date the deeds were processed?" Laura didn't have a clue and asked her mum to just tell her. "The day you were born."

"The day I was born?" Laura repeated. "It just gets worse doesn't it?" She felt the despair returning. How many more questions would be revealed but no answers found? "Is there any connection to this Walter Matthews and the man in the letter?"

"Not that they've found just yet," her mum continued. "Walter was an only child, his dad died in the First World War just a few years after he was born and his mum died in the Second. He had a daughter called Lauren in 1943 but we couldn't find the mother's name or a marriage certificate. Apparently it's not uncommon in times of war. Documents get lost or destroyed all the time."

"Perhaps Jack and I will find something out at the weekend." Laura wasn't looking forward to the trip at all.

Yes it would be nice to catch up with Beth who still lived there but the thought of returning to that house filled her with fear and trepidation. She'd virtually made up her mind that she was just going to put the house straight up for sale, but when she'd told Jack and her parents that on the Sunday afternoon they had all disagreed with her and persuaded her to at least go and see the house again and see how she felt then.

It was with a heavy heart and a suitcase full of supplies that she and Jack headed up to Coventry on Saturday morning. Laura knew the house had no power or water so had packed plenty of snacks and drinks. They were going to meet Beth for dinner that evening and then head home. Jack had other plans.

"I thought it would be a bit of an adventure if we camped out for the night," he explained as Laura opened the boot of his car to reveal sleeping bags, camping lights and a bag of firewood. "I bet there's a fireplace there. We can build a fire and toast marshmallows and then snuggle up together." The look of horror on Laura's face said it all. "Or not!"

"I don't think I can be there when it's dark, Jack." Laura was having a hard enough time facing the fact of going in the house when it was light.

"I know it's scary," Jack soothed her. "But he's long gone, dead and buried. He was just some poor old man. Maybe he thought you were his daughter or something like that. Maybe he knew your name because he'd heard you and your mates in the garden or in the house."

Laura had to admit it sounded plausible but that didn't explain the one big thing.

"How did he have a photo of me though?" She wanted Jack's explanation to be true, more than anything she needed to believe it was true.

"You said yourself it was dark." She nodded at this. "Then maybe it wasn't you in the photo at all. Maybe the lack of light and your heightened senses made you think it was you. Like I said perhaps it was his daughter he was talking about, his daughter may even have been called Laura, it's not an uncommon name after all." He shut the boot and they both made their way to the front of his car. "After all, you did say he was old, he was probably very confused, obviously dying, and I just think he'd wandered in thinking it was his old house and you were his daughter or something like that."

"You could be right." She clipped in her seatbelt and turned the radio on. "I haven't really thought about it these past fourteen years. I've tried my hardest not to think about it, never talked about it with anyone since it happened and never told anyone new until you last week. I hadn't considered any other possibilities except that it was me in the photo." She smiled feeling her mood lighten. "It still doesn't help solve who my mysterious benefactor is but at least I'm not so frightened of the house now."

"Then let's go see this mystery house." He shifted into first gear, took off the hand brake and moved into the narrow road. "I have to say, I'm actually a little bit excited, you know. It's not every day your girlfriend inherits an abandoned farmhouse. Who knows what treasures we might find?"

"You and treasures!" she teased.

"A man's got to earn a living you know."

Laura hadn't realised how much she'd missed Coventry until she caught sight of its famous three spires on the skyline. She always considered herself a London girl and had never been homesick for her birth city until today. She explained to Jack that the three spires were the old cathedral that had been destroyed by the Germans in World War II but somehow the tower, walls, and spire had survived. She explained about the charred cross that had been found made of two burnt timbers that had fallen in the shape of a cross after the bombing raid. The other two spires were of the old Christ Church which had also been destroyed in World War II leaving just the tower and spire, and Holy Trinity Church.

"Beth, Lucy, and I used to love sitting in the old cathedral ruins," she recalled. "It always felt so very peaceful there."

"Then you'll have to show me round one day." The Sat Nav interrupted them telling them to take the next exit off the ring road. It was just another ten minutes until they had reached Hampton Court Road. Laura had started feeling sick again as they had got closer and closer and now as Jack drove slowly down the road she thought she would throw up.

"I'm not sure I can do this, you know." Jack had pulled up outside the hedges of Hampton Cottage. The house was just as she remembered it except it was even more run down than before and all the windows and the front door had been boarded up. Stepping out of the car, Jack held her hand tight and they walked towards the gate. The hedges and garden were so overgrown it was hard to establish where a path might even have been.

"How do we get through here then?" Jack tried to open the gate but the grass and brambles behind it were so dense that it only opened an inch. "Shall I go and ask the neighbours if they've got any power tools?"

"Or we could just go home," Laura said hopefully.

"You're not getting out of it that easily." He walked off towards the neighbour's house, returned empty handed and went to the other side. While he was gone a white van with the words *Fallon's Ground Maintenance* pulled up and two men got out. One went to the back of the van while the other came over to talk to her.

"Miss Reynolds?" he enquired. Laura looked at him as if he was talking a different language. "Miss Laura Reynolds?" he asked again.

"Yes … yes … that's me." Laura almost had to convince herself that she was indeed Miss Laura Reynolds.

"We're here to clear the garden for you and get all the boards off the doors and windows." The other man had joined them now, armed with a rather lethal looking power strimmer. "Shall we get started?"

"Erm … yes, if you like." Laura didn't really know what else to say. The man with the strimmer started it up and quickly cleared the growth away from the gate while the other man brought out another strimmer and followed behind once the gate was open.

"I didn't have any luck …" Jack trailed off as he saw the two men in the garden. "What the hell?"

"They just turned up." Laura couldn't quite believe what had just happened. "They knew my name, my full name, and said they were here to clear the garden and take the boards off the doors and windows."

"I bet your mum and dad arranged it," Jack queried. "After all, they were the only ones who knew we were coming."

"I didn't even consider that." She smiled. "I just thought it was more mystery goings on. I'll text them to say thank you later."

"I have to say they're making light work of it." There was already a path to the door and one of the men had stopped strimming and had started to take the boards off the front door. "Shall we go and take a look?" Jack led her up the garden path and to the door, holding her hand tightly all the time.

Underneath the boards the door was open, the glass that had been in the top half was smashed and scattered on the floor. They were just about to step in when a car beeping its horn caught their attention. They turned round to see a short, bald man dressed in a navy-blue suit step out the driver's side of a white Jaguar.

"Miss Reynolds! Mr. Williams!" He called. "I'm so glad you're both here." He made his way towards them. "I've waited thirty years to meet you."

Chapter 5

"**R**aymond Maythorpe." The man held out a slightly chubby hand and shook each of theirs rather vigorously. "So very pleased to finally meet both of you." He reached into his jacket pocket and pulled out a card and handed it to Laura.

"Maythorpe, Maythorpe, & Maythorpe. Solicitors. Solihull," she read out loud.

"I'm the middle Maythorpe." He tapped the card as if to emphasise the point. My father is the first Maythorpe and we've just added the last Maythorpe for my daughter." He said the last part very proudly.

"Who are you?" Jack asked.

"Raymond Maythorpe," he repeated.

"We know who you are," Jack stated. "I mean why are you here? How do you know our names?"

"Of course that's what you meant." Laura had taken an instant liking to Mr. Maythorpe. He seemed incredibly jolly and easy to talk to. "It was me who wrote the deeds out for this place thirty years ago. I was so intrigued by it all that I left cards with all the neighbours a few weeks ago and asked them to ring me if they saw anyone coming. Luckily I was only down the road when Mrs. Rogers opposite telephoned to say a young couple were outside the house."

"You wrote the deeds?" Laura was excited. "Then you know who left me the house," she asked eagerly.

"Certainly I do." He nodded.

"Well?" Laura asked again after a long pause.

"Don't you know?" He seemed perplexed.

"No!" Laura was getting a little irate now. "I just received the deeds to the house and this letter last Saturday on my thirtieth birthday."

"Just how she planned it." Mr. Maythorpe smiled. "Although I don't recognise the letter."

"She?" Jack picked up on this piece of information. "Not he?"

"No, no, definitely a lady." Laura knew Mr. Maythorpe wasn't being deliberately annoying but her patience was wearing a little thin.

"Could you tell me her name?" Laura thought the direct approach might work. "And why she would leave me a house?"

"Mrs. Lauren Edwards her name was." His eyes glazed over as he seemed to reminisce. "Beautiful she was. Early forties I think, glorious dark auburn hair and bright blue eyes, not unlike yours I have to say, but striking against her hair and pale complexion. She came into the office, I hadn't long qualified so my father still didn't trust me with the complicated things. When she told me the details and dates I thought I'd misheard her, but when she calmly repeated them to me again I knew I'd heard her correctly." He stopped and looked around. "Is there anywhere we could sit down?"

"I don't think so." Laura felt sure the house would be empty of furniture, after all it had been boarded up since the morning after her prom.

"I'll just lean on the wall then." He stepped over the newly cut brambles, snagging his trousers on a thorn and plonked himself rather unceremoniously on the rather precarious looking wall; luckily it didn't budge. "Now, where was I? Oh yes, when I asked again if the dates and names were correct she got a little exasperated with me and got up to leave but I apologised and just filled it all out as she'd said. She came back a few years later and handed us an envelope addressed to you. She explained it was the deeds to the house and they needed to be delivered to you on the fifth of March 2016 and not a day before or a day later. Then she said I was to visit the house on the twelfth or thirteenth of March 2016 to meet Laura Reynolds and Jack Williams." He took an enormous deep breath as if the long tale had tired him.

"But why would she leave me a house?" Laura asked again. "How did she know about Jack? How did she know we'd be here this weekend?" Although the question of the mystery benefactor had been discovered all it had done was bring up more unanswered questions. "I thought the house belonged to a Walter Matthews?"

"Wait," Jack interrupted. "Didn't you say Walter Matthews had a daughter called Lauren?"

"Didn't I tell you that?" Mr. Maythorpe questioned himself. "I felt sure I'd told you that. Must have forgotten, silly me." Laura rolled her eyes at Jack. "Walter Matthews lived here with his daughter Lauren till she married sometime in the seventies and became Lauren Edwards. He left here sometime in the eighties to go and live with her and the house has been empty ever since, waiting for you to come and claim it. I have to say I didn't know whether you were real or not."

"But why me?" Laura asked a third time. "I'm no relation to the Matthews or Edwards family and okay she knew about me somehow but how on earth did she know I'd be here with Jack on this very day? I only met Jack back in January."

"You're not related to Mr. Matthews or Mrs. Edwards in anyway?" Mr. Maythorpe seemed to be grasping the situation finally. "And when you were born,

Mr. Williams here was in no way connected to your family or hers?"

"No to both of those questions." Laura sat down next to him on the wall and Jack sat next to her. "So you see Mr. Maythorpe, we are in a bit of a pickle. A complete stranger leaves me a house, but all the paperwork is dated on the day I was born. Somehow this stranger knows that thirty years later I will come and see the house with a man called Jack Williams. And to top it all off, when I received the deeds there was this letter inside dated December 1986." She handed the letter to Mr. Maythorpe who read it, re-read it, and read it again.

"My, my, what a mystery." He stood up quickly. "I shall go and open up the office right now and see what information I can find out for you." He shook both their hands again. "I'll be in touch." He walked off down the path, stopped, turned around, and walked back towards them. "It might help if I took your number," he said sheepishly, taking out his phone and carefully tapping in the numbers that Laura recited to him. He then headed back to his car and with a quick toot of his horn was gone.

"What an interesting fellow." Jack put his arm round Laura. "Let's get inside shall we? I know it won't be much warmer but at least we'll be away from this cold wind." He took her hand and helped her back over the brambles. "Do you think we should leave the boards on the windows for now?" he suggested.

"Why?" Laura wanted as much light as she could get in the house.

"Once the boards are off, there won't be much security for the house," he explained. "I mean, I know there's nothing in there for anyone to steal but if the door is anything to go by the windows are likely to be smashed as well and then the house will be far more vulnerable to the elements and animals, that sort of thing. We can board the door back up when we leave and I'll measure up for a new one and fix it next time we come."

"I didn't say there'd be a next time," she said, but had to agree that what he was saying made sense, so they told the gardeners to leave the boards on and just carry on clearing the garden as best they could. "Do you have any money on you?"

"About fifty quid for dinner later and my debit card for some petrol on the way home. Why?" Jack looked puzzled.

"Won't they need paying?" She nodded in the direction of the two men.

"Ah!" Jack started checking his pockets. "I've got a few quid in change as well." He smiled hopefully.

"I've got about the same as you so I hope it's no more than a hundred quid." She took out her phone. "I'll text mum now and see what the agreement is with them."

"Good idea." Jack suddenly realised that they were in the hallway of the house. They must have carried on walking while they talked. Laura was still texting her mum so she hadn't noticed where they were either.

"Hopefully she'll answer me quickly. I would have rung her but she never answers it straight …" Laura didn't finish the sentence; she was rooted to the spot and her mouth was bone dry.

"It's not as bad as I thought it would be." Jack squeezed her hand. The hallway was just how she remembered it except this time there was more light but even less wallpaper. The floor was thick with dust and bits of paper which made them cough as they walked down the hallway. As before all the doors were open or missing and the rooms all empty. Thin slivers of light penetrated through the gaps in the boards. Jack and Laura didn't speak, they just held hands as they walked round the downstairs and then more hesitantly upstairs.

Jack took her straight to the front bedroom, the door was wide open this time and standing just as she remembered it was the mirror. Jack went towards it and reached for the top of the sheet.

"Don't, Jack!" She hadn't meant to shout but the sudden fear that gripped her was overwhelming.

"You've got to face it sometime." He pulled off the sheet with one fast movement. "See. It's just a mirror." Laura took his outstretched hand and stood next to him looking in the mirror and then over her shoulder before looking back again. She felt much calmer now with Jack by her side.

"It really is a beautiful frame isn't it?" She resisted the urge to touch the wood as she had done before. In the light she could see that the carved frame was made from various flowers and at the top there was an oval shape that had been cut out, like something was missing. "What do you think this was for?"

"Maybe a plaque or something." Jack looked it over. "I've seen similar but none as well carved as this one. The plaque was probably removed by the last owners." Laura's phone beeped.

"I bet that's mum." Laura tapped her phone and read the message. "She says she has no idea what I'm going on about and have I been drinking?"

"We'll have to go and ask them then." Jack made his way out of the bedroom with Laura following close behind. The men had already finished the strimming and were collecting all the cuttings up into a jumbo-sized rubble bag. It was amazing how different the front garden looked. It still needed an amazing amount of work but at least now you could make out the boundary walls and the hedge at the front of the house. There were even some paving stones leading from the gate to the front door.

"Nearly done." It was the man that had first spoken to Laura that approached them. "If you want a quote for the rest of it or for doing the back just give us a ring."

"Erm …" Jack felt a little foolish asking his next question. "I know this might sound crazy but believe me, crazy doesn't even begin to cover where we are at the moment. But could you just tell us who told you to come and do this?"

"It was a lady that called us, just after Christmas. Asked if we'd come and sort out an overgrown garden for her when the weather got a little better in March. We should have been here last week but with all the rain we've been having we thought we'd best leave it till today."

"Can you remember her name?" Laura was hoping it would be someone she knew.

"Hang on a minute, I've got the diary in the van. I'll have it written down there." He went to his van and returned a few seconds later with a leather-bound red book. "Here it is." He flicked through the pages. "That's odd. I've got a number but no name. Not my writing either, looks like Chris', typical of him not to write the name."

"Have you been paid?" Laura was hoping that maybe whoever it was had paid by cheque and they could trace the name.

"Yes, the money was posted to the yard the next day after we gave the quote." Laura's face fell. "Cash in an envelope with just the address written on it. "Do you want me to ring the number for you?"

"Would you mind?" Laura watched as he tapped the buttons on his phone. "Can you put it on speaker?" The automated voice of the operator announced that the number was unobtainable. "Well, that's that then."

"Sorry Miss." He went back to help his mate pull the bag of waste into the van. "We'll be off then." Laura and Jack both thanked them before they drove off.

"I don't know about you but I think it's time we put one of those heaters on, boiled up some water on the camping stove and had a nice hot drink," Jack suggested. "My mind is in turmoil." Laura nodded as they loaded themselves up with all the things out of the boot and headed back into the house.

Chapter 6

"This wasn't how I thought we'd be spending our Saturday night." Jack took out another slice of pizza. "I was looking forward to meeting Beth and her husband."

"I just hope she's okay." Laura took a sip of tea. "She's only got a few weeks to go now and her midwife said she had to stay in the hospital because she's having contractions. They're hoping it will stop on its own because it is a little too early."

"Probably for the best we didn't go out though." He pulled at his clothes and looked at his hands. "I'm absolutely filthy."

They had spent the day cleaning out the house as best they could. The dust was unimaginable and without power to use a hoover it was all done using stiff brooms and a dustpan and brush. They swept downstairs first room by room, moving it all into the hall before filling countless black bags and lugging them outside into the garden. Then they cleaned the upstairs, all four bedrooms and the bathroom looked so much bigger once the peeling wallpaper and dust had been cleared. They left the mirror uncovered but Laura still checked the reflection in it every time she had her back towards it and in the end she put the dust sheet back on.

There were no carpets in any of the rooms and they could see that some of the floorboards were rotten. Jack had said that the whole place would need re-wiring, new roof, damp treatment, and of course a new kitchen and bathroom. He wrote things down in a little notepad he'd brought as they went through each room. Laura didn't stop him, but she didn't encourage him either as he made his list of things the house needed, putting them in order of urgency. She hadn't decided what she was doing with the house yet but she knew that even if she was to sell it she would get far more money for it if it was ready for someone to just move in and she liked the idea of restoring the house to its former glory even if she wasn't going to live in it herself.

She had to admit that the house had a certain feel about it. It was homely and despite the cold March weather it was quite warm inside. Just as she had on prom night she imagined it full of life with a large family living in it. She knew the reason she had felt so scared of the house was because of what had happened here that night so many years ago but now she was older and Jack was here with her she was beginning to look at it differently.

"We would have looked a bit of a sight in the restaurant wouldn't we?" She had to agree with Jack on this one. They were in what they assumed was the front room. It was on the left-hand side of the house with a large fireplace on the back wall. The mantelpiece was as ornately carved as the mirror upstairs and they wondered if they had been made by the same person. Jack had swept out the hearth as best he could, even trying to unblock the chimney but with at least thirty years' worth of goodness knows what up there the fire inevitably smoked like crazy when he had lit it and they'd put it out quickly.

Instead, Jack had set up the camping heater and a few battery-operated lanterns. They were huddled in sleeping bags enjoying a much-needed delivery of pizza and chicken wings washed down with a slightly warm bottle of wine drunk out of paper cups.

"You feeling a bit better about this place?" Jack was now on his fifth slice of pizza. "I like it you know; it certainly has plenty of potential."

"I have to say I am." Laura smiled. As they'd worked today she'd found herself feeling more and more at home. She didn't know why but there was something about the house that she hadn't felt before, like it was talking to her, pleading with her to make it a home again. "It's got a nice feel about it." She didn't know how to explain it to Jack, she felt sure that when he said potential he meant money but Laura could see far more than that.

"Luckily it's still basically sound as far as I can tell." He took out his notepad and flicked through his notes while still eating his pizza. "Some of this I can do and obviously the final decorating we can both do but electrics, plumbing, plastering, that kind of thing, is going to need the experts."

"How much do you think it will cost?" Laura was grateful she'd been saving these past few years for a deposit on her own house instead of renting for the rest of her life and her parents had always said they'd help her out when she decided to finally get her own place. She was sure she wasn't going to ever live here, her life was in London now, but getting this house up to scratch would be a wonderful challenge and a fantastic investment.

"I'm not an expert but it's certainly going to be well over ten grand, maybe even fifteen; depends on how much we can do ourselves." He continued flicking through his notes. "I probably haven't even got everything written down yet. We haven't even looked outside to see what's out the back, then there's rendering the walls outside, plastering inside …" Laura stopped him with a kiss.

"Enough talking about the house now." She unzipped his sleeping bag and placed herself on top of him, one leg either side and bent down to kiss him again.

"But what about …" Laura kissed him again. "Sod the house," he said throwing the notepad over his shoulder and pulling her down for another kiss.

"Jack!" Laura nudged him in the ribs. They'd zipped their sleeping bags together to make a double and keep each other warm. "Jack!" She nudged him harder.

"Ouch!" He rubbed his side. "It's dark still, why have you woken me up?"

"I can hear someone moving upstairs." Laura felt sure she could hear footsteps in the bedroom above them.

"Don't be silly." He turned on his side to go back to sleep. "This house has been empty for three decades and it's basically just had the shit kicked out of it today so of course it's going to be creaking, it's settling back down, that's all." Laura wasn't convinced so she wriggled further down the sleeping bag and hid her face against Jack's side. A loud creak upstairs made Jack shoot up. "Okay, I heard that."

"I told you." She couldn't hide a smug smile even if she was scared stiff. "Go and look, will you?"

"I'm not going up there." Jack's voice had become quite high pitched. There was another creak and they both stared up at the ceiling, it was right over their heads.

"Come on." Laura threw back the covers, grabbed a lantern and Jack's hand, pulling him up at the same time.

"Okay, but you're going first." He picked up a light himself. "It's your house."

"Some protector you are." She held the lantern right out in front of her, Jack following behind. They walked up the stairs and towards the front bedroom. The door was open just as they'd left it. Laura stepped a little way in lifting the light as high up as she could.

"What do you see?" Jack was hiding his head in her shoulder.

"Nothing." She continued scanning the room. "There's nothing here; just like you said, the house is just creaking ... Shit!" Laura shot back out of the room.

"What the hell?" Jack caught hold of her hand.

"I thought I saw something in the corner." Laura didn't know if her eyes were playing tricks on her or not but she was sure she'd seen something moving in the corner of the room. "You look!"

"Me? But ..." Laura pushed him into the room and followed behind as close as she could without tripping him up. "Which corner?"

"The one opposite the mirror." Laura suddenly remembered this was where the old man had died but she thought she had best keep that to herself for now.

"There's nothing there." Jack switched the light round to make a torch, its beam was far more powerful than the lantern. "Holy shit!" he screamed making Laura jump.

"What Jack? What is it?" Laura was certain he'd seen a ghost.

"It's okay." Jack let out a huge sigh of relief. "It's a cat." When he'd shone the bright light of the torch around the room it had caught the cat's eyes and he'd nearly shot out of his skin but then his brain had kicked in to tell him it was just a cat.

"A cat?" Laura peeked out from behind him. "Would a cat make the floorboards creak like that?"

"You haven't seen the size of him." Jack had moved over to the corner and put his light down before picking up the cat. "Hello boy." It wasn't scared of them at all, in fact it was already purring loudly in Jack's arms.

"How do you know it's a boy?" Laura stroked it behind its ears. Jack was right, it was one of the biggest cats she had ever seen with bright yellow eyes and long ginger fur.

"I can't be a hundred percent sure but as most ginger cats are actually males it's a pretty good guess." They started walking back down the stairs. "Something to do with the X chromosome I think and girls have two X chromosomes so they very rarely get two ginger genes, or something like that."

"Well aren't you the fountain of knowledge." Laura's heartbeat had finally returned to normal. "Do you think he's a stray?"

"From the weight of him I'd say he's definitely well fed and looked after somewhere." Jack laughed. "This is probably where he comes looking for mice."

"How did he get in?" Laura knew they'd put the boards on the front door, from the inside this time.

"I should imagine there are holes everywhere in this place." He put the cat down as they reached the bottom of the stairs and it immediately walked into the living room and stuck its head in the box of uneaten chicken wings. "Even ones big enough for him." He chuckled. "Let's get back to sleep shall we?" They snuggled back in their sleeping bags, the cat making himself right at home by the heater. Neither of them had noticed that one corner of the dust sheet covering the mirror in the bedroom had moved and when they awoke the next morning the cat had gone.

Chapter 7
April 2016

The difference in the house in just a few short weeks was amazing. It was the second week of the Easter holidays and Laura and Jack had travelled up to Coventry to see how progress was going. It had been three weeks since they'd last been there and with a little help from Mr. Maythorpe the house now had a new roof, new wiring throughout, the damp had been treated, and a shiny new bathroom sparkled upstairs. There was now electricity and running water as well as new windows and doors and the two men from Fallons had returned to clear the back garden.

"Wow!" Was all Jack could say as they drew up outside. "It looks like a totally different house." The walls of the house were still a dirty grey with some of it chipped off in places, the front hedge was still overgrown and the garden still in its basic state but just having the new roof, windows and doors fitted gave it a whole new lease of life.

The keys to the new doors had been left with Mrs. Rogers over the road who had been happily making the various workmen tea and coffee and plying them with biscuits. In fact she had made it her mission to 'keep an eye on the place' while Laura and Jack were away.

"I bet you don't recognise it, do you?" she asked as Laura had thanked her for her help.

"I didn't think just those few things would make such a difference." She had made to leave, eager to get started on the inside and have a look at what the back garden had to offer.

"Of course I remember Mr. Matthews." This piece of information intrigued Laura and she turned round. "Lovely man he was. A proper gent through and through." She smiled. "This was my mum and dad's house and my brother and I grew up here in the early sixties. He used to let us pick the apples from the trees out the back of the house. I moved away when I got married but came back after my parents passed." A quick sadness passed over her face before she pushed it away. "I remember my mum telling me he'd gone to live with his daughter. She said he'd never been the same since his wife had died after having Lauren in the 1940s and living in such a big house on your own must have been ever so lonely. When Lauren left to get married the house became more and more run down; it was like he'd given up."

"So no one came to the house in all that time?" Laura knew she would have to invite Mrs. Rogers round for a cup of tea one day and get some more information out of her.

"Not a soul. The local kids used to break in." Laura looked away at this point. "Then there was that incident with the old man. So sad, dying like that with no one ever knowing who he was, of course they had to board the house up after that." Laura made no comment. "So are you Mr. Matthews' granddaughter?" Now it was Mrs. Rogers turn to try and get some gossip. Laura's phone rang just at that moment.

"I'd best get that Mrs. Rogers. Thanks again for all you've done." She walked down the neat path and out of the gate as fast as she could.

"I thought you needed saving." Jack smiled as Laura hurried over the road to meet him by the gate.

"She used to live in that house as a child, said her and her brother knew Walter Matthews." Laura was excited by the news. "It seems his wife died in childbirth and when Lauren got married he went downhill and stopped looking after the house."

"We're going to have start writing all these little bits of information down you know." Jack knew it meant a lot to Laura to try and find out why Lauren Edwards had left the house to her.

"I already have." She pulled out a hardback book from her handbag. "I've written everything I know but you'll have to have a proper look over it later see if I've missed anything out."

"Has Mr. Chicken or Mr. Maythorpe found any more information?" Jack had a quick flick through the pages.

"Not a thing." Laura shook her head. "It's like all their records have been erased from the world. All either of them could find was Walter's birth certificate, no marriage or death certificates and just a marriage certificate for Lauren."

"I find it so intriguing." Jack said as he took Laura's hand. "Do you think we'll ever find out why she left you the house?"

"I hope we do." They started to walk up towards the house. "I don't know if I can just resign myself to never knowing." They unlocked the newly fitted front door and stepped in. Both of them just stood and stared. It was filthy again after all the workmen had traipsed backwards and forwards but the amount of light that flooded in through the windows was astonishing. All the dust particles seemed to dance in the sun beams that shone through.

They walked all over the house. Each room now had working lights and plugs. The kitchen had running water although the sink was still in dire need of a good clean, and there was now a fully functional bathroom. Mr. Maythorpe had even arranged for a chimney sweep to clear out the chimney in the front room and had a delivery of logs placed there ready for lighting later.

Laura still hesitated at the door to the front bedroom but now when she walked in it was light and bright, bearing no resemblance to prom night. The mirror had been moved, obviously the window fitters had had to move it away and its dust sheet now lay on the floor. Laura decided it was time to leave it off and told Jack she would give it a really good polish. He'd brought some wood treatment for the fireplace so he said he'd put some on the mirror frame at the same time.

"It doesn't look right here though." She went to lift the mirror but it was too heavy. "Give me a hand to put it back by the window." Jack took the other side and together they carefully placed it back in its original setting. "It gets much more light by the window." She stood looking at her reflection. "I wonder how many other people have stood here doing this?" Laura twirled round imagining herself in a long dress rather than her ripped and faded jeans.

"May I have this dance?" Jack asked, bowing deeply.

"Why of course, kind sir." They twirled and twirled around the room to imaginary music until they were both out of breath and collapsed onto the floor laughing. Jack's phone started ringing.

"Hi mate, what's up?" Laura watched him nod and make occasional comments before clicking off the phone and stuffing it back in his pocket. "Change of plan I'm afraid. I can only stay till Monday; we've got a big house clearance on Tuesday and Big Fred's gone and bust his foot so he can't help."

"But we were going to get the rooms all measured up and spend the week here together." Laura sulked a little. "Beth was going to visit with the new baby. She gets out of hospital on Monday."

"You can still stay here." Laura wasn't sure she liked the sound of that at all. "We'll get measured up over the weekend, I'll drive back Monday and come pick you up on Friday. You said you wanted to go and get wallpaper samples and look at carpets and stuff and that really isn't my kind of thing at all."

"I don't want to be here on my own though." She was adamant on that. "And I was looking forward to spending the week together, I'll just come back with you on Monday and help with the house clearance, it'll be fun." Laura was disappointed she wouldn't get to see Beth though. "I'll see if we can go to the hospital tomorrow afternoon to see Beth and the baby."

"You don't want to be coming with me and Pete." Jack tried to dissuade her. "It won't be very interesting for you."

"Of course it will." She was looking forward to it now. "I'll enjoy poking round someone else's house."

"If that's what you want to do." He stood up and then helped Laura up off the floor. "As long as you're sure you don't just want to stay here." She shook her head frantically. "Let's go plug that shiny new kettle and toaster in then shall we?"

Laura woke up on Monday morning, stretched out lazily then turned to nudge Jack awake. Finding an empty sleeping bag she assumed he must be in the bathroom or kitchen so she called out his name but there was no answer. Unzipping the bag, she wrapped her dressing gown around her and pushed her feet into her fluffy pink slippers. She called his name up the stairs before walking into the kitchen. Still no answer. She walked back into the living room and then noticed that his bag was missing. A sudden sense of panic gripped her. Pulling back the makeshift curtain from the window she saw an empty space where his car had been.

Now she really was confused. His bag was gone, his car was gone but worst of all Jack was gone. But where and why? It was then she saw a small piece of paper on his sleeping bag. It was a hastily scribbled note, torn roughly out of the notepad he'd been using.

Pete rang. Had to leave early. Didn't want to wake you. See you Friday. Jack xx

And that was all it said. He knew she didn't want to stay here on her own, knew she wanted to come back to London with him but still he'd left her here. She picked up her phone and rang him. Straight to voicemail. Well she wasn't going to text him, what she wanted to say was too long for a text.

She'd never felt so angry. She still couldn't believe he'd left her here. She stomped into the kitchen and switched on the kettle, threw a tea bag into a cup and slammed two pieces of bread into the toaster. All kinds of thoughts rushed through her head as she stood there waiting. Should she just go home on the train, but then spend the next few days doing nothing? She couldn't go and stay with Beth, that wasn't fair to lumber them with her in their first days with the new baby.

She smiled as she remembered her visit to the hospital yesterday. Jack had dropped her off and headed into town saying she didn't want him there getting in the way. Beth was sitting up in bed reading with a bundle of pink lying next to her in the plastic crib. Beth's face had broken into a huge smile when Laura walked in carrying a present and card for the new baby.

"She is beautiful." Laura daren't touch her for fear of waking her up. "And so tiny."

"She didn't feel tiny when she was coming out." Beth was opening the present, a tiny gold bangle. "That's so sweet."

"My Godmother bought one for me when I was born so I thought it only right I bought one for my Goddaughter." She sat on the side of the bed. "I'll get her name engraved on it when you've decided."

"We decided last night, actually." Beth put the card on the cabinet next to her bed. "Jessica Rose."

"That's lovely." She looked over again at the baby. "Suits her."

Jessica Rose spent Laura's entire visit fast asleep so the two old friends had had plenty of time to catch up. Laura told her all about Jack and the house, she hadn't seen Beth since before Christmas, they texted most days but the full details of the last few months could only be told face to face. Beth was as perplexed as all of them about the mystery goings on. She hadn't heard any more about the house except for the bit about the old man being found.

All too soon the bell to end afternoon visiting sounded and Laura gave Beth a hug and kissed Jessica Rose ever so gently on the forehead. With the promise of a visit one weekend soon, Laura walked out to meet Jack in the car park.

The toast popped loudly, making her jump slightly. She spread butter and raspberry jam onto it, grabbed her tea and walked back into the front room. The house was too quiet so she turned her iTunes on. A missed call from Jack was ignored with some fragrant words and she sat sipping her tea and eating her toast. It was then that she decided she would stay in the house until 'that bastard' came to pick her up, or maybe she'd tell him to piss off and make her own way home but either way she was going to do what she came to do and get this place resembling a home again.

A knock at the door made her remember that the plasterers were coming to re-plaster all the walls so she let them in, got herself dressed extremely quickly in the cold bathroom then made cups of tea all round. The house felt alive with all the commotion and noise so she decided to spend the day here. There would be enough time to visit the DIY store when the plasterers had finished.

She walked down to the local shop, marvelling at how much the area had changed since she was a child. The sweet shop that she, Lucy, and Beth had visited on numerous occasions for fizzy cola bottles and red liquorice was now a beauty salon. She walked past her old school; it still looked the same except someone had had the brainwave to paint it blue. *A very odd thing to do* she remarked to herself. She walked through the park remembering the many summer afternoons the three of them had spent ogling boys.

When she got back to the house she was feeling happy and content and all thoughts of Jack's abandonment of her had been forgotten for the time being. One of the plasterers called Will met her on her return.

"We've had a slight accident I'm afraid," he said rather sheepishly. "Nothing major, just young Ryan somehow put his foot through one of the floorboards in the front bedroom." Laura was relieved it was only a floorboard.

"Is he okay?" she asked. "It was probably rotten anyway, there's a few of them."

"He's fine Miss, thanks for asking." Will pulled a photo out of his pocket. "We found this in the hole though." He handed it to her, wiping the dust from it as he did so. "That's a pretty dress you're wearing I have to say. I didn't go to my prom, couldn't be bothered dressing up in a fancy suit." Laura wasn't really listening to him as she looked at the photo and saw her sixteen-year-old self, smiling back.

Chapter 8

"Are you okay Miss?" Will asked, concerned. "You've gone awful pale."

"You said this was under the floorboard in the front bedroom?" At least Laura now knew that she hadn't been seeing things that night, that the man had had a photo of her and that's why the police had never found it—because it must have fallen under the floorboards. She felt lightheaded and started swaying slightly so Will helped her into the front room and sat her down on the stool he'd been using to reach the ceiling.

"I'll go put the kettle on." Will walked off towards the kitchen. "You look like you could do with a nice cup of tea."

Laura just sat staring at the photo. Where had that man got it from? Why did it look so old? It was only taken fourteen years ago yet it looked closer to eighty. Her mum and dad had the very same photo in a frame on their wall and she had one at home in an album. There were only two copies so where had this third one come from? She turned the photo over and over idly as she thought. It was then that she noticed the writing on the back. *It will all make sense in the end.* It looked like her handwriting but she knew she hadn't written anything on the back of the photo, not even the date.

Will came back in with two steaming mugs of tea. He didn't speak, just placed it down beside her then made an excuse to check on the other lads upstairs. Laura was glad he'd left her alone. As nice as he seemed she wasn't about to explain all this to a complete stranger. How did you even start explaining it?

She sipped her tea and read the sentence again. She thought seeing the photo would bring back the old feelings of fear but for some reason it didn't. The familiar writing calmed her; of course she knew it wasn't actually her hand writing but the words seemed to hold a promise that one day everything would become clear. She was beginning to love the house; it had a peaceful feeling about it that seemed to envelop her every time she stepped inside. She was certain now that she wouldn't live there, but she couldn't see herself selling it either. Perhaps she would rent it for a few years and use the money towards a mortgage on a house in London.

"You feeling better now Miss?" Will popped his head round the door.

"Yes, thanks." She nodded. "I don't know what came over me." She stood up as if to prove to him that she was indeed feeling better. "I'll let you carry on with your work." She walked out of the room as Will picked up his trowel. She went into the kitchen where Jack had set up a picnic table and two chairs. She frowned as she thought of him.

She sat down at the table and placed the photo next to her book of facts that she'd been compiling. She had tried to write them in chronological order but as she seemed to find out things back to front and upside down this had long been abandoned. She re-read everything she knew on Walter and his daughter, the things she'd gleaned about the house; but nothing was making any sense, so she slipped the photo into the page where she'd written about prom night and added the fact *'photo of me in prom dress'* to the page. She wasn't even sure that the man on prom night was even linked to the house but somehow she thought it was significant so she'd written everything down that she could remember about that night.

A commotion upstairs, swearing and the words, *"Bloody hell, Ryan,"* brought Will running out of the front room and up the stairs.

"Everything okay up there?" Laura called, looking up from the table.

"It's fine Miss," Will shouted. "Ryan just tripped over his bucket of plaster." Laura chuckled at the obviously clumsy Ryan, shut the book, and went upstairs to see if she could make herself useful in anyway.

The plasterers left late that afternoon. Laura had nuked a microwave meal for her tea and was watching a film on her laptop when her mobile rang. It was Jack again. He'd rung a few times and each time she had ignored it but this time she answered.

"What?" was her short greeting.

"Don't be like that." Jack's voice sounded soppy. "I'm really sorry but it was like five in the morning when Pete rang and I really didn't want to wake you up."

"Didn't want to wake me up?" Her voice was high and angry. "Didn't want me to come back with you more like?"

"Don't be silly," he chastised. "Of course I did, but I knew how much you wanted to spend a few days at the house."

"Not on my own I didn't," she snapped.

"You'll be fine," he assured her. "We've spent a few nights there now and nothing's happened, there's no ghosts and you can have the lights on and the heaters."

"Jack, you left me here when I specifically told you I didn't want to be here on my own," she reminded him. "The plasterers found a photo of me in my prom dress under the floorboards so I wasn't seeing things that night, that man did have my photo."

"Shit! You're joking?" Jack still didn't seem to understand why she was so angry with him.

"No, I'm not joking; it really freaked me out to start with." She was finding the casual attitude to his disappearing act a little annoying now, when before his carefree attitude had been endearing. "I'm going to do some research on Wednesday but I've got to go into town to do it as I need the internet."

"We'll have finished the house clearance on Wednesday because we started earlier so I can be back Thursday." Laura couldn't believe he thought he'd already been forgiven.

"Don't force yourself," she said sarcastically.

"Stop sulking Laura, it doesn't suit you." Jack was fed up now. "I've said I'm sorry and I've said I'll be back to pick you up on Thursday; if you don't want me to just say so."

"Of course I want you to." Laura had to admit that although she was still extremely pissed off with him she did like him a lot and enjoyed his company. He was sweet and funny with a very dry sense of humour. He was attentive, most of the time, and made her feel special. Did she really want to finish with him when they'd only just started?

"Then I'll see you on Thursday." The tone of his voice was back to normal Jack. "Enjoy your research."

Laura clicked off the phone feeling like a wimp for letting him off so easily but she wouldn't forget this and if he did anything else in the future he'd best watch out. She thought a nice long bath would help relax her so she grabbed her washing bag, PJs, dressing gown, and slippers. All the lights were on in the house already, had been since it went dark. She didn't care how much the electricity bill was going to be, she just wanted every room to be nice and bright, it made her feel better somehow.

She turned the taps on full in the new rolled top bath and poured the lavender scented bubble bath into the water, it frothed and bubbled immediately, the smell filling the bathroom. There were no tiles on the walls or floor yet and Laura had been warned not to spill any water as there was nothing to stop it dripping into the room underneath, so she just filled it halfway instead of to the top as she would have done at home.

She sighed with pleasure as she lowered herself into the warm water, pushing herself down so that the water and bubbles reached just under her neck. The bath was as long as she was, not like the cramped one she had at home; that was the bonus of an old house, she thought to herself, everything was bigger in those days, made for large families. Not trying to cram as many homes as they could into tiny spaces.

She sat there till her fingers were wrinkled and the bath water had lost its heat. After a quick scrub she pulled out the plug, listening to it gurgle down the drain, dried herself off and put on her pyjamas. She felt hot after the bath so left her dressing gown where it was and padded softly down the stairs in her slippers. She made herself a hot chocolate and curled up in her sleeping bag to watch the end of the film.

She must have dozed off because the next thing she knew it was after midnight, well twelve twenty-two if you wanted to be exact about it. It felt chilly in the room and she shivered slightly. She decided to bring one of the other heaters in so trudged into the kitchen, unplugged it and trudged back into the front room, half dragging it half carrying it. She plugged it in, switched it on and *puff*! All the lights went out, the heaters went off, and Laura was in complete darkness.

"Bugger," she said, fumbling around trying to find her phone. It took a few minutes and a stubbed toe before finally she had her phone in her hand and switched on the torch app. She made her way under the stairs where Jack had explained to her all about the newly installed fuse box and how if one blew it tripped out everything else connected. There wasn't a door to the cupboard yet so ducking her head she peered in, located the tripped switch and flicked it back on.

"Would you mind telling me who you are and what the hell you're doing in my house?" Laura turned slowly at the male voice behind her, forgot about the low ceiling, stood up in shock, bashed her head and fell to the floor unconscious.

When she came to it was morning and she was lying in her sleeping bag. Her head ached and there was a huge lump where she'd knocked it. She touched it gingerly and winced. Recollection flooded her brain. The man had been tall, about six foot three she thought, short dark hair and brilliantly blue eyes. His voice had been calm but authoritative and Laura thought he was in his early thirties.

She dashed round the house checking all the doors and windows but every one of them was locked and shut just as they had been before she'd gone to bed. *Well, it must have been a dream* she said to herself, a very vivid dream she thought. She checked the time on her phone, realised that the plasterers would be here any minute and ran upstairs to get dressed. She walked into the front bedroom to check her appearance as it was the only mirror in the house. Again she marvelled at the beauty of the carving before looking down at her feet to tie her shoelaces. It was then that she noticed her cameo necklace lying at the foot of the mirror. She picked it up wondering how on earth it had got there, looked back in the mirror as she put it round her neck and saw the man from last night staring back at her.

Chapter 9

Laura spun round, but the room was empty. She looked back in the mirror and realised that it wasn't a reflection at all and the man wasn't actually looking at her. He seemed to be examining the mirror, pressing his hand against the glass and tapping it. He had an intense look of concentration on his face and was dressed in a smart shirt and trousers complete with a tie but they didn't look like anything she'd ever seen before. Laura waved her hand but he couldn't see it, didn't even flinch when she put it right in front of his face.

She looked behind him. He was in a bedroom, richly decorated with red floral wallpaper, long red curtains and she could see one half of a four-poster bed. There seemed to be someone in the bed and when she looked closer Laura could see a frail looking old lady fast asleep. To the side of the bed by the window was a rocking chair and curled up on the red cushion was a big fat ginger cat. Laura gasped, was that the same cat that had been in the house a few weeks ago? But how could it be? And how could this man have been in the house last night?

Laura scrutinised the layout of the room, the position of the door and window and realised it was a perfect mirror image of the room she was standing in. Was it the same room? But how could it be the same room? The room she could see was obviously lived in, not like this empty room that didn't even have any wallpaper let alone furniture, carpets, and curtains.

Taking out her phone she began to film the man, he seemed to be saying something, maybe he was talking to the lady in the bed she thought. Then he moved away from the mirror and the image was gone. All Laura could see now was her own reflection and the bare walls behind her. She clicked off her phone just as the plasterers knocked at the door.

Opening the door to them she noticed Ryan wasn't with them today, just Will and the other chap; Laura was sure his name was Colin. They went straight into the kitchen and began setting up so Laura went back upstairs. She stared and stared at the mirror but all that stared back at her was her own reflection. She replayed the video on her phone but instead of the man standing there it was just a video of her videoing herself. There was no trace in the mirror of what she had just witnessed and now she was beginning to think she was seeing things again.

Shrugging her shoulders helplessly she went back downstairs and into the kitchen. She made tea and toast for her and the two lads then went into the front room where she played the video again and again before deleting it, shaking her head and throwing the phone down in despair.

That night she couldn't sleep, she lay awake tossing and turning and listening for any kind of noise from above, she even went upstairs and sat in front of the mirror for nearly two hours but nothing happened and nothing changed. All she could see was herself staring back.

Wednesday morning came and went as finally she had gotten to sleep but had woken up just after twelve. Her stomach was growling and her throat was dry so she addressed both of those first before getting dressed and catching the bus into town. A quick check of the mirror before she'd left had shown nothing different.

She found an internet café just by the main bus station, ordered a large hot chocolate and a slice of carrot cake before sitting down next to the window with a large pad and pen by her side. She pulled out her book of notes and began searching the free birth, deaths and marriages online.

Her initial findings came quickly. Walter Matthews had been born on the third of October 1910 to Iris and George. By the looks of it he was an only child. George had died in 1915 and Iris in 1942. There was no sign of a marriage for Walter and no sign of a birth for Lauren but as she already knew she found Lauren marrying Graham Edwards in 1972.

As she exhausted the amount of information she could get from the free sites she then logged onto her *Genes Reunited* account, renewed her account from years ago when she had researched her own family tree and started again. On the 1911 census she found Iris and George Matthews and their son Walter living at the house with an older Walter Matthews. The 1901 census showed George Matthews living at the house with his father Walter and mother Gwen.

Laura didn't feel there was much point going back further than this so she searched and searched for a marriage for Walter Matthews and a birth for Lauren but there was nothing, not even anything close. She then switched to her own family tree, searching all the information she'd found out before, looking for any connection to the Matthews family; but again there was nothing.

Flicking onto Google she tried one last search. She knew that sometimes old photos or articles from papers appeared online so she searched *Walter Mathews, Lauren Matthews*, the house address, any and every combination she could think of until finally there in front of her was a black and white picture of the house. It was an article from *The Coventry Evening Telegraph*. The house stood pristine and a woman and young boy stood outside the front door, named as Iris and Walter Matthews.

The article was about when the new houses had been built on the street and although Mrs. Matthews had sold her land she refused to sell the house for re-development and that she and her son would continue to live there for many years to come. Laura had to admit that Iris looked like a formidable lady but there was a softness about her in the way she was holding her son's hand.

Walter must have been about ten in the picture. He was already as tall as his mum and dressed in neat shorts, shirt, and a tank top with long socks up to his knees and heavy shoes. His neatly combed dark hair was swept to one side and Laura thought he looked like he was dying to take off what were obviously his good clothes and go and play with his friends. Neither of them were smiling but Laura didn't think she'd ever seen anyone from earlier times smiling. All the old photos she saw of her grandparents and their families were all stern and posed: not like the silly faces you pulled nowadays.

Checking her watch she was amazed to find it was almost five and that the owner of the café had been cleaning up and stacking chairs on tables. She apologised as she packed up her things and headed to McDonald's on the way home.

The burger and fries were delicious as was the banana milkshake that washed it down. She mused over her findings in her head. *Still no nearer to an answer,* she thought; but a few more facts in the book couldn't hurt and it was nice to finally put a face to Walter Matthews, albeit a very young face. She rang Jack while she waited at the bus stop.

"Hello, Jack's phone," a giggly female voice answered.

"Erm ... Can I speak to Jack please?" Laura was a little perturbed by the woman's voice.

"He's in the shower." The woman giggled again. "Shall I get him for you?" Laura's mind was racing.

"No, no, it's fine." Laura didn't really know what to say. "Just tell him Laura called." She went to put the phone down but then heard Jack's voice in the background.

"Hi Laura." His tone was casual. "Don't mind Mercedes here, I'm at Pete's and she thinks it's hilarious to wind me up."

"Why are you in the shower at Pete's house?" Laura wasn't sure she believed him.

"I'm not." Laura felt sure she could still here Mercedes giggling and what sounded like two people having a play fight. "She's winding you up. I'll go in the other room so I can talk to you properly."

"Don't worry, I'll tell you later. The bus has come early." It wasn't her bus that had pulled up but Laura was grateful of the excuse. She hadn't heard mention of a Mercedes before, she was sure Pete's girlfriend was called Katie. Perhaps that was why Jack hadn't wanted her to come back with him, maybe he had another woman?

The thought angered Laura and she stomped onto the bus when it finally arrived. The house was cold and dark when she walked in and she spent five minutes turning all the lights on and firing up the heaters. Surely she was reading too much into it? She had begun to calm down on the bus ride home. She hadn't had any suspicions before and so what if another girl had picked up his phone, it didn't mean anything. Perhaps Pete had a new girlfriend or perhaps it was Pete who was messing around on Katie.

Feeling slightly better about the situation she rang Jack and told him everything she'd found out that day. He explained about Mercedes saying that she was an old girlfriend of Pete's who took great pleasure in winding other people up which was one of the reasons they'd broken up. She told him about what had happened Monday night and then Tuesday morning. Jack was a little freaked to start with but when she mentioned bashing her head he was a little worried and said maybe she should go to A & E in case she was a little concussed. She promised to see her doctor when she got back home if she continued seeing strange men and after a *see you tomorrow,* she got ready for bed.

She fell asleep early and easily after being awake the previous night. So deep was her sleep that she didn't hear the footsteps upstairs a little after midnight, didn't hear the stairs creaking. It was only when she felt something jump on her that she shot awake to find the ginger cat pawing at her and making himself comfy on her lap.

"Hello again." She stroked his head and as before he purred instantly. "Am I asleep still or are you really here?"

"I see you've met Chester before." Laura's head shot up at the sound of the man's voice. Here he was again, the man from the other night, the man from the mirror sitting cross legged on the floor at the end of her sleeping bag. Laura knew now that she was definitely dreaming and made a mental note to herself to take Jack's advice and see the doctor as soon as she got home. However, because this was a dream she didn't feel frightened in the slightest, in fact she thought she'd ask him a few questions.

"He was here a few weeks ago," Laura replied as Chester curled up in a ball and went to sleep. "So who are you and how did you get in here?"

"My name's Ben and I came through the mirror." He spoke without a hint of laughter.

"Of course you did." Laura was one hundred percent sure now that this was a dream. "I quite often walk through mirrors myself." He picked up on her sarcasm and smiled.

"So who are you and what are you doing in my house?" Laura hadn't expected the dream man to question her, but dreams were dreams.

"Laura Reynolds." She held out her hand and he shook it politely. "And this is my house."

"I don't think so." Ben looked around the room. "It looks very different but I'm pretty sure this was my house the last time I checked."

"And when was the last time you checked?" Laura felt a little giggly at the serious look on his face.

"You don't seem to be taking the situation very seriously." Ben was a little bemused by the silly look on her face. "There I am in my mother's bedroom watching Chester chase a mouse across the floor, when all of sudden he brushes past the mirror and disappears. Then when I put my hand on it to see where he went it goes straight through. Then I find myself here."

"You were here the other night, weren't you?" Laura thought she may as well go along with what he was saying, after all she could wake up at any time.

"I don't really know what happened the other night." He shrugged his shoulders. "The candles had blown out and I stumbled over the mirror. I heard a commotion downstairs and thought someone had broken in so I came to see what was going on. That's when all of a sudden I was blinded by light and saw you under the stairs." He pointed to the light on the ceiling. "Why hasn't that got a candle in? In fact where is all the light coming from?"

"Why would it have a candle in it?" Laura was baffled. "The bulb works perfectly well."

"You mean an electric light bulb." Ben stood up and stared at the light intensely.

"Don't look at it directly," she shouted at him. "It'll hurt your eyes."

"How fascinating." He looked away. "When I close my eyes I can still see the light." Laura shook her head in disbelief. "I've heard about some people having these in their houses, they work on switches don't they?" He started moving around the room examining the wall. "Is this it?" He asked when he found the switch by the door. "How does it work?"

"What do you mean how does it work?" She moved a rather disgruntled Chester, got up and walked over to him. "You just press it, like this." She turned the lights off and then on again.

"Fascinating," he said again, flicking the switch on and off over and over again. "Absolutely fascinating."

"Shall we have a cup of tea?" Laura walked off into the kitchen hoping he would follow. *I really must see a doctor soon,* she thought to herself as she filled the kettle and flicked the switch.

"What does that do?" Laura rolled her eyes as he dashed over to the kettle and then to the microwave.

"This is a kettle." She lifted it up. "Surely you know what a kettle is?"

"Of course I know what a kettle is," he scoffed. "I'm not stupid. But our kettle goes on the stove." A look of despair came over him. "Where's the stove? Where's the table? In fact where is all the furniture?" A sudden panic came over him and he almost ran over to the window. "Where are the curtains? Get the lights off before the warden sees."

"I'm going back to sleep now." She switched off the kettle hoping that if she went back to sleep in her dream this madness would stop. "Lovely to meet you Ben." She went into the front room and got into her sleeping bag. "Nice to see you again Chester." She gave him a quick kiss on top of his head, closed her eyes and ignored the sounds of the mad man running round the house turning all the lights off and muttering about wardens and blackouts. When she awoke the next morning everything was as it had been the night before and she sighed with relief before ringing her doctor to make an appointment.

Chapter 10

"**E**verything looks fine, Miss. Reynolds." The doctor sat back down at his desk. "The bump has virtually gone and you're not complaining of headaches or dizziness so as long as that continues I wouldn't worry any further."

"Thank you, Doctor Bloor." She shook his hand. "That's a great weight off my mind."

Jack was in the waiting room as they were heading off to lunch after the appointment. It was Friday and Laura was determined to enjoy her last day off before locking herself away for the weekend planning the next week's lessons. She sighed as she remembered how long the next term was. Easter had been early this year which meant that the next term was seven weeks.

"All clear?" Jack stood up as she came out.

"All clear." She nodded. "As long as I don't have any more visions or start getting headaches or feeling dizzy."

"Well, I don't know about you but I feel like a dirty, great, stuffed crust pizza." He rubbed his hands together as they headed to the bus stop.

"Sounds good to me," Laura agreed. "I need the stodge to get me through the weekend.

"Are you sure you have to work all weekend?" Jack turned to look at her with sad puppy dog eyes.

"You know I do." She kissed him on the end of his nose as they sat down at the bus stop to wait.

Sitting at her desk on Sunday afternoon Laura stared out the window at the early spring sunshine. She could feel the warmth coming through the glass and longed to be outside. She checked her watch, it was half past two, she could have a quick stroll around the park, grab something to eat, and then head back home and carry on working.

She had made good progress so far, only a few more numeracy books to mark and then some history planning so she knew she could afford an hour or so break. The sun felt wonderful and she lifted her face to feel the full heat. It was a picture-perfect day. The sky was bright blue with fluffy white clouds drifting slowly past.

She treated herself to an ice cream cone at the entrance to the park, licking it quickly to stop the chocolate sauce dribbling down onto her fingers. The park was busy, families were out in force walking off Sunday lunch or working up an appetite for Sunday tea. Children were playing on the swings, swooshing down slides and hanging like monkeys from the climbing frame.

She found an empty bench to sit at by the boating lake and watched the swan pedal boats and those braver souls who took out the rowing boats. A young girl was throwing bread to the ducks on the opposite side; Laura smiled as she watched her throwing huge chunks into the water and laughing as the ducks pecked at each piece. It brought back memories of her and her parents visiting Jefferson gardens in Leamington Spa when she was small. How she had loved to feed the ducks and swans, squealing with delight when the greedy geese came along to steal the bread right out of her hands.

The girl had turned to her mum who was standing behind a push chair with a small boy fast asleep. They walked away from the ducks and off towards the exit, stopping at the ice cream van on the way. They stood waiting for a few minutes; the girl had joined a man in the queue who Laura assumed was her dad. It was so lovely to see young families out together and she couldn't stop the quick daydream about having a family one day herself. The girl was happily licking her ice cream, pulling out the flake and dunking it back in again.

 The couple had their backs to Laura now and were walking off through the gate when something about the man's jacket caught her eye. She was sure Jack had a jacket like that. Come to think of it the man looked the same height as Jack with the same short brown hair and cropped beard. She got up quickly and walked as fast as she could round the lake and through the gate but by the time she had gotten outside the park the family were nowhere to be seen.

 Laura scanned the street but there was no sign of them anywhere. She walked home telling herself that plenty of men wore Nike jackets and as beards were in fashion at the moment lots of men had decided to grow them. She hadn't seen the man's face so why she would even think it was Jack. Besides, he lived on the opposite side of the city: why would he come to a park near her?

 By the time she was back home she was convinced it hadn't been Jack in the park and as there was a text on her phone from him asking if she was sure she couldn't spare an hour she knew for certain it hadn't been him. *He must have a twin brother,* she thought to herself then cursed as she remembered she'd forgotten food. Ordering a Chinese she sat back down at her desk and continued marking the maths books before tucking into Chicken Chow Mein in front of the television.

 Five weeks later and Laura was feeling frazzled. It was Friday and she was just tidying away after the day's lessons. Her class had been particularly fractious that day as it had been raining nonstop all week and they hadn't been able to get outside to burn off any of their excess energy. She couldn't believe there was still two weeks left of term but at least she had the weekend with Jack to look forward to.

It was his birthday and she had arranged a surprise weekend away for them both in Brighton. The forecast was finally for good weather and she couldn't wait to meet him after work in the car she had hired for their trip to the seaside. She wished Mrs. Bell a good weekend as she passed by her classroom on the way out and said goodbye to Mr. Busby the caretaker.

She made her way home, showered quickly then packed a bag before heading to the hire centre to pick up the Corsa she'd ordered. It was way past five when she was finally on her way to Jack and Pete's shop. It was called Serendipity and was the cutest shop Laura had ever seen. She'd only been there the once but remembered that it was tucked away in a little back street and was stuffed to the rafters with antiques, knick knacks, and antiquities.

She had spent hours wandering round the place and looking at the shelves. They had glassware, porcelain, books, jewellery, kids' toys, and even a small section of military uniforms. Laura had been fascinated by these especially the hat badges from so many different regiments. And it was amazing to see actual swords from past wars, shivering at the thought of how many people each one had killed.

She knew from her previous visit that the street the shop was on was called Camden Passage and as it was a pedestrian-only street she parked as close as she could before walking the short distance to the shop. It was almost six by the time she got there but luckily the shop was still open.

Laura pushed open the door to an antique bell ringing above her head. She'd forgotten how wonderful the smell of the shop was. A mix of dust and polish only added to the vintage atmosphere. She couldn't see Pete or Jack but knew they wouldn't be far away so she headed towards the counter.

It was then that she saw the woman from the park with the same boy in the pushchair and the same little girl standing by her side. Laura quick stepped behind one of the tall bookshelves and almost held her breath peeking through a small gap as she heard someone else come through the door.

"Daddy," the little girl screamed in delight and ran towards the man that had just come in. Laura watched as he picked her up and swung her round. She couldn't see his face but instinct told her exactly who it was.

"Hello pumpkin." It was unmistakably Jack's voice. "Have you had a good day with Mummy?" The little girl explained all about her day painting and how she'd made him a birthday cake. "Well, I shall look forward to eating that later." Laura knew he had never mentioned a daughter and presumably a son by the looks of it. Maybe he wasn't with the woman though, perhaps he had kids but hadn't told Laura about it yet, after all they had only been together a few months.

Laura knew she was kidding herself. Every part of her brain screamed at her to stop being naïve, to walk out of the shop as fast as she could but she felt rooted to the spot as Jack and the little girl came up to the counter.

"Hello, my little soldier." She watched as Jack bent down in front of the pushchair and then stood up to kiss the woman. "And hello my gorgeous wife." Laura felt sick at the words and had to put her hand to her mouth quickly. She dared not move.

"Are you ready to go?" Laura heard the woman ask.

"Yeah, let me just tell Pete." Laura watched Jack walk out the back before re-emerging a few seconds later. "Pete's going to lock up." He took the little girl's hand as they all walked out of the shop together. Laura waited just a few seconds before heading to the door. She didn't want Jack to see her but she also didn't want Pete to lock her in. She grabbed the bell above the door and moved it out of the way so she could make a silent getaway.

Scanning the street outside she cursed as she realised that Jack had walked in the direction she needed to go. Feeling like a criminal she ducked in and out of doorways before she was able to scoot off towards the car. She sat behind the wheel for almost half an hour before the shock of what she had just seen started to sink in and then the tears came; and once they came they didn't stop.

Laura presumed the woman in the shop was Mercedes but she had imagined Mercedes to be a rather ditzy blonde with big boobs and the woman in the shop was a very normal, and very pretty young woman and the voices didn't seem to match either. She had only heard her speak a few words but she had a sensible voice, not like the giggly voice Mercedes had had.

"Perhaps he was cheating on his wife with this Mercedes girl as well." Laura spoke out loud as she grabbed a tissue from her bag and dried her eyes. She decided that she would still go to Brighton as the hotel was booked and paid for and she always felt calmer by the sea. She plugged in the Sat Nav on her phone and started the engine.

Laura had been right to carry on with her weekend in Brighton. She had spent all of Saturday walking or sitting on the beach enjoying fish and chips, rock, and numerous ice creams. She wasted countless pennies in the flip machines and even won herself a teddy bear. The little niggles she had about Jack had all been explained. She had always wondered why he didn't have Facebook or Instagram and now she knew.

She wanted revenge, wanted nothing more than to tell his wife all about his little antics but did those two little kiddies deserve that? By the time she got home on Sunday afternoon she had made the decision that revenge wasn't the answer as she didn't think it would make her feel any better, would probably only make her feel worse. She hadn't answered his texts or phone calls and had now taken matters into her own hands, blocked his number and deleted it from the memory.

She wiped all the photos of him from her phone and changed her screen saver to her favourite Harry Potter quote, about Happiness being discoverable if one remembers to 'turn on the light'. In fact she thought it was about time for a bit of a Harry Potter marathon and dug out the first three films, watching them back-to-back while drinking a bottle and a half of her favourite red wine.

Feeling more than slightly drunk and realising that she had work in the morning she took a bath. Her choice of album to play had been wrong and as The Vamps' *Cheater* came on she felt angrier and angrier as they sang about a two-timing boyfriend.

Fuelled by anger and red wine she hastily got out of the bath and began flicking through her Facebook. She found Peter and in seconds had found Jack's wife. It was a closed profile but she was able to message her and message her she did. Laura told her everything including the part about Mercedes and without hesitation pressed send and then collapsed on to her bed fast asleep.

Over the next two weeks she made plans to go back to the house for the half term holiday. She was fed up with sleeping on the floor there so ordered a bed to be delivered on the Saturday. She brought pillows and a duvet, curtain pole and curtains to put up in the front bedroom. She thought it so bizarre that she wanted to sleep in that bedroom but it felt so comfortable to her now. The outside of the house would have been rendered and painted by now and she was looking forward to getting stuck into the garden.

She was so excited to be staying at the house again that she drove straight up to Coventry after finishing school on the Friday, the hire car stuffed with her recent purchases. The house looked brand new. Sparkling white paint gleamed in the evening sunshine. She parked the car out the front and unpacked the bags and packages she'd brought with her. She put the curtains up in the front bedroom, having to do this twice as she hadn't spaced out the hooks correctly the first time.

She stuck a few wallpaper samples she'd picked up on the walls and hung a pendulum shade on the ceiling light that matched the red curtains to perfection. It was only then that she remembered seeing red curtains at these windows before and wondered if that vision had influenced her choice in any way.

Deciding not to sleep in the room till the bed was there she set up her bed downstairs. This time she folded the new duvet in half to give her a softer base and the new fluffy pillows were heaven. After a busy school week and a long drive she fell asleep early only to be rudely awoken a few hours later by a familiar voice.

"Where the hell have you been?" Ben now stood at the bottom of her makeshift bed after shaking her roughly by the shoulders. His arms were folded and his face irate. "I've been here nearly every night waiting for you to turn up and I've got a few questions I wouldn't mind answers to."

Chapter 11
June 2016

"Are you real?" She stared into his blue eyes. "Am I dreaming again?"

"Of course I'm bloody real." He sat down on the floor. "I do wish you'd get some furniture in here. I'm fed up with sitting on the floor. I've tried to bring a chair through but it doesn't let me."

"What doesn't let you?" Laura was baffled. "What do you mean you've been here nearly every night?"

"The mirror doesn't let me," he said matter of factly. "Only me and Chester seem to be able to come through."

"Through the mirror?" Laura wasn't making any sense of his words. "You came through the mirror?"

"Well of course I came through the mirror." He looked at her as if she was speaking a different language. "It doesn't work in the day though and only after midnight." He didn't appear to be joking. "It took me a few days and nights to work it all out but I got there in the end." He smiled at her and she found herself smiling back, convinced that either he was completely insane or she was.

"Shall we have a cup of tea?" It was about the only thing she could think of to say at that moment in time.

"I'll make it." He shot up and dashed into the kitchen. "I've realised that I'm not in my time anymore," he told Laura as she came into the kitchen after him. "My street doesn't look anything like the one outside and some of the things I've seen and heard from people walking past would shock a priest. And the cars? Wow, the cars are amazing, like something from space."

Laura sat at the picnic table shaking her head. *Not his time,* she said to herself; well what time was his time?

"I've worked this kettle thing out though. I have to say it's amazing and so fast to boil. My mother would love one of these. She loves her tea does my mother." Laura watched as he picked two tea bags out of the box, ripped them open and poured the tea leaves into a cup. "I like the idea of these little bag things." He said quite innocently. "Just the right amount for the perfect cup but you haven't got a tea strainer."

"You don't rip the bags." Laura stood up, tipped the tea leaves into the bin, got two fresh cups and put new tea bags in. "The tea mashes through the bag, then you take the bag out and add the milk."

"And you keep the milk in these little, tiny things?" Ben held up one of the UHT sachets that Laura had been using as she didn't have a fridge yet. "Why doesn't it go off? Why haven't you got a refrigerator? They're quite a new thing I know, but absolutely remarkable. Keeps the milk, cheese, and meat fresh for so much longer. Mother won't have any of these new electric things in the house you know, but we have one at work."

"Erm …" Laura didn't know which question to answer first so she went with the fridge. "I haven't bought one yet; because I don't live here I don't need one."

"And about that." Ben watched in amazement as she squeezed the tea bags slightly against the side of each cup. "Why don't you live here?"

"I live in London." She handed him one of the cups and he stared at it.

"Unbelievable." He took a sip. "Not a single leaf floating about." He took another sip. "London you say. I've always wanted to see Buckingham Palace where the King lives and Big Ben."

"The King?" Laura queried. "You mean the Queen don't you? Queen Elizabeth."

"Don't be silly." He looked at her as if she was mad. "King George the Sixth, Elizabeth is his daughter." It was suddenly beginning to dawn on Laura that this man believed he was living in the past. She tried to remember when King George had been on the throne, she knew about his brother Edward abdicating in the 1930s and knew George had been King throughout the Second World War and then she remembered Ben talking about blackouts and wardens in her dream.

"Bloody hell."

Ben almost choked on his tea at Laura's words.

"Excuse me!" The look of reproach he gave her almost wilted her to the spot. "A lady doesn't speak like that."

"This lady bloody well does." Laura had just realised that she hadn't been dreaming that night weeks ago, that she had gone happily off to sleep with a mad man roaming around her house and here he was again. "What year do you think it is?"

"Back home it's 1942 but here I haven't a clue what the date is." Ben stood up and looked out of the window. "I mean, I know it's my house but some of the things in here I haven't a clue what they do." He gestured towards the microwave. "And when I look outside it looks so different."

"So you live here then?" Laura was wondering when she would be able to phone the police for them to come and pick him up. As pleasant as he appeared to be he was obviously delusional and in need of help.

"Aren't you listening to me?" he asked. "I live in the house on the other side of the mirror, which is this house, but not this house, if that makes sense."

"Makes perfect sense to me." Laura decided to just go with the flow, he seemed harmless enough. "So do you go back through the mirror?" She couldn't believe she was actually asking that question.

"Now that's what I can't work out." He turned round to look at her. "The mirror only lets me through after midnight and if I haven't gone back through of my own accord within a few hours then I literally get pulled back through."

"Would I be able to go through do you think?" Laura stood up thinking she may as well give it a try.

"I don't see why not." Ben put his cup in the sink. "Chester and I get through easy enough, but once I've gone back I can't come through again till the next night." Laura was amazed at how plausible it all sounded and before she knew it they were standing in front of the mirror. "You first." Laura felt absurd all of a sudden. "You just step through."

Laura looked at him and put out her hand to touch the glass. It was hard and cold.

"I don't think it's working." Laura wasn't sure what she had actually expected to happen. Did she really think she was going to walk through the mirror and be transported to another time?

"I don't understand it." Ben stood in front of her. "It always works for me." He took a step forward and Laura watched as the glass seemed to shimmer and shine. Ben put one foot through and it disappeared. "Perhaps I need to go first, just follow straight after me." Laura couldn't believe what she was seeing. Ben was gone, through the mirror just like he said he did. Laura reached out her hand but once again the glass was hard and cold.

Laura shook her head in disbelief at what she had just seen. She examined the mirror from top to bottom but it was just as it had been before, a normal mirror. She stood there for a while but nothing changed so she headed back downstairs and although she wasn't sleepy in the slightest she got back into bed.

Was she mad? Was her mind playing tricks on her? Everything screamed at her that it wasn't real but there was that little niggle at the back of her mind that said it was. That somehow the mirror upstairs allowed a man from the 1940s to walk through it and come into 2016. She tried to remember all the things he'd said. How the mirror allowed him and Chester through; didn't he say he'd tried to bring a chair through?

It obviously didn't work for her though, but why? Why could Ben come and go but she couldn't? This house was full of mysteries, just more to add to her current unsolved pile. But who was Ben? Was he related to the Matthews family somehow? But he'd said that he lived in the house with his mother. Maybe he was Walter's brother? But then Laura had never found anything about a brother in her research; in fact she was positive she had read he was an only child.

Taking out her notebook she turned to the back and began writing down all she could remember about Ben. He hadn't mentioned a surname, she would have to ask him next time she saw him.

"Next time I see him?" She repeated the words out loud and they sounded even more absurd. She was quite clearly imagining these things; perhaps it was her mind's way of blocking out the hurt she felt after Jack. Ben was a good-looking chap; in fact he was her ideal man in looks. Tall, dark hair and blue eyes. Definitely an apparition she had invented to divert her attention from Jack.

Reassuring herself of this fact over and over again, she eventually fell asleep; but when she awoke the next morning to find the four cups in the sink, the doubts returned.

Chapter 12

Laura made herself busy all of Saturday. The bed came early so she spent a while deciding whether to have it against the wall or by the window. Her gaze kept straying to the mirror and time and time again she found herself standing in front of it just staring. She asked herself over and over, was it really a portal to another time? And if so why didn't it work this way? Why could Ben come through to 2016 but she couldn't go through to 1942?

Shaking her head with annoyance she decided to just let it go for now, after all Ben said it only worked after midnight. She would stay awake and see what happened. She felt that the bed looked best against the wall opposite the window, it gave much more space this way. She unpacked the new sheets, marvelling at how much plastic and paper they were wrapped in, stuffed the pillows into their covers, and had a wrestling match with the duvet. She eventually won and after shaking it a few times, declared herself satisfied and stopped for lunch.

Sitting at the table with a Pot Noodle she began flicking through the kitchen brochures she had picked up from B&Q. Her savings pot was beginning to run a little dry but her parents had offered to pay for a new kitchen which should leave just enough for carpets, wallpaper, and paint if she did the decorating herself. Laura was finding the thought of selling the place almost heart-breaking. She had come to find a strange peacefulness when she was there, so different to her previous fears of the house.

The sun was shining bright and warm so she took a stroll into the garden after throwing her pot in the bin and quickly washing the fork and glass she had just used.

The garden stretched about twenty metres and was the width of the house. A small orchard of apple trees grew at the bottom, most were diseased and she put a reminder in her phone to look into treatment.

Luckily, the neighbours had kept the fences in good condition but she wanted to paint them and had brought a few tins of green fence care to get started on them this week. She had also purchased various pots and bags of soil and was looking forward to buying plants to add colour back in. She was enjoying owning her own house. She only had a little roof terrace back in London and as the flat was rented there wasn't an awful lot she could do to the place, but here she had full control.

She had even made a few sketches of where she wanted things to go. Ideally Laura thought a small patio alongside the house would look good. She wanted borders of sweet-smelling roses and a brick-built BBQ. She could imagine summer gatherings under a dusky August sky, people laughing and enjoying the warm evenings.

The sun was glinting off something a little way down the garden. It blinded her momentarily and she lifted her hand to shield her eyes from the glare. It was obviously something metal, maybe it was a drain cover. She walked over and stared at the ground. The gardeners had cut back the lawn as best they could but it was still overgrown. There were tiny spots of metal peeping through and an obvious outline about a metre squared, too big for a drain Laura thought.

Luckily she had brought a spade with her and she set about cutting around the outline. It took a while as whatever it was, was quite deeply buried. She cleared away the turf and gasped in wonder as a door made of a single metal sheet with a handle emerged from the grass. Kneeling down she pulled at the handle, it didn't budge, she tried again and again, and eventually it started to move. It took all her strength and a quick wedge with the spade for leverage to get the door open.

Dust flew up and made her cough. Wafting her arms in front of her face she could see a set of wooden stairs leading down into a small room. She stepped down carefully, unsure if they would support her weight, but the steps were sturdy and strong. The room was quite dark but with the sun shining in from outside it gave sufficient light for Laura to see that she was in an old air raid shelter.

There were a few shelves on the walls with candles and a box of matches. There were two small beds, one on either side each with a pillow and blanket stacked neatly at the end. A table stood in the middle with a rusty gas lamp, a pack of cards and a few copies of *Woman* magazine. Laura flicked through them, they were dated June and July 1942 with lots of articles about women at war and on the home front.

Laura marvelled at the hairstyles and fashions, wondered what on earth utility clothing was, and pondered on how people managed with such meagre rations. *So this was Ben's time,* she thought to herself. *Had he lain on one of these beds? Had he sat playing cards waiting for the all clear to sound so he could go back home?* She shivered at how frightening an air raid must have been. To sit there, listening to the bombs dropping and not knowing if your street or house would be there when you came out again.

An intense feeling of *deja-vu* come over her and feeling icy cold and, suddenly, depressed, Laura stepped back into the sunlight, closed the door on the shelter, and headed back into the house. She would decide later what to do with it but for now she needed to listen to some very loud music which she could sing along to very badly.

Laura had butterflies in her stomach all evening. She hadn't felt this nervous since going on her first date with Jason McClusky when she was thirteen. She had a limited amount of clothes to wear and wished she'd brought something smarter than the old everyday stuff she had packed for working around the house. Her mind wandered to her wardrobe back home and she longed for her low cut sparkly red top and skinny black jeans. Then remembered that Ben was from 1942 and would probably freak out if she was to dress like that.

She smiled when she remembered how shocked he had been when she had sworn yesterday. If she hadn't seen him disappear through the mirror with her own eyes then she would still be sitting here thinking he was an escaped patient with severe issues. But as absurd as it sounded, he lived in this house back in 1942 and somehow he was able to come through the mirror and into this time for a few hours every night.

After checking her hair and makeup for the hundredth time, she stood in front of the mirror and once again examined it. She checked the frame, running her fingers over the carvings and into the gap at the top where the oval shape was. She pressed all over the glass but as before it was a completely normal mirror.

Her phone vibrated in her pocket and she pulled it out. The alarm she had set for midnight was flashing at her and she felt sick to her stomach. Why did she feel like this? Yes, he was good looking, but up until now she'd thought he was either a madman or an imaginary friend.

Her palms felt damp and she rubbed them on her jeans, wishing yet again that she had something else to wear. She sat on the bed, then moved and sat on the edge. She moved again and sat at the bottom. She stood up and paced around the room, checking her phone every few seconds for the time.

Where was he? Why hadn't he come through? Her phone told her it was twenty past twelve now and hadn't he said the mirror only worked after midnight? Maybe he wasn't coming, maybe he'd had enough of 2016. She shrugged her shoulders slowly with despair and walked out of the door.

"I hope you're off to put the kettle on." Ben's voice from behind her brought a huge smile to her face. She turned around to find him standing in front of the mirror, dressed in his usual shirt, tie, and trousers although today he didn't have his jacket on.

"I thought you weren't coming." The disappointment she had felt a few moments ago had been replaced with overwhelming happiness at his appearance.

"So you believe me now?" His voice was slightly teasing.

"I always believed you," she lied.

"No you didn't," he chastised. "You didn't believe me for a second. I didn't even believe me to start with. It was only when it kept happening that I realised I wasn't actually dreaming and that I could travel into the future."

"So you know it's the future then?" Laura had walked back towards him.

"Of course it's the future." He turned to look around the room. "I see you've finally put some curtains up and bought a bed." He pointed to the wallpaper samples. "I like the beige one with the big red flowers."

"I like that one too." Laura smiled. "It matches the curtains perfectly."

"Well that's strange." Ben was looking at the mirror.

"What's strange?" Laura asked, coming to stand next to him.

"It's missing." He ran his fingers over the oval gap at the top of the frame just as Laura had done earlier.

"What's missing?" Finally she would know what was supposed to be there.

"The cameo." He turned to look at her. "Where's the cameo?"

Chapter 13

"**W**hat do you mean *where's the cameo*?" Laura looked at the oval shape in the frame. "Do you mean a blue cameo?" She didn't wait for his answer. "This cameo?" She made to pull the necklace from around her neck then remembered that she hadn't brought it with her. It was sitting on her dressing table back at home.

"Have you seen it?" Ben asked eagerly as Laura started searching through the photos on her phone. "What is that?"

"It's a phone." Laura forgot momentarily what era Ben came from.

"That's not a phone." Ben snatched it out of her hand. "Where are the wires? Where's the receiver and the dial? How are all these pictures on there? And in colour?" Laura watched Ben flip the phone over and over in his hand, looking at it from every angle possible.

"Let me show you." She held out her hand and he put the phone back into it. "It's called a mobile phone. It means you can take it everywhere and call whoever you want." She pressed the photo button. "And it has a camera in it as well that takes and stores photos. Colour photos became popular a few decades ago."

"But it's so small." He took the phone again, copying what he had seen Laura do and swiped his finger rather heavy handed over the photos. "I've got a Box Brownie, only a basic one and the photos don't come out anywhere near as clear as these."

"Pass it back a minute." Ben handed her the phone. "Say *cheese*." She clicked the button and then turned it round to show him the image.

"Wow." He stared at his grinning face on the screen. "That's incredible." He touched his finger to the photo. "That's me. Right there." He smiled like a child that had just been given a present.

"Where is it?" Laura was frantically scrolling through the photos now. "Why can't I find it?"

"What are you looking for?" Ben was curious and still incredibly fascinated by the tiny phone.

"I'm looking for a photo of me." Then she remembered how she had deleted all the photos of her and Jack and that she didn't own the cameo before her birthday. Then suddenly there it was, round her neck in a photograph Jack had taken of her with her mum and dad on her birthday. "Is this it?" She showed him the screen once again.

"That's it." His eyes were wide in wonder. "How on earth did you get my mother's cameo?"

"It's your mother's?" Laura couldn't believe it. "But Jack gave it me for my birthday."

"Well that is definitely my mother's cameo." He scrutinised the photo. "It was given to her by my father when they got married. I'd know it anywhere." He paused for a moment as if digesting what she had just said. "Who's Jack?"

"A mistake." That was all she felt like saying. "Well, not a mistake I suppose because without him I wouldn't have the cameo."

"But you don't have the cameo." Ben reminded her. "It's just a photo on that mobile thingy."

"I left it back home in London." She explained. "It reminds me too much of him at the moment so I don't wear it."

"But it should be in the frame." His voice was slightly chastising. "When my father went off to fight in the war he made the mirror for my mother using an old Oak tree that had fallen down in a storm the previous October. He had already made a new fireplace for the house with the same wood. He was so clever, my father, I wish I'd known him more." A wistful expression crossed his face. "Alas, that was not to be. He carved my mother's favourite flowers into the frame and placed the cameo into the top and made her promise that she was not to wear it again until he came back from the war. Unfortunately he died a few months later and she has never worn the cameo since. In fact I don't think she has even taken it out of the frame."

"What a beautifully sad story." Laura wiped a solitary tear away. "They were obviously very much in love."

"They adored each other." Ben looked at the mirror again. "They were childhood friends and until the war separated them I don't think they spent a day apart from each other. Mother was heartbroken when he died and she hasn't ever recovered properly but she had me to look after and I was a bit of a rascal growing up." He smiled cheekily. "I was always into mischief."

"I bet you were." Laura could see him as a little boy getting into all sorts of trouble. Then she remembered the writing on the back of the cameo, surely his father must have inscribed it for his mother. "Did your parents get married in 1902?"

"Don't be silly." He scoffed. "They were only thirteen. They were married in 1909 and I came along the following year. Why do you ask?"

"Is there anything special about the fifth of July 1902?" Maybe it was when they first met, Laura thought but hadn't Ben said they had been friends since childhood?

"Not that I'm aware of." She could see him trying to think.

"Then why are the words *please remember me* and the date *July fifth 02* written on the back of the cameo?" Laura was hoping he could shed some light on the matter.

"There's what written on the back?" Ben was suddenly angry. "Who would do such a thing?"

"It was there when I got it." Laura was quick to exonerate herself from any blame. "I thought it was something to do with its previous owner."

"Well there is nothing written on the back of my mother's cameo. I know that for a fact." He was quite adamant. "Perhaps it isn't the same one, after all I'm sure there was more than one made."

"I suppose you're right." Laura wanted to move on to the other subject that was bugging her. If Ben lived here then why was there no record of him in her investigations? "So, you live here with your mum?"

"Not this again; I thought you believed me now?" He turned to look at her. "For the last time, I live in 1942 with my mother and I come through the mirror into your time."

"Yes, I know that but …" Laura wasn't quite sure it was the time to be explaining all about Walter Matthews and inheriting houses from strangers. She believed everything he was saying but it didn't match with any of the information she had found out. She decided to just keep it all to herself for now and see what other things came to light.

"Are we having that tea then?" Laura hadn't noticed that he was now by the door. "And I hope you've got some more of those hobnobbly biscuits, they were delicious."

"I haven't got any more HobNobs," Laura corrected and watched his face fall. "But I do have some chocolate digestives."

"Chocolate biscuits?" Ben's face stretched into a huge grin. "We can't get chocolate biscuits anymore. We can't get a lot of anything anymore to be honest with you."

"It's a good job I bought a few packets then." She laughed as he almost ran down the stairs and she could hear the packet being ripped open before she had even reached the bottom.

"Delicious," he said, spraying crumbs as he spoke, one biscuit in his mouth and another already in his hand. "You don't know how good these taste."

"I heard these were in short supply as well?" Laura had a flash-back from a history lesson back in primary school about the scarceness of bananas and pulled out a bunch she had brought with her. His eyes lit up like a child on Christmas morning.

"I love you." He grabbed a banana and took alternate mouthfuls between the biscuits and the bananas.

"I'll put the kettle on then shall I?" He nodded his agreement and carried on stuffing his face, his cheeks bulging with pleasure.

They spent a very amiable if somewhat strange couple of hours together. Laura found Ben to be extremely good company; he made her laugh and smile and he was easy to talk to. She had already decided not to discuss certain things with him; Jack was still very raw and the details about the house might upset him. She would have to do some more digging in the daytime when he wasn't around.

Instead Ben told her about his life. He was a building foreman so hadn't been called up as he was in a reserved occupation but he felt frustrated that he couldn't go and fight for his King and Country. Laura found this very strange, why would anyone want to go to the front line? She knew all about the horrors of the Second World War and the horrendous conditions that the men at the front had to endure, so what would make someone want to do this if they didn't have to?

The passion in Ben's voice when he spoke about the fight against Hitler was mesmerising and soon Laura could see how the whole country was rallied together in the fight against the Nazis. She now knew what made all these people give up their lives and subject themselves to such hardships all in the name of freedom.

"Do we win?" She had been waiting for this question.

"I can't tell you," was all that she could say.

"Why can't you tell me?" He pleaded. "I won't say anything."

"There are lots of things I'm not going to be able to tell you." She thought it best to try and explain. "You're from the past and I'm from the future, imagine if I told you things and you let them slip to someone back home, the events could be catastrophic." She had seen enough episodes of *Doctor Who* to know what disasters could enfold if the past was disrupted. She knew it was only a fictional programme but surely those facts were still true? Surely if time travel was possible, which clearly it was owing to the presence of Ben here in her house, then altering past events would surely affect the future?

"It's time." Ben suddenly stood up and started walking towards the stairs. "Two fifty-eight exactly, the same time every night."

"What do you mean it's time?" she asked, then realised what he meant before he had chance to answer.

"Time to go?" He nodded. "So what would happen if you just stopped walking?"

"It doesn't let me." He was halfway up the stairs now.

"What do you mean it doesn't let you?" Laura thought this statement was absurd.

"It literally doesn't let me." He was now outside the bedroom and stopped walking but as he did so he continued to move. His legs were still, yet somehow he was still heading towards the mirror, like an invisible force was pushing him or pulling him. "See. There's no use fighting it. Believe me I've tried." He started walking again. "I'll see you tomorrow night?" He asked just as he stepped into the mirror.

"I'll be here," she answered just in time as he disappeared once again back into the mirror.

Chapter 14

The house felt bereft and empty once Ben had left it and Laura's mood felt the same. She went back downstairs, washed up the mugs, and threw the biscuit wrapper and banana skins in the bin, before returning upstairs and getting into bed. She knew she wouldn't sleep so instead she propped herself up against the pillows and pulled out her notebook and pen. She read and re-read the pages about Walter Matthews and his daughter Lauren.

All the information about his childhood was the same as Ben's but how could that be? They were two separate people but with the same story and living in the same house at the same time.

"How can that be possible?" Laura spoke out loud but no answer came. She knew she had never seen any mention of a Ben living here but how could his story be exactly the same even down to the year of his birth?

Turning to the back of the book where she kept her notes on Ben, Laura wrote down some questions she needed the answers to. She would have to go carefully though as she got the feeling he thought she still didn't believe him. Firstly she wanted to know his surname and date of birth. His parents' names would also be useful and she was determined to find out more about the cameo. Ben had been convinced it was the same one, but if it was then why and when had the writing appeared on the back of it?

She could have kicked herself for leaving it back in London. If only she had brought it with her. But it was no good worrying about that now. She would bring it with her next time she came. She laughed at this comment. Only a few months ago the thought of this place sent shivers down her spine but now she was planning visit after visit. She had to admit the presence of the extremely handsome young man in the house helped allay her fears.

Laura began to wonder about the mirror, did it have to be in this room to work? Did it have to be in the house to work? Could Ben even leave the house? She added these questions to the notebook as well then switched off the big light but left the lamp on and wriggled down under the covers.

She slept surprisingly well and awoke to a bright spring morning. The birds were chirping outside the window, some still busy with their babies, others just enjoying the sunshine and letting everyone know about it. It was already ten o'clock and Laura cursed herself for not getting up earlier.

Dragging herself out of bed she ran a bath, just a small one today as she didn't have the luxury of a soak. She had planned to get on with painting the fence, but she felt the irresistible urge to go and buy some slightly more flattering clothes and headed into town instead.

She drove past the retail park then doubled back and impulsively bought a fridge which just fitted in the boot of the car once she had worked out how to fold down the seats and remove the parcel shelf. She took it straight back to the house, unpacked it and plugged it in. Then instead of clothes shopping she headed off to the supermarket.

After a quick flick through google she made a list of all the things that Ben would be missing or would never have even seen and she bought as many of these things as she could. Exotic fruits, meat, chocolate, cakes, and even the humble white loaf was scarce in the war, she discovered.

Laura began planning a kind of indoor picnic in her head with all the delicious finger food that came with it. Mini sausages, pork pie, little cakes, sandwiches, and a couple of bottles of wine. She even purchased new wine glasses and a posh picnic hamper for authenticity. She felt like she was preparing for a date, which in a way she was. She was beginning to enjoy Ben's company, now she knew he wasn't a random madman but a perfectly sane thirty something who just happened to live in the 1940s.

The fridge was bulging with all the newly purchased goodies and as it was only two o'clock she decided to start on the fence after all. Pulling on her really old tracksuit bottoms and tatty shirt she popped open the first tin, gave it a stir and got busy. It was oddly therapeutic painting panel after panel. Her iPhone shuffled its way through the playlist and she sang along, sometimes adding in the odd twirl or quick step if it was a more upbeat song. Justin Timberlake's *I Can't Stop the Feeling* came on and she found herself shimmying and swaying her hips as she painted.

She finished the last panel just as the light was beginning to fade and headed back into the house. She had a few hours till Ben would be here again. Not for the first time that day she found herself wondering what he was doing back in 1942. Had it been such a sunny day there as well? Had he been to church or for a walk in the park? Had he had Sunday dinner? Was it even Sunday in his time? What if he wasn't hungry when he came? Then she remembered the biscuits and bananas and knew that even if he had eaten he would probably still find room for more.

The butterflies were back in her stomach and she cursed herself again for not going and buying a new top and some jeans, so she wore the same thing she had worn the night before, hoping that as he was from a time when people had very little of anything he wouldn't mind that she was wearing the same outfit two nights in a row. She was ready far too early so put a film on her laptop, an old favourite, *Dirty Dancing*. She knew it off by heart and had watched it so many times, but that just made her love it more. She found herself yawning, she hadn't realised how tired she was after all that painting this afternoon so she closed her eyes just for a second.

"What the bloody hell are you watching?" Ben's raised voice startled her awake and for a few seconds she was a little confused. "What is that thing?" He pointed to the laptop. "And why is there pornography on it?" Laura shook her head trying to wake up.

"This is called a laptop." She paused the film, then turned it off as she realised the paused screen was of Patrick Swayze kissing Jennifer Grey's bare shoulders. "It's a small, portable computer which you can watch films on."

"What's a computer?" He examined it closely. "Looks like a typewriter." He picked it up and began pressing buttons. Patrick and Jennifer came back on the screen. "Jesus, Mary and Joseph will you get rid of that filth. What is a young girl like you doing watching something like that? Don't tell me you're all sexual delinquents in the future?"

Laura ejected the disc which Ben instantly took out of her hand.

"That is called a DVD." She explained, knowing that this didn't actually explain anything to him at all. "You watch films at the cinema using a projector right?" Ben nodded, still in shock from what he had just seen but intrigued by this new technology. "Well this little disc has all the information on it, like the reel of tape at the cinema. When you put the disc in here it projects the film onto the screen like the projector does at the cinema."

"Is that all it does?" Ben was fascinated. "I mean the fact that you can watch a film in your own home is amazing enough although your choice of film leaves little to the imagination. But can it do anything else? What are all the keys for?"

"There are worse films than that, I can tell you." Laura wondered how he would've reacted to something like *Fifty Shades of Grey* and giggled.

"I don't think it's funny in the slightest," Ben said rather prudishly.

"It's only a bit of sex." Laura was still giggling; in fact it was threatening to turn into laughter if she wasn't careful.

"A bit of sex!" His voice was raised again. "Are you really that flippant about sex in this century?"

"It's just sex!" Laura remarked. "Everyone does it." She wished she hadn't said this last statement as a look of disgust came over Ben's face.

"Do you do it?" She didn't know how best to answer this.

"Yes … no … sometimes." She shrugged her shoulders. "Do you?"

"I most certainly do not." He folded his arms crossly. "I'm not married and neither I believe are you."

"It's very different now." The laughter had completely vanished at the stern look she was now getting. "Has been for quite a few decades. People have sex because they love each other whether they are married or not." She didn't think explaining drunken one-night stands would go down too well at this point so stuck to sex in relationships.

"Well I've never heard the like of it." He handed her back the DVD he was still holding. "I think I'll head home for now."

"Don't be like that." Laura pleaded. "I've got a surprise for you."

"I think its best I just get home for tonight." He started heading for the mirror.

"I've brought us a picnic." He stopped walking. "With sausages, pork pie, cakes, and biscuits." He turned round. "Just come and see." He followed her downstairs to where she had laid out a picnic blanket on the table in the kitchen and the hamper was open with all the food she had bought earlier on display.

"I suppose it would be rude to refuse after all the trouble you've obviously gone to." He sat down; his eyes wide with delight but still he restrained himself.

"Ham sandwich?" Laura handed him a plate of neatly cut finger sandwiches of which he daintily took one, bit gently into it before forgetting the earlier unpleasantness and stuffing it all in quickly followed by a couple of sausages and a piece of pork pie.

"Where did you get all this?" He picked up a piece of chocolate cake before continuing to eat sandwiches.

"From the supermarket. There aren't any food shortages anymore." She didn't think this would tell him either way who won the war, just that the war was obviously over.

"They have those in America." He had paused to take a sip of wine. "Wow, that's good." He downed the glass quickly before pouring another. "Do we have them here now?"

"Hundreds of them." She wished she could show him. "Have you tried going outside? Maybe I could take you one night?"

"I've been to the end of the back garden and I've walked to the front gate but I didn't seem to be able to go any further." He was munching crisps now. "Why do you think this is happening?"

"I really don't know." She wished she did. "Has anything like this happened before?"

"You mean have I walked through mirrors into different centuries before?" He laughed gently. "No, this is my first time." He smiled at her with raised eyebrows and just a subtle hint of innuendo.

"Is it hot in here?" Laura felt her cheeks going red and stood up to open the window, fanning herself as she leaned up against the wall.

"Perhaps it was when you came here." He got up and walked towards her. Placing each hand on the wall, one either side of her he leaned closer. "Perhaps we're connected in some way," he whispered in her ear.

His voice sent a tiny shiver down her neck but she wasn't cold. Dear God, she wasn't cold in the slightest. Where had the prudish man from earlier gone? Here he was almost kissing her. Then she remembered the two bottles of wine he had almost devoured on his own and vowed to get him drunk more often.

"Maybe," she squeaked, not trusting her voice as he caressed her cheek with the back of his hand then ran his thumb over her lip.

"So beautiful," he murmured bringing his mouth closer and closer to hers. Laura shut her eyes in anticipation, her breathing shaky.

Hurry up and kiss me already, she thought to herself then opened her eyes when no kiss came. Ben was nowhere in sight so she called his name.

"Bloody timing eh?" She followed his voice to find him heading up the stairs and after checking her watch found it to be two minutes to three. "Shall we continue this tomorrow?" He held out his hand towards her and she took it, falling into step beside him.

"I shall look forward to it." He raised her hand to his lips and kissed the back of it so softly that she hardly felt it but the slight touch left her tingling all over. "There was something I wanted to ask you." Laura suddenly remembered all the questions she had written down earlier.

"You'd better hurry then." They were almost at the mirror.

"What's your surname?" She tried to hold onto his other hand to stop him going through but it was no use, half his body had already vanished.

"I thought I'd already told you that." His head was the last thing to disappear. "It's Matthews."

Chapter 15

"**D**id you say Matthews?" Laura shouted after him but it was no use, the mirror had once again returned to normal and Ben was nowhere to be seen. "He can't have said Matthews?" She continued talking aloud even though nobody could hear her. "How can he be Ben Matthews? There's no Ben Matthews living here in 1942 or even before that or since." She threw herself on the bed in exasperation knowing she had to wait till tomorrow night to be able to question him further.

She changed into her pyjamas and brushed her teeth but she knew sleep would be impossible so she opened up the laptop and loaded up Genes Reunited, patting herself on the back for remembering to purchase a dongle with mobile internet. She searched and searched for a Ben Matthews but nothing even vaguely familiar or bearing any resemblance to the facts she already knew came to light and she slammed the laptop shut in frustration.

The sun was already beginning to shine and the birds were singing their dawn chorus so she decided against sleep and went downstairs to tidy up. She wrapped up what few bits of food were left and put them back in the fridge, folded up the blanket and washed up the plates and glasses.

She took the two empty bottles of wine to the recycling bin outside smiling as she remembered the kiss that had almost happened. He had been so close to her that she could feel his breath on her lips. It had felt so natural to want to kiss him as if part of her already knew what it would feel like.

There was still a whole week of the holiday left and lots of daylight hours to fill so she poured some cereal and milk into a bowl, grabbed a glass of orange juice, and sat at the table flicking through the free newspaper that had been delivered on Saturday morning. It was interesting to read about all the local goings on, some of which were in this area, and it made her remember her childhood days.

There was an article about a long serving teacher from her old primary school. The face in the photograph was familiar to Laura and then she realised that the lady retiring was her old teacher Mrs. Jones who had taught Laura, Lucy, and Beth in their last year at St. Josephine's. It also mentioned that the school was now looking for a replacement teacher to start in September as Mrs. Jones would be retiring at the end of the summer term.

Laura felt like destiny had stepped in and without a second thought she updated her CV, attached a covering letter, and sent it off to the Head Teacher. It was then she realised that she wanted nothing more than to live in this house and make her home back in Coventry. Even though it was a large city, in comparison to London it was a tiny village. The pace of life was so much slower, less traffic, less hustle and bustle, and a more relaxed way of life.

Decision made, she applied for a few more job vacancies in the local area, sent a letter of resignation to her current Head, and then set out a plan of action. The furniture in the flat was hers and although it would look lost and out of time in the house it would have to do for now. The most important thing was to get a kitchen fitted and then decorating could be done a room at a time over the summer.

Relishing the prospect of a new challenge she headed off to the retail park she had visited yesterday, then sat in the car waiting for B&Q to open as it was still only half past eight. She was the first in the store and headed straight to the kitchen department. Here she chose country cottage style cabinets to complement the house. She would have loved an Aga but money wouldn't stretch that far, so a combination oven and separate hob were purchased instead. She had an American-style double fridge freezer back at the flat, it took up most of the kitchen there but would fit perfectly into the corner of the kitchen in the house.

She picked out various roses and bedding plants for the garden and even found a spray treatment for the apple trees. She considered buying a mower but as the gardeners had offered to cut the grass every other week for a very reasonable price she decided against it, relieved that that chore had been taken out of her hands.

Pushing her trolley full of goods and armed with more wallpaper samples and tiny pots of paint she filled the boot of the car and also the back seat before heading back home. The kitchen fitters were due to start in two weeks' time and Laura popped in to ask Mrs. Rogers if she would open the door for them when they came, keep an eye on them, and lock up after they'd gone. Mrs. Rogers said yes straight away, eager to be the centre of anything that was going on in the street. She invited Laura in for a chat which she declined due to wanting to get out in the garden and somehow found Mrs. Rogers following her over the road to give her advice on the best positions for the various plants.

Laura found her knowledge extremely valuable and enjoyed showing her the old air raid shelter. Mrs. Rogers was of course full of information.

"Mr. Matthews built this, you know?" They were sitting on the two beds after having bashed as much dust out of them as they could. "Being a builder he wasn't content with just your ordinary Anderson shelter: he wanted a proper one where they'd be as safe as they could be." Laura listened intently. "He told me and my brother all about it this one autumn day when we'd been over for some apples for Mum to make a pie."

"It must have been exciting for you to see a real air raid shelter?" Laura had only ever seen the mock up one in the Transport Museum in town.

"It was 1965, I was eight and my brother Bobby was ten. We'd always had apples from Mr. Matthews' trees for as long as I can remember but we'd never seen the shelter before." Mrs. Rogers gaze drifted away as she shared the memory. "I don't know whether it was because it was twenty years since the end of the war, we'd had a little street party to celebrate not long before, maybe it had brought back memories for him but when me and Bobby popped our heads over the gate we could see this big old door wide open." She pointed to the gap left open by the metal sheet. "Of course it was on proper hinges then, it didn't just lie on the ground like it does now, but inside hasn't changed a bit." She scanned the place with her eyes. "Those were his mum's." She tilted her head towards the magazines on the table. "He told us how he used to have to carry his poor mum down here once she became bedridden and then when she died he would sit here on his own and play cards."

"I thought he had a wife?" Laura was enjoying the story immensely.

"Oh he did, lovey," Mrs. Rogers confirmed. "But he didn't marry her till after his mother died. In fact he told us that they had their first kiss in here on the night of Coventry's last air raid."

"What a strange place for a first kiss." Laura looked at the bleakness of the walls.

"Better than some places, I can tell you." Mrs. Rogers stood up. "Well I must be off dear; Wilf will be wondering where I've got to." Laura helped her up the stairs. "Built it with his own hands you know." Mrs. Rogers started another part of the story once she was outside. "Bobby was fascinated by architecture and engineering so Mr. Matthews told him all about it. He dug the hole by hand then laid a load of cement on the bottom, built thick steel walls with more cement round the sides and on the top then covered it with soil and turf. But don't ask me how he did the air holes because I'd lost interest by then and started picking apples."

"You'll have to come round again and tell me some more stories," Laura said as Mrs. Rogers headed out of the gate and back over the road.

"That would be lovely, dear." She stopped just before her gate. "I think there are some photos of the street party we had back in '65, I'll see if I can find them for you."

"I'd love to see them," Laura shouted as a car went past and waved as Mrs. Rogers headed into her house.

The rest of the morning was spent digging and planting but by one o'clock she was flagging and remembering that she hadn't slept last night she headed in for lunch and a quick nap. She set her alarm for three o'clock, determined this time to go and buy a new outfit before Ben visited again.

She headed into town and straight to River Island. Her eyes were instantly attracted to a teeny tiny black dress that left very little to the imagination but she didn't want to shock him too much just yet so instead chose a pretty floral dress that reached just below her knees and had little cap sleeves.

Feeling very pleased with herself she went straight back to the house via Burger King and jumped straight into the bath. She spent a good hour pampering herself before logging into her emails. There was already a reply from her current school who said they were very sorry to see her go but understood her desire to return to her childhood home.

No turning back now then, she said to herself before going round the house sticking bits of wallpaper here and there and dabbing paint from the little pots onto the walls. She measured the windows and floors, noting them down in the book that Jack had started. A small feeling of anger threatened to bubble up inside at the thought of him but she pushed it back down and continued with her plans.

By the time midnight came she was dressed, hair neatly plaited, and a small amount of makeup applied to enhance rather than mask; a few squirts of her favourite Calvin Klein perfume finished off the look. At twelve twenty-two exactly the mirror turned into its puddle appearance and out strutted Chester.

"Hello boy." Laura picked him up and nuzzled her face into his head. "Where have you been? You've been away ages. Not enough mice for you here in 2016 eh?" She continued stroking him but the mirror had already turned back to its normal state. Letting the cat fall gently out of her arms she walked over to the mirror and touched it slowly. It was as it usually was, cold and hard. "Ben?" she called his name. "BEN?" she shouted the second time but even using her best teacher voice she knew she couldn't make herself heard back in the forties.

She sat on the bed cuddling Chester until he was forced back through the mirror just before three. Realising Ben wasn't coming and with the most immense feeling of disappointment she threw herself under the covers in a kiddie tantrum before remembering that the poor man was living in the middle of World War Two with a sick mother and had probably just got caught up with something far more important. She felt better after that and promptly fell asleep.

Tuesday flew by once again in a blur of gardening and decorating plans and before she knew it she was waiting for Ben to appear. The time ticked on and on, no Ben, no Chester, nothing. The mirror stayed flat and unyielding. When this happened again on Wednesday and Thursday night Laura decided enough was enough and on Friday morning she packed her things, locked up the house, left a spare key with Mrs. Rogers, and drove back down to London vowing to stay off men for good.

Chapter 16
July 2016

The last of her things were packed into the back of her newly acquired Vauxhall Astra. She had waved off the removal van and was now waiting for the landlord to finish inspecting the flat so she could have her deposit bond back and hand him the keys. She was a little sad to be leaving London but also excited by her new job and the new house.

Laura hadn't been back to Coventry since the half term holiday. She had had an interview over Skype with the Head Teacher at St. Josephine's and they had offered her the teaching position the next day which she had immediately accepted.

There had been lots of tears on both sides yesterday afternoon as the children had said goodbye at the end of the summer term. This was usually the case as she always grew attached to her students, but this time had been different as she knew she wouldn't be seeing them again.

Mrs. Rogers had phoned her the other week to say that the kitchen was fully fitted and she'd been over and tested all the appliances for her, *and had a good nose around the house too*, Laura thought to herself but didn't begrudge her, after all the house had been a part of her childhood.

It wasn't long before she was on her way up to Coventry, the stereo blasting out in the car. Laura had tried not to think of Ben over the past few weeks. She was sure there was a rational explanation for why he hadn't come back after that eventful night but surely he must have known she was waiting for him and could have at least just popped in to tell her what was going on.

One of her current favourite songs came on, Justin Bieber's *Sorry* and she turned the volume up even louder, singing along and tapping her fingers on the steering wheel. She passed the removal truck just on the outskirts of London and had a traffic- and stress-free run all the way to Coventry, arriving a little after eleven a.m.

It was already warm and the weather forecast promised the hottest day of the year so she flung open all the windows in every room before inspecting the new kitchen for herself. She didn't know if Ben had been here or not as the workmen would have made hot drinks for themselves, and as everything was neat and tidy she assumed that Mrs. Rogers had cleaned up after them.

"Yoo hoo!" came a voice from the front door.

"Speak of the devil and he shall appear." Laura recognised Mrs. Rogers' voice instantly. "Come on in Mrs. Rogers, I'm just putting the kettle on."

"How lovely dear." She was in the kitchen quicker than her slightly chubby frame should have allowed. "I won't stop though; I know you'll have lots to do. I just wanted to show you these." She handed Laura a packet. "Just a few old photographs I looked out for you. And I thought this would interest you as well." She gave her a book about the Coventry Blitz. "There's an article in there about Mr. Matthews and his air raid shelter. I'd forgotten all about it." Laura wanted nothing more than to sit down and look at the photos and book straight away but politeness restrained her.

"Are you sure you wouldn't like a cuppa?" She secretly hoped she would say no.

"No, no dearie." Mrs. Rogers headed back into the hallway with Laura following. "I must get back to Wilf;

he does worry when I'm not there." She had just stepped out of the front door when she turned back round. "Before I forget, I'm sure it's nothing but I have seen the lights on a few times in the middle of the night."

"I set them on a timer before I left." Laura thought quickly and Mrs. Rogers seemed satisfied with the answer.

"Well I'll be off then." And with that she was down the path, through the gate, over the road, and back in her own house. Laura shut the door and dashed back to the kitchen. Instead of the fold up table and chairs that Jack had brought with them that first day there was now a black marbled top breakfast bar and two black high-backed stools. She grabbed the photos first and began flicking through them.

There were pictures of Mrs. Rogers and someone who Laura assumed to be her brother Bobby playing in the street. Some were in colour and some black and white. A few photos of them were in the garden of Laura's house, climbing up the trees and even one of Bobby popping his head out of the air raid shelter waving a Union Jack flag. Then she saw the ones that she had been waiting to see.

The street was festooned with flags and a long trestle table was set up in the middle of the road, she could see the odd car parked up and even these had been bedecked with bunting. The table was groaning under the weight of the food and drink and all the children had party hats on. Laura recognised Mrs. Rogers and her brother instantly but no one else in the pictures were familiar to her at all.

"It's me again, dearie." Mrs. Rogers' voice came through the letter box. "I forgot you wouldn't know who anyone was in those photos." Laura had already opened the door to her, photographs in hand. "Now I don't remember everyone but that's me and Bobby right there, next to us is Martha and Mary Simpkins, Johnny Neville is right on the end, and that there is Lauren Matthews." Laura's eyes focused on the tall girl standing near to the front of the picture.

She was around twenty years old with dark red hair and even through the camera lens you could see startling blue eyes. *So this is Lauren Matthews who becomes Lauren Edwards and gives me this house.* Laura was glad to have a face to the name now but it still didn't help solve the mystery as to why.

"Is Walter Matthews in any of these?" Laura would love to know what he looked like as an adult; she only had the vision of him as a young boy in her head.

"Walter who dear?" Mrs. Rogers looked at her confused.

"Walter Matthews." Laura repeated again. "Lauren's father, the man who owned this house?"

"I don't know any Walter Matthews, dearie." Mrs. Rogers scanned through the photos quickly. "Thought as much." She nodded to herself. "Mr. Matthews took all these pictures, that's why he isn't in them." Silence followed.

"Walter Matthews?" Laura asked a third time.

"Why do you keep asking about a Walter Matthews?" Mrs. Rogers gave her back the photos.

"Because Walter Matthews was Lauren's father." Laura was getting exasperated now but intended to keep her cool.

"No, no, no my dear." Mrs. Rogers shook her head. "Mr. Matthews wasn't called Walter." A lorry pulling up outside heralded the arrival of the removal van. "Well, I'd best let you get on dear, you'll have so much to do now all your furniture has arrived." She was already down the path and through the gate despite Laura's attempts to stop her. "Don't be silly dear, you don't want me in the way. I'll pop over in a few days when you've settled in." And with a quick 'hello dearies' to the removal men she was gone.

The day passed in a blur of tea making, unpacking, and moving stuff around. Luckily her small amount of furniture didn't fill all the rooms in the house. Lacking a table and chairs, the dining room became the dumping ground for empty boxes and unsorted crates. As she knew it would, her small sofa looked lost in the living room and without shelves she just left the books and DVDs stacked up in their boxes.

She pushed the mirror against the wall in the front bedroom so it didn't get damaged while her dressing table was moved in and her suitcases full of clothes and shoes were unceremoniously dumped on the bed and floor. Once the removal van was empty and the two men had had their final cup of tea, Laura started on the bathroom. It took half an hour to find all her toiletries even though she had made sure she'd packed them in the box marked *bathroom*.

Then she unpacked the boxes marked *kitchen*, loving the cupboards and wishing she had bought all new stuff to go in them instead of the tatty old, mismatched plates and cups that she owned. The house was definitely meant for a family, far too big for her on her own and again she found herself wondering if she would ever settle down and have children.

Shaking herself out of the pessimistic mood she had just sunk into she looked at her watch, and realising it was almost six o'clock and she hadn't eaten since the hastily snatched slice of toast this morning, she popped a chilli con carne into the microwave and sat at the breakfast bar while she waited for it to ping.

The Coventry Blitz book that Mrs. Rogers had given her caught her eye and she flicked through it. The pictures of the destroyed buildings amazed Laura and she couldn't believe how people had continued to live their normal lives with all the destruction and never-ending threat of further bombs looming over their heads.

She came to the section about air raid shelters and how people had built the government-issued Anderson shelters in their gardens. Laura couldn't imagine how people spent hours and hours, night after night in these dark and damp conditions. There was even a section about the Morrison shelter which was for people without gardens. This was even more terrifying to Laura. It was 2 metres by 1.2 metres and just ¾ of a metre high and you crawled into it when the air raid siren went off.

Again, Laura was in awe of this generation and how they endured hardship and sacrifice day after day, week after week, month after month. Even after the war had ended it took years for their lives to return to normal, and for most, the loss of loved ones meant even more suffering. Turning to the final chapter in the book Laura stopped dead at the man staring up at her from the page.

She scanned the article quickly; it was about a Coventry man who had built his own air raid shelter and kept it in perfect condition as a tribute to his late wife as they had shared their first kiss in there on the night of Coventry's last air raid the third of August 1942. The article named the couple only as Mr. and Mrs. Matthews but the man in the photograph, standing by the entrance to the air raid shelter in his garden, even though he was older and with slightly greying hair, was undoubtedly Ben.

Chapter 17

Laura grabbed the book and went straight over to see Mrs. Rogers.

"We were just finishing the washing up, wasn't we Wilf?" She beckoned Laura into the house as she called down the hallway to the kitchen.

"Yes dear," came the male reply.

"What can I help you with, dearie?" Mrs. Rogers showed her into the extremely floral and overly cluttered front room. Flowers were everywhere, on the carpets, the curtains, the wallpaper, and the cushions. There were even pictures of flowers on the walls and numerous vases full of fresh flowers. The clashes of scents and colours assaulted Laura's nose and made her eyes water.

"The man in the book … Mr. Matthews?" She began tentatively, opening the book to the relevant page.

"There he is." She smiled adoringly. "Lovely man he was, so kind to me and Bobby. Mum always said what a proper gent he was, so sad about his poor wife though."

"What was his first name?" Laura wanted the answer to this question before any others.

"Ben," Mrs. Rogers stated. "We always called him Mr. Matthews of course but my dad called him Ben. We never knew his wife, she died in 1943 I think Mum said and they moved here in 1954 just after they got married, so Lauren would have been eleven I think." Laura's mind was working overtime. So if Ben was Lauren's father who on earth was Walter Matthews? And why was there that photo in the *Evening Telegraph* of Walter Matthews with his mother Iris outside the house if it was Ben Matthews that owned the house?

"I don't suppose you remember his wife's name or his mother's name do you?" Laura was clinging on to straws here.

"I'm ever so sorry I don't, before my time you see, and before Mum and Dad's as well." Mrs. Rogers sat down in one of the soft looking chairs. "Do sit down dear, you look worn out."

"I'm okay thank you Mrs. Rogers." Laura stayed standing. "I'll get back now, so much to do."

"Please call me Agnes." Mrs. Rogers got back up and walked her to the door. "Far too formal to be calling me Mrs. Rogers all the time, especially now we're neighbours."

"I will do, Mrs. Rogers … I mean Agnes." Laura paused just before she opened the door. "So you don't remember a Walter Matthews living at the house or even visiting the house at all?"

"Never heard of him." Agnes shook her head. "Only ever saw Mr. Matthews and Lauren and then her husband to be … oh what was his name … Graham, that's it, Graham Edwards."

"Thanks again, Agnes." The name felt unfamiliar on her tongue and she hesitated as she said it. "Bye Wilf," she called to the still unknown man in the kitchen and received a muffled goodbye in return.

The chilli was still warm when she got back and she ate it quickly. Her mind was alive with the new questions that her conversation with Mrs. Rogers … *Agnes*, she corrected herself, had uncovered. So Ben was Lauren's father, not Walter? Or had Walter died and Ben adopted her? Was Ben a long-lost cousin? Her head ached from the thinking. All she knew for certain that if the dates were true then Ben would soon be sharing his first kiss with his wife-to-be who would then die the following year. Poor man, to have such a fate before him. Did he already know his wife? Was it someone he saw every day or were they yet to meet?

Laura took the book and photos to her car; she couldn't risk Ben seeing them, and how could she tell him he had that future to look forward to? She wanted a long soak in the bath before tackling her mountain of clothes, so she headed upstairs, filled the bath as high as she dared, and lay there for what felt like hours, letting the warm water and bubbles soothe her aching muscles and head.

She begrudgingly dragged herself out around half past nine, wrapped a towel around her head, and pulled on her rabbit onesie with the fluffy bunny tail and floppy ears on the hood. She emptied each suitcase onto the bed in turn and hung clothes up or put them in drawers and placed her shoes neatly on the new shoe rack she had bought specifically to fit in her new much larger wardrobe.

A sudden thud from behind made her jump and she turned to find Ben lying in a crumpled heap on the floor, half of him up against the wall.

"A little help, please?" He looked over to her and she immediately dashed over, dragging the mirror back a little way to allow him to move. "Why's the mirror there?" He brushed himself down and rubbed his arms and head where he had knocked them against the wall.

"I'd moved it out of the way so it didn't get broken." Her heart had skipped a beat at the sight of him.

"Bloody stupid thing to do." He turned the mirror round and put it back in its normal place.

"I thought it was quite a sensible thing to do actually." Laura was a little miffed that his first words after two months apart were a rebuke. "If the removal men had broken it then you wouldn't be here, would you."

"Removal men?" He looked at her, a slow smile creeping over his face. "Have you moved here? Permanently?"

"Just today." His smile was contagious and she soon found herself grinning like a Cheshire cat. "I've got six weeks before I start my new job teaching at my old primary school."

"You never told me you were a teacher." He started looking around the room, picking up things and examining them with interest.

"You never asked." She watched with amusement as he tried to figure out the iPod player that was sitting in the dock and laughed as he shot backwards when it turned on, blasting out *Candy Man* by Christina Aguilera.

"Well, I like the tune," he said after it had finished. "The words are a little risqué though." Laura laughed. "And what on earth are you wearing?"

"It's called a onesie." She twirled round to show him the fluffy tail on the back. "Do you like it?"

"And what's the purpose of this onesie?" He flicked the tail and pulled at the ears. "Looks like a fancy-dress costume to me."

"They're like pyjamas but all in one so they're much warmer." Then she remembered it was the summer. "And comfy too."

"You do have some strange things in this century." He looked on the bed where she had just been unpacking her underwear. "What in God's name is this?" He picked up one of Laura's tiny, black, lacy thongs.

"Erm …" Laura snatched it out of his hand and hastily threw the duvet over the rest of her things. "Would you believe me if I said pants?"

"Those teeny things were pants?" Laura nodded. "But they wouldn't cover anything."

"That's kind of the point." She couldn't believe she was explaining what a thong was. "It's so you don't see them under your clothes."

"Mind boggling." Ben looked baffled. "How on earth would you see pants under clothes?"

"If they're tight fitting." Laura desperately wanted to change the subject. "So, where were you before? I waited night after night for you."

"I'm so sorry about that." The thong was instantly forgotten. "Mother took a real bad turn and I couldn't leave her. Dorothy from down the road was a Godsend. She used to sit with Mother in the night for a few hours so I could get some sleep, still had to go to work you know and I couldn't really be popping in and out of mirrors in front of her could I?"

"That's awful." Laura felt instantly guilty. "Is your mum okay now?"

"She died on the twelfth of June." Ben wiped a tear from his eye.

"Oh Ben." She flung her arms round him. "I don't know what to say."

"It's fine." He hugged her back. "She'd been poorly for a while so it was a blessing for her in the end. I couldn't stand to see her in so much pain." They pulled apart awkwardly. "At least I was with her when it happened. Dorothy had been sitting with her again while I'd gone to work but she'd sent her son to fetch me as Mother had taken a turn for the worse. I just made it back in time to say goodbye."

"Lucky that Dorothy was there." Laura couldn't help the small stab of jealousy.

"She has been amazing." Ben's voice was full of enthusiasm. "Her husband was killed in action last year leaving her a widow with a young son to look after, yet she stayed day and night with Mother and has looked after me since she died." Laura had the immediate thought that Dorothy was Ben's future wife. "I don't know what I would have done without her."

"I wish I'd been able to help." She knew this would have been impossible but it didn't stop her wishing it.

"That would have been nice but I'm not sure how Mother would have reacted to a stranger looking after her." He went quiet all of a sudden. "Where have you been for the past two months? I've really missed you."

"I've been so busy sorting everything out for the move here that I just didn't get time to come back." She knew this was a lie but he didn't need to know that. "I missed you too." There was a long pause before either of them spoke again. "I've got the cameo if you want to have a look." His eyes lit up. "I know you said it probably wasn't the same one but at least we can rule it out." She walked off down the stairs with Ben following behind.

"You've got a lot of stuff." He remarked as he looked at all the boxes still to be emptied in the dining room.

"It's amazing what you accumulate over the years." She searched through the boxes. "Where is it?"

"What are we looking for?" Ben asked. "Maybe I can help?"

"It's a small black case, about this size." Laura mapped out the shape with her hands. "Has a little handle on it. All my jewellery is in it." Ben started lifting boxes and moving things around.

"Is it inside another box maybe?" He asked after they'd been looking for ten minutes.

"No." She put her hand to her head. "I distinctly remember putting it on the shelf by the front door of the flat to bring with me in the car as I didn't want it getting lost. Maybe I left it in the car." She unlocked the front door and headed to the car before coming back empty handed.

"No luck?" Ben asked.

"I don't understand it." She was struggling to remember what happened then it dawned on her. "Shit!"

"What's the matter?" Ben ignored her swear word.

"My mum called just before I was leaving to check everything was okay," Laura recalled. "I had to go outside because the signal was awful." She wasn't about to explain about mobile phones and signals even though Ben looked a little lost in the conversation. "I got straight in the car after speaking to her and drove here."

"So you've lost the cameo?" He was able to pick up this piece of information from her words.

"It's not lost exactly," she reassured him. "I'll just have to ring the landlord in the morning and pay for it to be sent up here."

"Well, how long will that take?" He had found her box of photos and was starting to look through them, sitting himself cross legged on the floor.

"Only a few days." She sat down next to him explaining who everyone was and where they were taken. "One thing that has been bugging me since we last saw each other is your name."

"What's wrong with my name?" He put the photos down. "I chose that name, you know."

"What do you mean you chose it?" Laura was perplexed. "You mean Ben isn't your real name?"

"I wasn't born Ben if that's what you mean." The conversation was taking a strange turn. "I chose Benedict as my confirmation name and shortened it to Ben. I much prefer it to the name my parents gave me."

"You're Catholic then?" Laura didn't know much about the Catholic religion but she did know that they usually took a Saint's name when they were confirmed. Ben nodded. "So what name were you christened with?"

"Walter." Laura knew he was going to say it but it was still a shock when he actually did. "My full name is Walter George Benedict Matthews."

Chapter 18

Sunday morning dawned bright and clear but Laura hadn't slept. She had made general small talk and chit chat with Ben till the time had come for him to return to 1942 then she had sat in the kitchen with her notebook and pored over all the information she knew before and all the new information she had discovered.

Ben was Walter Matthews and Lauren's father, but that still didn't explain why she wanted her to have this house. Did she play such a big part in Lauren's life that she felt the need to leave the house to her? Why didn't it just pass to Lauren's children and grandchildren? Why hadn't Ben sold it when he no longer wanted to live there? She felt so frustrated that every time she got a question answered another two seemed to take its place.

And then there was Dorothy, she was the obvious candidate to be Ben's wife and Lauren's mother yet in all the searches Laura had done there had been no trace of her or in any of the photos that Agnes had shown her but then if she'd died in 1943 Agnes and her brother would never have known her.

Laura slammed the notebook shut in frustration and headed off to bed where she slept on and off till about ten o'clock. The bright sunny dawn had changed to a rainy morning which didn't help lift her despondent mood. She continued unpacking her clothes and then made a start on the boxes in the dining room. An unexpected knock at the door around one brought a most welcome surprise visit from Beth.

"It's so lovely to see you!" Laura hugged her tightly. "Come in, come in."

"Wow, it's a bit different to the last time I was here." Beth looked around in wonder. "I can't believe how light and airy it is." Laura showed her round the downstairs and then up into the bedrooms. "That's not the mirror is it?"

"The very same." Laura nodded.

"And this was the room that he was standing in?" Beth shivered slightly.

"Just in that corner." Laura pointed. "Right opposite the mirror."

"I don't know how you can be so calm about it." Beth went over to the mirror. "You were petrified that night."

"I know I was but things have happened since." She watched as Beth examined the mirror. "Have you got some time?"

"I have all the time in the world," Beth replied. "My wonderful husband is looking after Jessica all afternoon so I'm all yours."

"That's good news, because I have so much to tell you." They went back downstairs and over numerous cups of tea and an entire packet of shortbread biscuits Laura recounted the whole tale to Beth who listened avidly.

"This Ben that comes through the mirror is actually Walter Matthews?" It was more a question to herself rather than to Laura. "And his daughter Lauren, who hasn't been born yet in his time is the one that leaves the house to you?" This question was directed to Laura.

"By then she is called Lauren Edwards." Laura opened up her notebook. "But what's really strange is that the deeds to the house were drawn up on the day that I was born and to be given to me on my thirtieth birthday. I mean, how did she know me? And the letter that was written to me, how did they know about Jack?"

"You've got to remember that all this is the future to them and the past to you." Beth had always been the most pragmatic one. Even something as unbelievable as this she had taken in her stride and hadn't even batted an eyelid. "But now it's kind of your future as well. I mean your future and his future are obviously linked somehow but his future is also your past as well."

"You watch too much science fiction." Laura's head was beginning to hurt with all the past, present and future tenses.

"And what about the cameo?" Beth was intrigued by how this had come into Laura's possession. "It has to be the same one surely? But how on earth did it end up with some woman called Carmichael and then get given to Jack who didn't even know you then for you to happen to turn up at an antiques sale where he happened to be at that very moment. They can't all be coincidences."

"Well what else can they be?" Laura picked up the two mugs and started to wash them up. "I'm not related to Ben Matthews or Lauren Edwards. Ben is more than likely dead now and Lauren would be in her seventies. I have no connection to either of them."

"Except for the blindingly obvious fact that you are just the tiniest bit in love with him." Laura turned round sharply at Beth's comment.

"I am not," she said harshly.

"Oh come off it, Laura," Beth laughed. "I've known you long enough now to know when you like someone."

"Well, maybe just a little bit," Laura admitted for the first time.

"And you keep thinking two-dimensionally, you've got to think in the third dimension remember." Beth drew some lines and dates in the notebook.

"Although the 1940s until now are all the past to you, its Ben's future and soon to be Lauren's, and you have somehow crashed into that future but it's in your past but also your future." Her hand swirled all over the page drawing lines backwards and forwards. "Who knows what will happen in the future? I mean the past."

"Have you been drinking?" Laura was more than slightly confused at Beth's explanation and diagrams.

"You've got to think out of the box Laura." Beth shook her head. "You've got to think out of the box."

Laura thought out of the box for the next few days. She found it hard to talk to Ben because she was trying not to tell him anything about his future but desperately wanted to tell him all about her past. She had begun to decorate the rooms beginning with the living room and then her bedroom. This was easier said than done having never wallpapered before and many sheets were wasted as she tore them down in anger when the patterns didn't match.

Luckily Ben proved a dab hand and he showed her how to draw a plumb line and match the pattern before pasting the paper, not afterwards as she had been doing and then finding that the length she had cut was too short to reach the skirting board.

Before she knew it more than a week had gone by and she was finding herself enjoying Ben's company more and more but despairing as to how she could have a proper relationship with him if they could only ever see each other for a few hours every night. It was okay staying up late while she was off work but when the term started again how on earth could she miss out on sleep and still function properly in the day?

Her body had already adjusted to the later nights and she found herself sleeping in till after ten most mornings but as she would need to be up at six come September there was no way she would be able to continue with her current bedtime of three a.m., even weekends would prove difficult as she needed time for lesson planning and marking.

Even the ever-resourceful Beth didn't have an answer for this current situation and no amount of third dimensional thinking brought a solution any closer.

Using yesterday's paper, Laura taped it to the floorboards in the dining room before beginning to paint the skirting boards. She was happily singing along to Adam Lambert when the date on the paper caught her eye. It was the second of August so that meant today was the third of August, why did that date seem familiar?

Balancing the paint brush on top of the tin she sat back on her heels and rattled her brain. She went through everyone's birthdays that she knew, anniversaries, anything that might be familiar to her but nothing came to mind so she picked up the brush again and resumed her painting.

She was just coming to the end of the first wall when she heard a van pull up outside. She stretched a little to look out of the window to see the familiar brown van of UPS parked up and watched as the delivery man opened her gate and walked up the path, a brown cardboard box in his hand.

"Delivery for Miss Reynolds?" He smiled as she opened the door. Laura knew exactly what was in the parcel and she was almost rude in her excitement to shut the door and rip it open. Her jewellery case was here, it was finally here. It had taken her two days to get hold of the landlord then another two days before he confirmed that the case was indeed still in the flat, then she had to arrange for its collection and delivery to Coventry.

She clicked open the latches in anticipation and there staring at her was the little box and inside was the cameo. Laura grabbed it and virtually ran up the stairs to her bedroom. Hesitantly she held it up against the oval gap in the mirror and instantly she could see the bedroom on the other side.

Ben was standing there with his back to her and she shouted his name but he obviously didn't hear her. She was just about to see if the cameo fitted in the gap when a movement at the door caught her eye. She drew her hand back slightly and watched as a tall, slim, dark-haired woman walked into the bedroom wearing a man's dressing gown and rubbing her wet hair with a towel.

Laura couldn't take her eyes off of her. She was stunningly beautiful and walked with a sway of the hips that Laura envied. She threw the towel onto the bed and sauntered up to Ben, the dressing gown revealing more than an eyeful of ample cleavage. The woman reached up to caress Ben's face and as Laura pulled the cameo away, the image instantly faded as did Laura's hopes.

Chapter 19
August 2016

*W*ell, *what on earth were you expecting to happen?* a little voice inside Laura's head asked. *He's not going to fall for someone who swears, watches rude films, and wears scanty underwear.* Laura shook her head as if to stop the voice from speaking. *You always knew it would never work; how could it have worked?* the voice continued. *You live in different centuries and can only see each other at night: how could that have even begun to work?*

She put the cameo on her dressing table with a tinge of sadness. She had been so eager to see if it was the same cameo; it obviously was but she wasn't intending to see what happened if she put it back in its rightful place at the top of the mirror: well, not right now she wasn't anyway.

Thinking back to the last time she had seen Ben in the mirror, she had been holding the cameo that time as well but as soon as he had moved away the image had faded, maybe it only worked when he was close to the mirror on the other side. Well, she would try later when Ben came through and she knew he was on his own. She had no desire to watch him being seduced by Dorothy.

This thought was like an arrow through her heart. She hadn't realised how strong her feelings for him had grown. *He obviously wasn't as innocent as he made himself out to be,* she thought to herself. *There he was unmarried, as was Dorothy if she recalled correctly, and where was her son? Why wasn't Ben at work? Why was she wet in the middle of the day?* Laura was fed up with questions. She went back to her painting and tried to push the image of Ben and Dorothy out of her head every time it crept in.

The day passed so slowly that Laura had even had time to make a brief plan of action before Ben appeared at precisely twelve twenty-two. He beamed from ear to ear when he saw her sitting on the bed and all her careful planning went out the window.

"Had a nice day have you?" She felt like a jealous wife.

"Lovely, thank you." He plonked himself next to her on the bed.

"Seen anyone special, have you?" She couldn't help the small amount of malice that crept into her voice.

"Not really." Ben looked at her quizzically. "Are you okay?

"I'm fine." She gave a wry smile. "I've been here on my own all day painting." She emphasised the on my own part.

"Have the paint fumes given you a headache?" He gently laid a hand on her forehead. "You feel a little hot, are you sure you're feeling okay?"

"I'm fine," she repeated a little harsher than she intended.

"I think I'll go home." Ben stood up. "You're obviously not feeling very well." He gave her a quick peck on the cheek. "I'll see you tomorrow." And with that he was gone, back through the mirror.

Laura stood up, cursed, stomped her feet, and cursed again. Why had she acted like that? He didn't owe her anything, they weren't a couple, if he wanted to see another woman he was a free agent, and after all, she knew he would soon be meeting his wife. A light bulb went off in her head.

"The third of August 1942, of course." She spoke out loud and reached for the Coventry Blitz book. "The day he shared his first kiss with his future wife." So that was obviously why Dorothy had been there. There must have been an air raid, perhaps it was raining and she'd got wet in the downpour. Feeling guilty about her treatment of Ben she took the cameo from the dressing table and held it to the mirror; nothing happened.

"Well, here goes nothing." She placed the cameo into the hole and it clicked into place. Instantly the hard glass turned into a puddle, as it did when Ben came through. Laura stared at it for a few minutes and as it shimmered and shone she could just make out the bedroom behind. Taking a deep breath and with eyes tight shut she stepped through.

She opened her eyes one at a time and looked around. The bedroom was as it had been the very first time she had seen it that day through the mirror. Heavy red curtains were shut tight, a large ornate dressing table stood under the window and a four-poster bed stood in the middle of the room against the back wall. It was so strange seeing the room from the opposite angle. She turned back to check the mirror. It had returned to its hard glass form but her room was clearly visible on the other side and when she reached out to touch it, the shimmering began again.

Not knowing how long she had before it wore off, she called out for Ben. He was there almost instantly.

"How on earth?" He looked at her, then at the mirror. "The cameo?" Laura nodded.

"It came earlier." Laura looked at the cameo on this side of the mirror for the first time. It was unmistakably the same one. "I saw you and … erm … a friend in here." She didn't quite know what else to say.

"You mean Dorothy?" Laura nodded. "She'd locked herself out of her house and it was pouring it down earlier. She keeps a spare key here but I was at work so she waited till I came home for lunch and I let her in. She was soaked to the skin by then so I made her a hot drink while she dried off."

A sudden wailing noise pierced the air and Laura put her hands on her ears.

"What the hell is that?" But Laura already knew what it was and she was terrified.

"It's the air raid siren." Ben took her hand and almost pulled her out of the bedroom and down the stairs. "We have to go to the shelter." The sound was deafening and Laura's mind was racing. She'd only gone and popped into 1942 when Coventry was experiencing its last air raid. Why hadn't she waited? Why had she come through today of all days?

"Let's just go back through the mirror?" She pulled against him. "We can go back to my time where it's safe." She started to run back up the stairs but Ben had grabbed her hand again and was frantically pulling her out towards the back garden.

"It's too late. Can't you hear them?" Laura could hear nothing but the shrill siren going on and on. They were in the garden now and Ben had managed to open the door to the shelter with one hand while ushering her inside with the other. Then as quickly as the siren had started it stopped.

"We can go back in now." Laura breathed a sigh of relief.

"What do you mean?" Ben looked at her confused. "That's just the start. We have to wait for the all clear. And you seriously can't hear them?" The door to the shelter was still open and she was standing on the top step. She strained her ears and could hear the very quiet rumble of an engine. It grew louder and louder and was joined by numerous other rumbles. Then the distinct whizz of something flying through the air and landing with a huge thud filled the sky and Ben pulled her in, bolting the door behind her.

"We're in an air raid." Laura was in shock as Ben carefully led her down the steps to one of the beds. "We're really in a real air raid." She was shaking so he placed a blanket round her shoulders before lighting the candles and lamps. They gave a spooky glow to the room and cast eerie shadows on the wall. The thuds and whizzes continued outside and one in particular made Laura jump so Ben put his arm round her.

"I know they sound close," he reassured her. "But they're a good few miles away. Nothing like the ones back in 1940."

"That was when the cathedral was destroyed." Laura felt better with him so close.

"And half the town." He held her hand with his free hand. "But I suppose you know all about it?" Laura nodded.

"I'd love to have seen the cathedral before it was burnt down," she said. "The new one is lovely but it's so sad to see the ruins of the old one." She spoke without thinking.

"They build a new one do they?" This was the first time she had let anything slip about the future.

"Yes, right next to the walls of the old one." She'd said it now and didn't think him knowing about the new cathedral would affect his future in anyway.

"What's it like?" His eyes were shining with interest.

"Very modern really. Lots of glass and a huge ceiling." She was trying to remember as much as she could. "I haven't been there since we visited with the school when I was little, but I know that the real charred cross is kept in the new cathedral."

"The charred cross?" Ben was thoughtful for a while. "You mean the two burnt timbers that fell from the roof into the shape of a cross during those first few raids. Imagine keeping that all this time." He let go of her hand and reached over to the table. "Dorothy left a couple of magazines in here; do you want to read them? It might take your mind off the noise." She smiled as she realised they were the exact copies of the ones in the shelter back in her time only here they were in pristine condition, so they hadn't been his mother's magazines after all.

"I'm okay." The noises outside seemed to have quietened down.

"Looks like it might be over." Ben stood up and Laura followed. "They'll sound the all clear in a minute." He took her hand again and turned her to face him before taking her other hand in his. "Are you sure you're okay? I don't just mean with the air raid, you were very strange earlier, you got me worried."

"Must have been the paint like you said." She was enjoying standing there holding hands with him in the candlelight. It was so surreal to be in the aftermath of an air raid yet so calm. But Ben had remained calm the whole time while she had been, well, petrified was the only word to describe it.

For a while they just stood there, holding hands in the flickering light, not saying anything but it wasn't awkward, it just felt right. Ben leaned towards her, closer and closer and then boom. The whole shelter shook and they were knocked backwards onto the bed, Ben lying on top of Laura.

"Are you hurt?" He examined her face closely.

"I don't think so." She was a little shocked by the ordeal but not hurt.

"Must have been a stray." He brushed a strand of hair away from her eyes. "It felt a bit close for comfort that one." He made to move away from her.

"Don't move just yet." She coiled her arms round his neck and pulled him in close. "Not just yet." She arched her back up towards him so their lips were almost touching. "Isn't there something you'd like to do first?" Her voice was a whisper against his skin and without hesitation he touched his mouth to hers, gently at first, so gently, then with a surging passion that they'd both been fighting for weeks.

Chapter 20

The 'all clear' siren broke them apart and Ben hastily disentangled himself and stood up.

"I am so sorry," he apologised. "I shouldn't have taken advantage of you like that."

"I think you'll find that I took advantage of you." Laura took his hand as he helped her up off the bed. "It's okay you know; it was just a kiss." *Just a kiss*, she thought to herself, but what a kiss. It had turned her insides to jelly and transported her far, far away from the damp and dark room they were actually in.

"But …" She silenced him with another kiss; this time he smiled as they drew apart.

"Does that mean we can go back in the house now?" She was starting to feel a little chilly down in the shelter, even if it was August.

"Yes, I told you it wouldn't be long." He looked at his watch. "Wow, maybe not, we've been down here nearly four hours."

"Four hours?" Laura looked at her own watch. "Crikey, it's five o'clock." They both looked at each other as the realisation of what was happening dawned on them at the same time.

"Why haven't you gone back to your time?" Ben blew out the candles but took the lamp to light their way up the steps. There was an orange glow to the left of the house, a little in the distance. "Looks like there's a few fires burning tonight. Bastards!" This was the first time she had heard him swear and it surprised her a little. "I'm thinking of signing up, you know, now I no longer have Mother to look after."

"But I thought you weren't allowed?" Laura's heart fell to her stomach at the thought of him heading to the front line and all the horrors that she knew would be waiting for him.

"I'm in a reserved occupation if that's what you mean, but now I don't have Mother to look after I could just give a different name and occupation. They'd never know, the army needs as many men as it can get." They were back inside the house now and Laura looked around for the first time.

The kitchen was as she had imagined it would look. A large table and chairs in the centre of the room with a few stark white cupboards on the wall. The floor was black and white tiles and the walls were half tiled in white with a black dado rail and then white-washed walls above. *It was certainly very bright and clean,* Laura thought to herself. Ben had closed the door, pulled a curtain over and switched on the light.

"I thought you said you didn't have electricity?" Laura distinctly remembered the night he had run round the house playing with all the light switches.

"I had it installed not long after Mother died." He headed to the stove, lit a match, and held it to the gas ring before placing a large copper kettle on top and shaking the match out. "She was very nervous of anything new and modern but I'm all for it, especially after seeing what the future holds."

Ben made himself busy making tea and slicing huge chunks of bread from what appeared to be a freshly baked loaf, lightly spreading them with butter and jam. Laura felt guilty about how much butter she would normally use on one slice, probably as much as Ben had in a week.

"So why do you think I'm still here then?" She returned to the original question after demolishing the soft bread with a hunger she hadn't realised she had.

"It must be having the cameo there, perhaps the link is permanent now." Ben was still nibbling at his slice of bread, pulling little bits off at a time and savouring each tiny morsel. Laura felt guilty again, she was so used to having whatever food she wanted whenever she wanted it, and it hadn't occurred to her that a simple piece of jam and bread would be such a treat. "From what you've said and what's been happening, I would say that the portal only opened my side to start with as the cameo was only on the one side, why I only came through for a few hours I don't know, and why there is a time portal there in the first place I don't know either."

Laura found it strange to hear him talk about time portals and thought he'd get on very well with Beth.

"And when I held the cameo near to the mirror and you were on the other side, it seemed to make a link as well." She sipped her tea instead of gulping it as she would have done at home.

"But now the cameo is on both sides, it seems to have completed the circuit so to speak." Ben was still only halfway through his slice of bread.

"I just find it so intriguing." Even though she had sipped her tea, it was almost gone. "Why us? Why here? Why now?"

"Just mysteries of the universe I'm afraid." He had finally finished his slice and started on his tea. "I'm dying to see if I can go through. Imagine if we can just come and go as we please. We'd be able to see each other whenever we wanted to." He put his cup down. "That's if you want us to see each other." He looked over at her with puppy dog eyes.

"I want nothing more." She placed a hand over his, thankful that he had obviously been thinking the same things as her. "It will be a bit strange, what with you in the forties and me in 2016 but I'm sure we can make it work if that's what we both want."

"At least we can spend the whole night in bed again." He smiled at her and she found herself laughing.

"Can we indeed?" she teased.

"I don't mean together," he said, realising what he had just said. "I mean we can sleep all night, in our own beds and see each other after work like normal people do."

"I knew what you meant Ben, I was just teasing." Laura watched a relieved smile spread over his face. "So shall we see if the mirror works both ways now?" They walked up the stairs hand in hand, Laura still coming to terms with everything being the opposite way round. The hall, stairs and landing flowed perfectly through the house with highly polished wooden floors and large flowery wallpaper.

Laura took a sneaky peek into the bathroom as she passed. It had the same black and white tiles as the kitchen with a huge white roll top bath and sparkling clean silver taps. Laura wondered how Ben had the time to keep the house so neat and tidy while working full time as well.

"Shall I go first?" They were standing in front of the mirror now, its glass already shimmering as if it sensed their presence.

"Yes, let's see if it works for you out of the normal hours." Laura watched as Ben stepped through the mirror, then hesitantly she followed. She need not have worried, there she was safely back in 2016 with Ben standing waiting for her, grinning like The Cheshire Cat.

"I can't believe it." He stepped back through the mirror and then back again. "It's amazing. One minute I'm there then I'm here." Backwards and forwards he went like it was the first time it had happened.

"You have done this before, you know?" Laura was a little bemused by his behaviour.

"I know, but not like this." He stopped on her side of the mirror. "Not to just come and go as and when I want to."

"Do you think it's only us that come through?" She had a sudden vision of Dorothy somehow finding her way through. "After all, Chester comes through."

"Well, yes, but everyone knows cats are magic." He said this with such seriousness that Laura knew he wasn't actually joking. "Why do you think witches always have cats?"

"Witches?" She hadn't thought he would believe in magic and witches and wondered what he'd think of watching the Harry Potter movies one day. "But Chester isn't black."

"That's such a stereotype Laura." Ben was almost reproachful in his tone. "Witches aren't green and warty with black cats and broomsticks. You wouldn't even know a witch if you passed one on the street. My father's family are from a long line of witches and druids, you know."

"Really?" Laura was starting to think he was pulling her leg now. "Do you think maybe he was a witch?" She was trying not laugh.

"I'm being serious, Laura." The look on Ben's face wiped the grin off of hers. "My father's sister Vivienne told me all about it when I was little, but we lost touch. We were even at the Salem witch trials but obviously we were never caught, real witches usually weren't."

"Do you think maybe your father put some magic in the mirror?" There was such sincerity in Ben's face that Laura was trying to believe him; and there had to be some kind of magic in it otherwise how did you explain the time travelling?

"If you think about it, it kind of makes sense." Ben could tell she wasn't fully believing his story. "Perhaps my father intended the mirror to be some kind of time portal to enable him to come back to my mother, after all he carved it himself just before he went off to war."

"Anything is possible I suppose," Laura agreed. "We'll never really know, but I like the idea of it being a magic mirror made with true love." She had always been a romantic at heart.

"I think it's best you keep the cameo away from the mirror." Ben was suddenly harsh.

"But then I won't be able to come through to you and you'll only be able to come through after midnight." Laura was a little perplexed by this turn around.

"I don't mean all the time." Ben quickly reassured her. "Just in the day maybe." He was thoughtful for a few moments. "Like you said, we can't risk anyone having an accident and falling through."

"Who would be in the room though?" Laura didn't want to take the cameo out in case it broke the link. "I live on my own, you live on your own now except for Chester and he's welcome anytime."

"Well …" Laura sensed she wasn't going to like the next sentence. "I've sort of employed Dorothy as my housekeeper and after today I've given her a key so I wouldn't want her accidently coming into your time; she isn't the kind of woman to understand that I'm afraid."

Laura wanted to answer with *I know what kind of a woman she is,* but instead she stayed silent; at least she knew now who was keeping his house so clean and tidy.

"And then there's her son, Jimmy. Imagine an eight-year-old finding a portal to the future, it would be all round his school in no time." Laura had to agree this was true.

"But they won't be there all day and night will they?" She was hoping for some time with Ben at least.

"No, no, of course not." Ben was adamant. "It's only a few hours a day while I'm at work but she did say she'd make dinner for me each night. She does make delicious dinners you know."

"I'm sure she does." Laura envisioned Dorothy greeting Ben at the door after work wearing nothing but a frilly apron and holding out a steaming hot pie she'd just baked.

"Speaking of which," Ben had noticed the time and with a quick peck on Laura's cheek he headed back to the mirror. "She'll be round soon to make breakfast and I've got to get to work."

"But you haven't slept." Laura knew she couldn't function with no sleep.

"Don't worry." He was halfway through the mirror. "It won't be the first time." Then he was gone. Laura felt somewhat deflated after the initial high of the evening and went over to the mirror to remove the cameo. "Put it back in about seven o'clock." Ben's head and shoulders popped back into view just before she had taken it out. "I'll make sure the house is empty." He reached a hand up under her chin and pulled her in for a lingering kiss. "I'll see you tonight." And with a wink he was gone.

Chapter 21

Laura was in turmoil for the rest of the day. She couldn't eat or sleep, working on the house was impossible, and reading a book was far too relaxing for her current state of mind. Instead she wondered aimlessly around, pottering about from room to room and resisting the urge to step into Ben's house and meet this Dorothy face to face.

She didn't know why she felt this strongly about a woman she'd never met and a woman she knew was to become Ben's wife very soon. She knew it wasn't going to be her, had always known it, but she liked him, really liked him, and the thought of another woman with him made her blood boil and put rather disturbing thoughts of violence into her head.

Dorothy was obviously making a play for Ben. Acting the helpless widow to the handsome lonely bachelor. Looking after him while he'd been looking after his mother, no wonder he was falling for it. Men could be so naïve sometimes. Laura had only seen her that once but already her judgement was made. Clearly Dorothy had set her cap at Ben; he was a man of means, good looking and kind, hardworking, just what you'd look for in a potential husband.

But you know what happens after they get married. The little voice inside her head was back. Yes, she did know. She knew that Dorothy would die in the not too distant future, that Ben would then be left to bring up a young boy and a baby daughter all on his own. A son? Laura's thoughts almost somersaulted in her head. There was never any mention of a son in Walter's future. She still found it hard to think of Ben as Walter; the name really didn't suit him.

Fetching the notebook and photos from their hiding place in the car she could find no mention of a son, but then hadn't Ben said Jimmy was eight? That would mean he would have grown up and probably moved on long before Agnes' family moved into the street or maybe he went to live with other relatives when his mother died. *That poor boy.* Laura was full of sympathy. To lose your father and your mother in such a short space of time.

Not for the first time she pondered on the futility of war. She remembered the week long project the whole school had been involved in back in July 2014 for the hundredth anniversary of the start of the First World War. They had learnt all about modern warfare and life in the trenches. Then the following May they had spent another week learning about the Second World War and the hardships that the people at home had endured.

Laura had found herself fascinated by World War II, especially the Home Front. The Land Girls had particularly inspired her and she had petitioned for a small vegetable garden at the school which the Head had instantly agreed to and the children had enjoyed immensely. *I hope one of the other teachers is looking after it*, she thought with a little pang. Perhaps she could start the same thing here, after all, the garden out the back was huge.

With a renewed optimism she headed into the garden and started to sketch a plan. She knew she couldn't plant anything as it was harvest time rather than sowing season but she could get some digging done and decide what she wanted and where. She'd always liked the idea of a garden that was split into different areas with screening between them and a pathway weaving through.

She went into the house around six o clock to sit down and talk with her mum on the phone, then feeling extremely tired thought she would grab forty winks before putting the cameo back in for Ben.

"Thank goodness for that." Ben's voice and a gentle shake of her leg woke her up. She looked around the room, the curtains were open and it was now pitch-black outside. "I've been worried sick you know, when the mirror didn't change I thought something had happened to you, I've sat staring at it for hours."

"I'm so sorry, I've been in the garden all day and what with not sleeping last night ..." Laura knew this sounded lame; he hadn't slept last night either and would have been to work all day as well yet here he was fresh as a daisy and she looked like something out of *Bill and Ben the Flower Pot Men*. "I must look a sight." She knew she had streaks of mud on her face and hands and her hair must be all over the place, it hadn't seen a brush all day.

"You look beautiful." He sat down beside her on the sofa and leaned over to kiss her. "This could do with a good brush though," he joked, messing up her hair even more.

"Oi!" She whacked him gently with a cushion. "I'll have you know this particular hair style took many hours of meticulous planning."

"I'm sure it did." He kissed her again. "I'm just not used to how the ladies in this century have their hair you know."

"I still find it strange when you mention different centuries like that." She snuggled up against him and he put his arm round her, placing a soft kiss on her head as he did so. "How are we ever going to work?"

"By doing exactly what we're doing." She felt his chest rumble as he spoke. "We're no different to other couples you know."

"How can you say that?" Laura said with disbelief. "You were born in 1910 and I was born in 1986."

"I never told you when I was born." He turned her to look at him. "What else do you know about me?" He wasn't angry, just intrigued.

"Only a few things really." Laura had to think on the spot about what she could tell him and what she couldn't. "I was interested to find out who used to live here so I looked it up on the internet."

"What's the internet?" Ben was baffled.

"Erm …" *How did you explain the internet to someone from a time where television was the most modern invention?* "It's like a massive library of information that travels through the air to various devices."

"Travels through the air?" She could see his mind working overtime. "Like radio waves?"

"A bit like that, yes." She pulled out her phone. "Ask me a question."

"Who won World War II?" She looked at him with raised eyebrows.

"Okay, Siri." She spoke to the phone much to Ben's amusement. "Who won World War I?" After a few seconds the automated voice of Siri came through.

"Okay, I found this on the World Wide Web." She showed the list of answers that had suddenly appeared on her phone.

"Wow," was all Ben could say.

"Anything you want to know these days; you just tap it in and it's there at your fingertips." She was careful to close her phone down and lock it.

"Don't you read books anymore?" He had taken her phone and was busy pressing the button like he had seen her do. "Okay, Siri." The phone stayed on the lock screen. "Why won't it work for me?"

"Because it only works for my voice." He wouldn't know that wasn't true. "We still have books but mostly just for reading novels and things like that. It's just so much easier to ask the internet and have the answer in seconds rather than going to the library to find the answer in a book."

"It's amazing." He handed the phone back to her. "All that information just in that tiny little thing."

"You would be in your element with all the technology we have these days." She knew this was true. He was so interested in the future, not just because it was all new and exciting but because he had a natural curiosity.

"Do you think you can show me some of it?" He was hungry for more knowledge. "Like those video things you showed me before."

"You'll love this." She took out the laptop and grabbed her Harry Potter collection from the stack of DVDs in the corner, took out *The Philosopher's Stone* and sat back with him on the sofa. The familiar music came on and Laura found herself watching Ben rather than the film. He was silent throughout, a look of wonder on his face.

Harry, Ron, and Hermione had just got past Fluffy the three headed dog when Ben got up.

"Time to go." Laura hastily paused the film. "We forgot about the cameo."

"I'll run up and do it now." She moved past him and up the stairs into the bedroom, pushing the cameo into the mirror. Ben instantly stopped moving. "I want to leave the cameo in all the time, Ben," she said, meeting him halfway up the stairs.

"But we can't," he reminded her. "Not with Dorothy around."

"Do you like her that much?" Laura was prepared to let him go if he did.

"Of course I do." He saw her crestfallen face. "But not in that way," he hastily added. "She's a lovely woman who has been through a hell of a lot and Jimmy is a smashing lad but I can't be what she wants me to be."

"What does she want you to be?" Laura thought she knew from the scene the other day in his bedroom exactly what she wanted Ben to be.

"She wants us to get married." He said this matter of factly. "And I have to admit I was tempted. She's beautiful, good company, an excellent housewife, and wonderful mother. But …"

"Well go and marry her then." Laura stormed past him down the stairs but he grabbed her arm and pulled her back towards him.

"You didn't let me finish." Laura wouldn't look at him, so he stepped down a few stairs so his face was level with hers. "But … how can I marry her when I am totally and utterly in love with you." She threw her arms round him with such force that they stumbled backwards down the stairs, landing in a heap on the floor.

"I feel the same," Laura gushed, sitting on top of him. "I don't know how it happened so quickly and without sounding like a cliché, I think I fell in love with you that night you went round turning all the lights on and off. I thought you were some mad man and I was dreaming."

"It was when you knocked yourself out for me." He laughed remembering the look on her face. "I carried you to that absurd sleeping bag you called a bed at the time and sat watching you. I didn't know how I'd got there, or even where 'there' was but I knew I'd never seen anyone as beautiful as you. You were so different from anyone I'd ever met before and my heart just melted at how vulnerable you looked; I just wanted to wrap my arms around you and take care of you and the feeling hasn't gone away since."

She leaned down to kiss him, her hair forming a kind of curtain on either side of his face. It was a different kind of kiss, full of promises and an unknown future. All Laura wanted to do was hold this moment tight and never let it go. She pushed all thoughts of Ben's future wife and child out of her head along with all the problems of an interdimensional relationship. Wow, that was a big word she thought to herself as she started to kiss his neck, down his chest, opening each button at a time.

Ben had gone quite still, yet his breathing was heavy.

"Are you okay?" Laura looked up at him, her chin on his chest.

"Girls from my century don't do this kind of thing." He was struggling with his words.

"Luckily I'm not from your century." She kissed him deeply on the lips. "And girls from my century do this." She slipped her top off and watched his eyes grow wide with desire.

"Well that's nice to know." He reached up to wind his hand in her hair and pull her back down for another kiss. "I'm beginning to like this century."

Chapter 22

The next few weeks passed uneventfully. Laura and Ben spent as much time together as they could. Usually it was in 2016 decorating or gardening or lounging in bed. They spent the 1942 weekends in Ben's time as Dorothy always visited her parents in Birmingham. As 2016 was two days ahead it meant that his Saturday and Sunday were Laura's Monday and Tuesday but as she was still off work it didn't matter.

They had discovered that they could only venture as far as the property boundary, why they didn't know, but each could walk right up to the front gate in the other's time but some invisible force stopped them going any further. This was more disappointing to Ben than Laura as he would have dearly loved to see Coventry in the future.

It was the August Bank Holiday, well it was to Laura anyway, and the Monday was gloriously hot with not a cloud in the sky. She decided to get started on the front garden and began digging and weeding round by the front wall.

"Good morning." Ben crept up behind her and kissed her gently on the neck, a slow shiver spreading down her spine despite the heat.

"And good morning to you." She turned round and kissed him fully on the lips. "I hope you're ready for some more hard labour?"

"I can't believe how much work this place has needed." He stood with his hands on his hips. "The people who owned this before you need shooting for letting it get so bad." He knelt down and began pulling up weeds as Laura moved along twisting them out with her hoe. "Do I die, then?" This was the first time he'd asked a question like this in a long time. "Well, of course I die," he said matter of factly. "And I'm either dead now or extremely old." He sat backwards onto the grass.

"Don't think like that." She sat down next to him. "You're very much alive here and now. Who cares about the future? The future will be what we make of it."

"But how did it get so run down?" It was obviously a question that had played on his mind. "Don't I get married and have children? Don't they want the house?"

"If I tell you something, will you promise not to press me for any more information?" Laura knew she could tell him a few things but not all the facts. He nodded eagerly. "I'm not telling you names or dates or places."

"That's fine." Ben smiled in anticipation.

"You do get married, you do have a child or children, I'm not saying how many." No one should know all about their future. "And I know you move away from here at some point."

"But who do I marry?" Laura gave him a warning look. "When do I move? Where do I go?"

"Ben …" She stood up and went back to her digging.

"Okay, okay." He knelt back down, content for now with just a little bit of information.

"Hello, Laura." Agnes had walked over and was now leaning on the wall. "What a beautiful morning. I can see you're getting to grips with the weeds."

"Good morning." Ben popped up and offered his hand to Agnes. "Pleasure to meet you, I'm Ben."

"But … what … who …" Agnes was lost for words. "It can't be. You look just like Mr. Matthews." She shook his hand, staring at him, her mouth wide open.

"I am Mr. Matthews." Laura groaned. "Ben Matthews." And with those words Agnes fell forwards onto the wall in a crumpled heap.

"She's fainted." Ben was shocked.

"Of course she's fainted." Laura ran round the front and tried to get Agnes to wake up. It was no good, so using all her strength she half carried, half dragged her into the kitchen, Ben helping once she was inside the front gate.

"But why would she faint at my name?" Ben was confused.

"Because," Laura was busy fanning Agnes with a paper trying to revive her, "She knew you when she was a little girl." Laura had been dreading him meeting Agnes. "She lived in that house with her parents and brother in the 1960s so seeing you looking younger than she would have known you would be a bit of shock I should imagine."

"Should I fetch the doctor?" Ben didn't know if that was still the practice but felt sure that they would still have doctors in this century.

"I'll go and get her husband." Laura dashed off over the road as quickly as she could and banged on Agnes' door. It seemed an eternity before it finally opened to reveal a very thin, very frail but extremely kind looking bespectacled man with wispy white hair. He was a lot older than Agnes and half her size and Laura was reminded of the Jack Sprat nursery rhyme.

"Can I help you?" Wilf asked in a surprisingly posh but very slow voice.

"It's Laura from across the road, Wilf." Laura found herself speaking slowly as well even though all she wanted to do was grab him and whisk him over the road.

"Agnes has fainted I'm afraid and I can't get her to wake up."

"She does that quite a lot." Wilf shuffle turned to walk down the hallway. "I'll go and get her smelling salts; they'll soon bring her round." Laura watched as he continued his agonisingly slow shuffle down the hall and into the kitchen. She heard drawers opening and closing. "Now, where are they?" A cupboard door opened and closed. Laura kept tapping her foot and checking her watch.

"Can I help, Wilf?" *Please let me help* she thought to herself.

"No, no it's fine." Wilf had re-emerged in the hallway and Laura breathed a sigh of relief. "I've remembered where they are now. Last time she fainted she was in the bedroom so I'll pop up there and get them for you." Laura didn't think he was capable of popping anywhere but she just smiled and watched him climb into his stair lift and ascend the stairs at the speed of a tortoise.

Laura looked anxiously back towards the house. What if she'd woken up? What if she told Ben all the things she knew about him? What if Ben told her who he was? It just didn't bear thinking about so she shoved it out of her mind and waited for what felt like an hour for Wilf to appear with a small brown bottle.

"Now my dear, you just take the lid off and waft it under her nose." Wilf did exactly that and Laura pulled her head away repulsed.

"Wow, that would wake the dead." She rubbed her nose trying to rid it of the smell.

But Wilf had already closed the door and Laura could see his little figure retreating back down the hallway through the frosted glass.

When she got back in the house it was to find a much-revived Agnes sitting opposite a very smiley Ben. Both were sipping tea and sharing biscuits like old friends.

"Well, fancy you courting Mr. Matthews' great grandson and you not telling me." Agnes turned to Laura as she walked back into the room.

"Apparently I am the absolute spit of him." Ben smiled knowingly. "Or so Mrs. Rogers would have me believe."

"Agnes, please." She tapped him playfully on the arm. "He is a devil, your young man."

"Oh he is that." Laura leaned on the door frame and stared at Ben. "Wilf will be worrying, Agnes, shall I help you home?"

"No need for that dearie." She stood up. "I'm quite alright." She waddled past Laura, who handed her the bottle of smelling salts as she passed. "And anytime you want to know more about your great grandad just come and ask me." This last comment was for Ben and as Agnes shut the door behind her Laura sat down next to him.

"What do you think you're playing at?" She couldn't believe what had just happened; *how much did he know?*

"It's all I could think of to explain why I looked so much like him." Ben pushed a cup of tea towards her. "I thought it was quite clever of me really." Laura had to admit it was quick thinking on his part.

"And she believed you?" Laura was sure Agnes had been completely taken in by Ben and his easy-going charm.

"Why wouldn't she?" He poured another cup of tea from the pot. "So much better without tea leaves floating about."

"I suppose she didn't have any reason to think you were lying." Laura knew she had believed him; well what other option was there? "And what things did she tell you?"

"To be honest, not a lot really." Laura found that hard to believe. "She wasn't awake that long before you came back: look, she hasn't even finished her tea." Ben showed her the cup with just a few sips taken out. "She came to and I told her who I was which seemed to calm her down no end. Then she just said how she and her brother used to come and play in the garden and pick apples in the autumn. She also said how lovely I was."

"How lovely your great grandad was you mean?" Laura teased.

"But that's me in the future so it means I'm lovely now." He smiled cheekily.

"Nothing else?" Laura thought Agnes must have had more to say than that.

"Well, she did ask who my grandparents were and didn't seem impressed with the answer, mentioned something about that not being right but she didn't elaborate and I was about to ask her what she meant when you came back in." Laura felt he wasn't telling her everything but didn't push it. "I've got a surprise for you tonight." His eyes were twinkling.

"Have you indeed?" She raised her eyebrows saucily.

"Come to mine about five o'clock." He stood up and gave her a peck on the cheek. "I'm doing tea." And with that he was gone and away leaving Laura to ponder on what Agnes had actually told him about his future.

Laura headed down the stairs in Ben's house at precisely five o'clock to find the table elegantly laid with a white linen cloth, serviettes, and silver candle sticks with red candles burning brightly even though it was still light outside. He was dressed smartly in a full black suit, crisp white shirt and black tie. Laura was grateful she had worn her little black dress and black heels and was greeted by a terrified but hungry look from Ben as if his morals went against what she was wearing but his mind was saying *Oh baby*.

"This way *mademoiselle*." Speaking in a diabolical French accent he pulled out a chair for her. "Dinner will be the finest *poisson et frites*."

"You mean fish and chips?" She laughed as he pulled open the oven and placed what appeared to be a wad of newspaper on her plate and his.

"But of course." The French accent continued. "Only the best for my *mon aimee*."

Laura unwrapped the newspaper to find a golden piece of fish and chunky chips drowning in salt and vinegar. She had forgotten that they used actual newspapers in the past. She took a bite and found them to be delicious.

"Would *mademoiselle* care for *un verre de vin*?" From the fact that there was a bottle of wine on the table and from her limited school French she nodded and watched as he filled each of their glasses in turn. "I've had this bottle a few years."

"It's delicious." Laura took a quick sip and then another. The fish and chips tasted divine and she wondered how much they had cost him in money and rations. Were fish and chips even rationed?

"They batter a mean fish round at Fergal's." He hadn't used his knife and fork and was busy getting stuck in with his fingers. The rattle of a key in the front door made them both look up the hallway.

"It's only me, Ben," came a woman's voice as the door opened. "I couldn't get to Birmingham today as there's some problem with the line and they've cancelled the trains till further notice so Jimmy has gone to his friend's house and I thought I'd come and keep you comp…" She didn't finish the last word as she came into the kitchen and saw the scene before her.

"Dorothy." Ben shot up. "I wasn't expecting you."

"Clearly." Laura felt naked as Dorothy's brown eyes scrutinized her from head to toe.

"This is Laura." Ben made the introduction. "Laura, this is Dorothy." Laura stood up and immediately wished she hadn't.

"Why is there a woman in her nightdress in your kitchen, Ben?" Laura sat back down. Just the tone of this woman's voice was enough to get you to do as you were told but the withering look she gave her made her feel like a child.

"Because she's my girlfriend," Ben almost stammered.

"Girlfriend!" This didn't appear to sit well with Dorothy and she immediately turned to Laura. "I don't know what he's told you, dearie, but I wouldn't believe him. We're getting married as soon as it can be arranged."

"Now, Dorothy we've talked about that." Ben moved round the table to stand next to her. "We're not getting married. We're just friends." Laura watched as Dorothy's immaculately made-up face turned red.

"Friends!" she almost screamed. "Friends!" Then she seemed to remember herself and was composed once more. "Well, I suppose you could call us friends now, but I don't know what people round here will call us when they find out I'm having a baby and you won't marry me."

Chapter 23

Laura didn't know who was more shocked by Dorothy's statement, she, or Ben. He seemed to stagger backwards, a look of sheer horror on his face before looking at Dorothy, then to Laura then back to Dorothy.

"But? How?" he stammered.

"Oh Ben, do I really need to tell you about the birds and the bees?" Dorothy moved over to him and linked an arm through his. "Now, why don't you tell this lovely young lady to go and put some clothes on and leave us alone?" Her face had a smug smile and her voice was condescending.

Laura didn't wait to be told anything, she walked as dignified as she could up the stairs hoping that Dorothy thought that was where she had left her clothes; after all she couldn't exactly escape out the front door—well, she could; but she wasn't about to sit in the front garden for hours. She stepped through the mirror and with huge tears streaming down her cheeks she pulled out the cameo, knowing that Ben would still be able to come through in a few hours but at least it would give her time to compose herself.

So it was Dorothy he married and had a child with. Laura had known deep down that this was true but some little part of her had hoped it was her. Impossible as it sounded she wanted to be the one that Ben married, had hoped that due to the different centuries that was why Ben's wife and Lauren's mother were missing from everything. After all, how could you name someone in the 1940s that hadn't been born yet?

Yet again, she had allowed a man to hurt her. What was wrong with her? Did she have *idiot* written on her forehead in big, massive letters or was she just a magnet for unfaithful men? But Ben had seemed so genuine, so innocent and such a gentleman, it didn't match what Dorothy was making him out to be.

The thought of Dorothy angered Laura once again. She was the epitome of how 1940s women were portrayed in the films. Her hair was immaculately coiffed with not a strand out of place, her face impeccably made up, and her clothes fitted in all the right places to accentuate every curve. Laura wondered how a widow with a young son could afford such luxuries or even where they would come from but then she remembered that the black market was rife during the war and assumed that Dorothy must be getting her clothes and makeup from there.

She stripped off her dress and roughly wiped the makeup off her face before brushing her hair so hard it hurt. She changed her mind time and time again as to whether she should be here when Ben came later or should she be out? Would he even come? She knew he would though, he was too much of a gentleman not to; and she sat on the bed waiting for him to appear.

It was twelve twenty-two exactly when a very anxious looking Ben walked into the bedroom.

"Why did you take the cameo out?" He came straight over to the bed and knelt in front of her. "I've been trying to get through for hours."

"I don't want you coming through anymore, Ben." She had decided that would be her opening line after hours of going over and over what she would say to him. "You've played me for a fool and I don't want to see you anymore."

"Why are you talking like that?" Ben couldn't stop a stray tear from falling.

"Because you've lied to me." She couldn't look him in the eye and kept her gaze downwards. "You told me Dorothy meant nothing to you yet clearly she does as you're having a baby together."

"It's not mine." Laura's head shot up in relief and disbelief.

"What do you mean it's not yours?" She looked into his eyes, he seemed to be telling the truth.

"I mean it's not mine," he repeated. "I was a …" He paused. "That is to say that I hadn't …" Laura didn't know what he was trying to say and he could see the puzzled expression on her face. "Oh for crying out loud. I was a virgin till I met you." He looked away from her, embarrassed.

"Well you wouldn't have guessed." Laura recalled his expert hands on their first time.

"I said I was a virgin not a monk." He sat up on the bed next to her. "I don't know why she's saying the baby's mine. We haven't even kissed. Well, that's not strictly true, she tried to kiss me that day after she'd been locked out but I stopped her."

"I know why she's saying it." Laura was angry now and wanted nothing more than to smash the face in of the perfect Dorothy. "She's trying to snare you. I bet she isn't even pregnant."

"No, she is." Ben corrected her. "She showed me the bump through her blouse."

"I bet she did." Laura couldn't sit still and started pacing up and down the room punching her fist into her palm. "Evil bitch!" Another punch. "I bet she's up the duff by some random man who won't marry her and she's trying to pin it on you." Ben didn't understand the phrase 'up the duff' but he got the gist of what she was saying.

"So if you haven't slept together how is she planning to make you the father?"

"We got drunk a few months ago." Ben looked a little sheepish. "It was the anniversary of her husband's death and she was very down. We woke up in bed together the next morning, but I swear we didn't do anything. I wasn't that drunk."

"How do you know for sure though?" Laura had had many forgotten nights due to alcohol.

"Jimmy had fallen asleep on the sofa so we covered him up with a blanket. I made up the bed in the spare room for her and headed into my own room. It was just before dawn that she crept in beside me." Ben shook his head as if telling himself off. "I should have said something then but I thought she was sleepwalking and as she didn't speak I just left it. She hasn't even mentioned it since but now she's saying I took advantage of her and if I don't marry her she'll tell everyone. I'll have to move away, you know."

"That's a little dramatic." Laura stopped pacing.

"Is it?" He stared up at her. "I'd be called goodness knows what in the street. The neighbours would refuse to talk to me and I'd be ostracised by the very people I've known all my life. They will think I've used her and thrown her aside. I've told you before sex before marriage is a sin."

"So how come we've had sex then?" Laura couldn't believe people could be so narrow minded about sex.

"Because I want to marry you." It wasn't a question, just a statement.

"You what …" Laura was almost dumbstruck.

"I know we haven't known each other very long but it's like destiny has brought us together; and I don't know how we'll manage it as we can't leave the house in each other's time so we'd never get to a church, but I want to marry you Laura, and spend the rest of my life with you." She flung herself at him with such force that he fell back onto the bed.

"You really want to marry me?" Her anger had changed to immense joy.

"Yes, Laura Reynolds. I want to marry you." She kissed him all over his face squealing with happiness. "Is that a yes then?" She kissed him on the lips this time.

"All we have to do is work out who the father of Dorothy's baby is and how we are actually going to physically get married then we'll be all sorted." Laura wasn't sure which one of those was the more impossible.

"I could ask around about Dorothy." Ben knew he would have to be discreet; he couldn't risk Dorothy finding out what they were up to.

"I could see what I can find out on the internet." Laura wanted to get started right away. "Tell me everything you know about her, full name, date of birth, who she married that kind of thing."

"How will the internet thingy help with that?" Laura kept forgetting he didn't really have a clue when it came to technology.

"I'll show you." She opened up her Genes Reunited account yet again and put *Walter Matthews* into the search. "There you are." She pointed at the screen showing the 1911 census of him living in the house with his mum and dad.

"Wow." He touched the names of his mother and father almost reverently. "And you can do that for anyone?"

"To a certain extent." She cleared his name from the screen. "You can search the UK census from 1801 to

1911 and it will tell you who lived where and with whom, it's invaluable for tracing your family tree." Ben looked fascinated. "But you can also look up births, deaths, and marriages if you know what you're looking for." She typed Dorothy into the search space. "Do you know her maiden name?"

"No, she only came to live here when her husband died." Laura looked disappointed. "Her husband was James Carter though, Jimmy is named after him. And she must come from Birmingham because that's where her parents are from."

Laura put James Carter, Dorothy, and Birmingham into the various spaces with an approximate date range. Luckily there were only two matches. One was in 1933 in Aston and the second also in Aston was in 1946 but this time the groom was Jonathan Carter.

"There she is." Laura did some more clicking to discover that Dorothy's maiden name was Styler. Ben watched in silence as she typed and clicked before discovering that Dorothy Styler was born in 1909. This meant that she would be on the 1911 census. A few more clicks and she found her living in what appeared to be an orphanage but what was even more surprising to Laura was the name of two of the other occupants. Jonathan and James Carter aged six and four respectively. "It's her brother-in-law." Laura cleared all the searches again and this time focused on Jonathan Carter. "Oh my God, the little whore." Ben, who had gone into a daze watching all the screen changes, shook himself awake at the word 'whore'.

"What?" He questioned. "What have you found?"

"Dorothy grew up in an orphanage with James Carter and what must be his older brother Jonathan. Jonathan marries a Christina in 1932 and the following year Dorothy marries James. We know that James dies but Jonathan is very much alive. His wife died in January 1946 and the following month he marries Dorothy. I wonder how long it's been going on."

"You found all that out from there?" Ben still thought the World Wide Web lived inside Laura's laptop and phone. "And you're telling me that Dorothy has been having an affair with her dead husband's brother?" Laura nodded. "For how long?"

"The internet's good Ben, but it's not that good." She closed down the laptop. "It could have been before her husband died, after, or they may have been carrying on all their lives but I bet you any money Jonathan Carter is the father of Dorothy's baby."

"I'm going round there right now to tell her." He stood up. "How dare she try and frame me for something I haven't done and pin another man's child on me." He was virtually at the mirror before Laura had an idea.

"Ben, wait." He turned to look at her. "If you go in all guns blazing she'll just deny it and anyway you don't have any proof, it's not like you can whip out my laptop and show her the facts, is it. We need to think about this carefully. Dorothy thinks she's being clever but she doesn't know what we know and we have to be cleverer. Pop the cameo back in then come and sit back down."

Ben did exactly as he was told and together they formulated a plan on how to catch Dorothy out, their earlier conversation about marriage on the back burner as this was a far more important issue at the moment.

Chapter 24
September 2016

It was a few weeks before Ben had the opportunity to catch Dorothy out in her lies and even then they weren't sure that it would go to plan. It was nearly the end of September and Ben and Laura had hardly seen each other which was a good thing considering Laura had started her new job and they had agreed that Ben should go along with Dorothy at the moment and play the loving fiancé.

The thought of Ben cosying up to Dorothy brought a jealous side out in Laura that she didn't know she had and even though it was only pretend, she found keeping busy was the only way not to think about it. The new term had started uneventfully at St Josephine's and Laura had immersed herself in her new class. Walking the halls brought back so many happy memories of her own school days. Just the smell of the place was enough to evoke vivid images of Beth, Lucy, and herself walking to assembly or that superior feeling of being chosen to ring the heavy bell to signal break or lunch time.

Ben and Laura had rarely spent any time together, partly because Laura was working again and had lessons to plan but mainly because that was how they had planned it. It was the last Sunday of the month for Laura and as normal this found her marking maths homework in the kitchen when she heard Ben's footsteps. Her stomach did a little flip as it always did when she thought of him and she stood up, straightened her clothes and went to meet him at the bottom of the stairs.

"I've missed you." She threw her arms around him, breathing in the smell of him.

"I've missed you too." He hugged her back just as tightly. "I can't wait for this to be over so we can get on with building our life together." And at this he pulled out a small box from his trouser pocket and got down on one knee. "Laura Reynolds: will you do me the great honour of becoming my wife?" Laura's hand flew to her mouth as he opened the box, inside was a beautiful diamond ring. "I know I should have asked your father's permission but as I've never met him and can't actually leave these four walls I thought I'd just ask you instead."

"It's okay, we don't do that sort of thing now." He had taken out the ring and was about to put it on her finger.

"You haven't actually answered my question." He looked up at her with teasing blue eyes.

"Yes, yes, a hundred times yes." Ben slid the ring on her finger and got as far as her knuckle but the ring would go no further.

"I was afraid of that." He stood up. "It's a family heirloom you see, and the last woman to wear it was my grandmother and she was a tiny lady."

"Are you saying I'm fat?" Laura pretended outrage at his words.

"No, of course not." He was immediately apologetic. "You're anything but. You're absolutely perfect in every way: it's just my grandmother was five foot nothing and ate like a bird."

"I was teasing, Ben." She took the ring and placed it back in its box. "I can get it altered at the jewellers in town."

"You like it then?" He was waiting for her approval.

"I love it." She kissed him as if to prove the point. "I'm so glad the mirror allows us to bring things through now."

"Yes, but only if it's on your person so to speak." They had spent a few hours one day testing their theory and had discovered that as long as the object was personal to the carrier and it was in a pocket or in their hand it could come through.

"How's things with Dorothy?" Laura had been avoiding this issue for days knowing what was to happen.

"She's wild with excitement." They walked into the living room and plonked themselves on the sofa. "What if it doesn't work? I'll have to marry her, you know."

"Of course it will work." Laura had gone over and over the plan in her head. "You've sent the letters, haven't you?"

"I wrote two just in case the first ones didn't get there." His voice had a tiny hint of worry in it. "And a third in case those went awry."

"Then it will be fine." She patted his arm reassuringly. "I might live in another century but women are basically the same. When Johnathan's wife finds out about the affair she'll go mad and the first thing she'll want to do is confront Dorothy because she won't be able to shout at her husband since he's away at war."

"But if he's away fighting then how has Dorothy been seeing him?" Ben could see so many flaws in this plan.

"I've told you before, he worked at RAF Stratford." Laura had had to do a lot of digging to find this information. She had been very lucky to discover one of Johnathan Carter's relatives on Genes Reunited and with a little white lie pretending to be related he had allowed her access to his extremely thorough family tree. The information on there had been so enlightening and invaluable.

Laura had discovered all about Johnathan and James Carter and the now infamous Dorothy. Both Carter boys had joined the RAF at an early age but Johnathan had soared through the ranks and had managed to avoid active service during the war unlike his brother who had been shot down during an air raid over France.

It was armed with this information that Laura had formulated her plan of action which relied heavily on the reactions of Johnathan Carter and his wife Christina. An anonymous letter had been sent to Christina telling her about the ongoing affair between her husband and his sister-in-law, the impending birth, and the up-and-coming wedding to an innocent man. Laura was hoping this part would prick at Christina's conscience.

Another letter had been sent to Air Marshall Carter informing him of the forthcoming marriage of Dorothy Carter to Walter Matthews. Ben was still at odds with this plan and had refused to go through with it to start with but when Laura insisted it was the only way, he had booked the registry office and allowed Dorothy to organise a very small party for a handful of guests at the local social club.

"I still can't believe this is the only way." Ben wasn't convinced it would work.

"I told you it has to be this way." Laura tried again to reassure him. "She has to be confronted in public otherwise there won't be any witnesses and she'll just wheedle her way out of it and you'll be trapped forever."

"I hope you're right." He still wasn't convinced.

"Of course I am. Now off to bed: you've got a big day ahead of you." She gave him a long lingering kiss then watched him trudge off up the stairs. "God, I hope I'm right."

Monday dragged and dragged for Laura. She couldn't concentrate on anything. Her normally well-behaved class seemed to pick up on this and not one piece of useful work was done all day. Her mind was awhirl with possibilities, what if the plan didn't work? What if Johnathan's wife didn't really care if he was having an affair? What if she already knew?

Laura consoled herself with the knowledge that she knew Ben didn't marry Dorothy as she married Johnathan in 1946 but then what if their meddling changed all that? What if Laura's plan changed the past? What if right now Dorothy was Mrs. Matthews?

The bell rang to signal the end of the day and Laura breathed a sigh of relief. She stood by the classroom door as all the children met their parents in the playground and then remembered there was a staff meeting after school to discuss the now overdue Ofsted inspection.

It was half past six before she got back home and it was to find a rather relaxed looking Ben standing at the cooker, saucepans bubbling and steaming away, and a recipe book open on the side.

"How was the meeting?" He spoke without turning round.

"How did you know I had a meeting?" She put her bag on the work top and walked over to him.

"It's on your calendar." He nodded in the direction of the back door where her Harry Potter calendar had pride of place.

"What the hell?" It was as he turned that she saw the tell-tale signs of a black eye appearing.

"It looks worse than it is." She clasped his face in her hands for a better look.

"Why did Johnathan Carter hit you?" Laura was perplexed: what had Ben done to deserve being thumped?

"It wasn't him." He said rather sheepishly. "It was Dorothy."

"What?" Laura couldn't help laughing a little but soon stopped at Ben's stern look.

"She didn't take too kindly to what I'd done." He started dishing out pie, mashed potato, and peas.

"Well I wasn't expecting that." They sat down at the breakfast bar and in between mouthfuls Ben filled her in.

"We'd arrived at the registry office just before twelve. Dorothy had invited two of her friends to act as witnesses, so we head inside. I'm sweating by now. I hadn't seen anyone outside waiting for us, there was no one inside either. There we are standing in front of the registrar about to begin when suddenly the door bursts open." It was at this point he paused. "More gravy?"

"No, thank you," Laura answered as politely as she could and tapped her foot as he poured more steaming hot gravy over his dinner.

"Well, there stands Air Marshall Carter in his full uniform demanding to know what on earth is going on. Honestly Laura, I was a little scared, the man was enormous. He stomps down the aisle towards us and I look over at Dorothy who is shocked to say the least. *'Why didn't you tell me about the baby?'* He booms at her. *'I'll look after you, haven't I always looked after you?'* Well Dorothy starts to sob in his arms and I'm feeling more than a little relieved but then who turns up but Mrs. Carter." Ben took a short breath. "She comes in shouting and screaming at her husband and Dorothy, brandishing the letters I'd sent her and when Dorothy recognises my handwriting, she goes mad and wallops me one."

"I told you it would work." Laura was busy picturing the scene.

"You didn't tell me I'd end up with a black eye though." He touched it gingerly and winced.

"Well, I can't know everything, can I?" She smiled. "Then what happened?"

"Then the registrar asks if the marriage is going ahead as he has another wedding in half an hour and of course I say no, so he leaves. Mrs. Carter is still shouting and screaming, her husband is trying to calm her down and Dorothy has had to sit in one of the chairs. Her two friends are in absolute shock asking me if I knew the baby wasn't mine and how could she have done such a thing." Ben shook his head. "I just feigned innocence and headed home. I don't know what happened then but it's already round the street so she won't be able to show her face."

"Serves her right." Laura was busy scraping the last of her meat and potato onto her fork.

"It's Jimmy I feel sorry for." Ben was helping himself to more mash and peas. "He's a lovely lad."

"He's not your responsibility, Ben." She put her knife and fork down on the plate. "Look what I picked up on my lunch break?" She reached inside her bag and pulled out the engagement ring. "It's all ready to go."

"Shall I do the honours?" He took it from her and placed it lovingly on to her finger. "It's official then."

"It's official." The ring fitted perfectly. "Now all we've got to do is work out how we can actually get married."

"Is that all?" he said leaning over to give her a kiss. "After today, defying the laws of physics will be child's play."

Chapter 25
December 2016

Laura had broken up for the school holidays and was looking forward to spending a few days with Ben over the Christmas period. He had told her that Dorothy had done a moonlight dash one night with Jimmy and had heard that she was living closer to the air base near Stratford. *Good riddance to bad rubbish*, was all Laura had to say.

She hadn't yet told him that her parents were coming on Christmas Eve and staying until Boxing Day. This would be the first time they would meet and it was also the first time her mum and dad had visited the house since Laura had moved in. Her mum wasn't one for visiting, instead she liked to be the hostess and apart from holidays she spent her time in her own home.

It had taken a bit of persuading and only the prospect of meeting Ben had been enough incentive for her mum to actually spend Christmas somewhere other than London. And even then Laura had had to insist that due to his work he couldn't make the journey to them. She didn't think her mum would understand that actually he couldn't leave the front garden.

The house was now completely finished, all the rooms decorated and furnished. New carpets had been laid and curtains hung. The house looked wonderful and Laura couldn't wait to show it off.

There was still just over a week till Christmas and Laura had been out and bought a tree, baubles, and goodness knows how many decorations. She started by winding the holly garlands through the banisters and up the stairs. She loved Christmas, always had, and this year would be even more special as she was spending it with

Ben. Maybe next Christmas she would be Mrs. Matthews. This thought stopped her in her tracks: Mrs. Matthews died next year.

She sat on the stairs suddenly downhearted. How could she get over that fact? If she married Ben she'd die. But then, maybe Ben didn't actually marry, after all she never found any proof of his marriage, it was just what Agnes had told her. And the facts about Lauren's mother, again no actual proof, just what she had been told. She smiled suddenly. *That was it, of course*, why hadn't she realised?

There was no record of Walter Matthews marrying because they couldn't actually physically get married, but that didn't stop him saying he was married. He had no close family to say otherwise and with regard to Lauren's mother, well if it was to be Laura, she would never be able to walk around in 1943 so it was probably easier to say that she'd died.

A huge smile crept over her face as she realised that at some time next year she'd be pregnant. Her mum and dad were certainly going to be shocked. Their long-unmarried daughter engaged and then a grandchild the following year. They could have a long engagement, she thought, after all some people never got married and it didn't really matter in her time, it was just Ben's era where it was still unheard of for a man and a woman to live together without being wed. It would be awkward at times that Ben would never be able to go anywhere or join her at parties or family gatherings, but if that was the price to pay for being with him she was more than willing to pay it.

Humming Christmas songs she carried on weaving the garland in and out of the banister. Then she headed into the living room and had great fun trying to get the

Christmas tree to stand up straight in its stand. It took her four times to get the lights looking just right before she added her silver and blue baubles and tinsel and ceremoniously plonked an angel on the top stem. She looked slightly drunk as the stalk was bent from Laura forcing it into the back of the car but after a little tweaking she finally stood tall and proud.

The wreath on the front door was the final decoration and when she opened the door to knock the nail in she found Chester sitting on the doorstep.

"Hello boy, been on your travels have you?" She picked him up and as usual he purred instantly. "Do you want something to eat?" The wreath was forgotten as she went into the kitchen and opened a pouch of cat food which was demolished in seconds. She stood staring at him as he washed himself after his meal. She still found it hard to believe he was magic, surely he was just a fat old tom cat. But there was something about the way he looked at you, as if he knew something you didn't.

Ben had told her that he couldn't remember a time when they didn't have Chester; he had been there when he was a boy, a teenager, and now a grown man. Laura wondered if his mother had bought a new cat each time the previous one died but surely it would be hard to match Chester's markings exactly, and how could you guarantee the same temperament? And those yellow eyes of his …

"It was you, wasn't it?" Laura had a sudden flashback. "It was you upstairs that night all those years ago." She couldn't believe she hadn't recognised him before but then she had only seen his eyes in the darkness. "Perhaps you are magic after all." Chester stopped his washing and looked at her with such intensity that Laura actually thought he understood what she was saying. "But why were you there?"

"Laura?" Ben shouted down the stairs.

"In the kitchen." She walked over to the cooker and poured two glasses of mulled wine that she'd put on to warm earlier.

"Wow, you've been busy." He was dressed in his usual attire of shirt and trousers and Laura had a sudden thought that he would have to have some more modern clothes for when her parents came and she made a mental note to show him the joys of online shopping later on.

"I wanted our first Christmas together to be special." She kissed him 'hello'.

"I'm not bothering with a tree this year." He shrugged his shoulders slightly. "Seems a bit silly to decorate the house twice so to speak and anyway I'm spending Christmas with you, just the two of us." He pulled her into his arms for another kiss.

"About that." He had started to kiss her neck. "My parents are coming." Laura didn't think he'd heard her so she said it again, a little differently. "My mum and dad are staying here for Christmas."

"They're what?" He stopped kissing her and looked her full in the face. "How's that going to work? I can't exactly sleep in your bed with your father here and I can't go home at night. What am I supposed to say? Oh do excuse me while I just pop through the mirror back into my own time. They'll think I've had too much sherry."

"They're coming late Christmas Eve and going Boxing Day morning." She tried to reassure him. "I've already told them you're staying here as well and they're really looking forward to meeting you."

"But what if I slip up?" He was panicking now; he hadn't thought he'd ever have to meet Laura's parents. It was hard enough trying not to say the wrong thing in front of the neighbours for just a few minutes at a time let alone nearly two days of watching what he was saying and how he was acting.

"You'll be fine." She slapped him playfully on the cheek. "They're not ogres you know and I so want them to meet you." She looked at the ring sparkling on her finger. "And we can announce our engagement properly as well."

"But then they'll want to know our plans and where we're having the ceremony." He started pacing up and down the kitchen. "You really haven't thought this through Laura. How can we even begin to explain how we met, where we go, all the normal things that normal couples do."

"Don't worry I've thought it all over." She had done nothing but think about how she could explain Ben to her parents. "If you have to lie, you stick to the truth as much as you can. We met here when you came to help me with the house. That's not too far from the truth." She poured herself another glass of wine. "We don't have to say anything about the wedding; couples stay engaged for years and years, sometimes they don't even get married at all."

"But I want to get married." He seemed horrified at the thought of them staying engaged forever. "We can't have children if we don't get married."

"So you want children then?" They'd never talked about raising a family and Laura still didn't know exactly how it would even work. Would the baby be able to come and go through the mirror? Surely it would, otherwise how were there pictures of Lauren in the 1960s? because there was no way she was having a baby in the 1940s, the National Health Service hadn't even started yet and she'd watched *Call the Midwife* every Sunday and the conditions that some mothers gave birth in made you wonder how babies had even survived in those days.

"Of course I do." He looked sad for a moment. "I wish my mother could have seen her grandchildren but with the war and looking after her there was never time to meet anyone and now I know why."

"Because you've been waiting for me all your life," Laura joked, placing a hand to her heart in mock adoration.

"Indeed I have." He took the hand off her heart and placed it over his. "I've never met anyone like you, Laura, it's not just because you're from the future. You're funny and kind, warm and generous and so beautiful it makes me forget myself sometimes." Laura was speechless all of a sudden. "I will be so proud to call you my wife." He raised her hand to his lips and pressed a kiss to the back of it.

"Well …" Laura's insides had melted and her power of speech had failed her. Men from this century just didn't talk like that. Not one of her previous boyfriends had ever said anything even remotely like that, it was things like 'you look fit in that' or 'your boobs look great'. "Thank you." The words seemed inadequate somehow and she kissed him as well.

"Haven't you taken Agnes and Wilf's card over yet?" Ben asked as his eyes noticed a red envelope propped up on the work top.

"Bugger." Laura grabbed it and walked off down the hall. "I'll go and do it now; she'll think we don't like her."

"In your slippers?" Ben queried.

"I can't be bothered changing them just to pop over the road and back." She wriggled fluffy green Elf shoes complete with bells on at him. "I'll have you know all the best Christmas Elves are wearing these this season."

Ben shook his head in amusement and stood by the door chuckling as she dashed down the path and over the road, bells ringing as she went. It was already dark even though it was only six and frost had started forming on the cars and the road was shiny in the moonlight. He watched her open Agnes' gate quietly, tiptoe down her path and post the card as silently as she could. Looking at him with her finger to her lips in a shushing motion she came back up the path and ran over the road.

Ben then watched in horror as she skidded on the ice, Elf slippers weren't the best for winter and she landed with a thud, in a heap in the road. He dashed to the end of the path and stood helplessly at the gate.

"Laura, are you okay?" He could only just see her face in the dark but he sighed with relief when he saw she was laughing.

"I'm fine." She giggled trying to stand up but the mixture of laughter and no grips failed her. "I can't get up." The laughter was uncontrollable now and she lay back on the road despite the chill on her back.

"Turn onto your front and use your knees." Ben advised, smiling at her. "I told you to change your shoes." A rumbling noise from up the street made Ben turn his head. Two bright lights were heading down the road. "Laura, you need to get up now, there's a car coming." He looked to the car and back to Laura, the driver wouldn't be able to see her where she was, there were cars parked on both sides. "You really need to get up now," he shouted.

"I can't!" she screamed. "Shit! Ben, I can't get up." Laura tried and tried to get to her feet but each time she slipped and fell back down. Panic was setting in now and making everything worse.

"Laura!" Ben screamed as the car came closer and closer. It was just a few metres away now and without even knowing what he was doing he raced across the road and grabbed Laura, depositing her not very gently on the pavement. The car screeched to a halt, stopping a few yards past where Laura had just been.

The driver wound down his window and swore at them, called them drunk arseholes, and drove off.

"Wanker!" Laura shouted after him.

"Are you okay?" Ben was feeling her arms and legs. "Nothing broken?"

"No, I'm fine." He helped her to stand up. "Ben!"

"What?" He looked at her worriedly. "What's the matter? Are you hurt?"

"Look!" she simply said. He shook his head in confusion. "Look around."

"I'm outside the house!" he almost squealed in delight. "I'm outside the house."

Chapter 26

"**H**ow did that happen?" Laura couldn't believe it, after months of being confined to the house he could now walk around. Was it just a one off? Could he go further than the street?

"Shall we go for a walk?" Ben was eager to see the futuristic world he'd only glimpsed from the window.

"I think I should change first." She looked down at her slippers. "And maybe get a coat, it's freezing out here." They walked back to the house but Ben wouldn't go past the gate. "What's wrong?"

"What if this is my only chance?" He started pacing a little. "What if I only broke the barrier or whatever it is, to save you? I don't want to go back in and then find I can't get out again."

"But you can't stay outside forever." She completely understood what he was saying and she knew she'd be the same if it was the other way around.

"I know that. You go change into your boots and grab a coat; can you get mine from my bedroom please?" He was starting to feel the chill himself and as much as he wanted to stay outside he didn't think he'd last long without a coat.

"Course I will." She headed into the house, up the stairs and through the mirror into Ben's house.

She'd never been in the house without him before and it was pitch black. She fumbled around for the light switch and bashed her leg into the bed in the process. He'd moved into this room a few weeks ago and with the help of Laura they had re-decorated it and changed the curtains and bed covers.

Chester was curled up asleep on the bed and Ben's long black coat was next to him. He must have come in from work, took off his coat and headed straight to Laura. She picked it up and draped it over her arm before giving Chester a quick stroke behind the ear. It was then she noticed something else on the bed, a small wooden box.

Putting the coat back down she sat on the bed and lifted the box onto her lap. Torn between curiosity and not wanting to invade his privacy she sat for a few minutes. Curiosity got the better of her and she opened the lid. Inside were a few black and white photos who she assumed were his mum and dad. A photo of a young man in uniform and some medals which Laura guessed to be his father's from World War I.

At the bottom she noticed something strange, underneath all the black and white was a colour photo peeping out. She picked all the other photos out of the box and found herself staring at her prom picture.

"How did that get in there?" She asked Chester who had woken up and was busy nudging her hand for more attention. She put it back with everything else, placed the box back on the bed and picked up the coat again. Ben must have taken the photograph out of her album, but why? It didn't really matter, if he'd have asked she would have let him have it but now she couldn't ask him because then he would know she'd looked in his private things.

"Where on earth have you been?" Ben was stamping his feet and hugging himself when she finally re-emerged outside.

"I couldn't find my gloves." She pushed all thoughts of the photo to one side; it wasn't important anyway, perhaps he just wanted a picture of her to keep and that was the only one of her on her own; she didn't really like having her photo taken so they were a rarity.

"So where are you taking me then?" He took her hand as they walked down the street.

"Seeing as we haven't had dinner yet, we'll go to the pub." He looked horrified at this suggestion. "Pubs aren't what they used to be," she reassured him. "Well, some aren't anyway."

It was a short walk to the pub but it seemed to take forever. Ben was fascinated by everything. All the different makes and models of cars, the Christmas lights; you name it and he had to stop and look at it. They even spent an hour in the little Tesco Express a few streets away because he had to look at every shelf in every aisle.

They finally arrived at The George and Dragon nearly two hours after they'd left the house. It was an old white house with a thatched roof and looked so out of place in amongst the modern houses but once you walked in you were whisked away to the olden days. Ben had instantly recognised it from the outside but the inside was remarkably different. He told her how dark it used to be and full of men smoking cigarettes and pipes but now it was light and airy, smoke free of course due to the new laws that Laura explained to him, with a mixture of men, women, and a few families dotted around.

They found a little table by one of the windows and Laura sat him down while she went to the bar. After all, he wouldn't know about the money they used today. She ordered two glasses of house red and headed back over. Two women were standing by their table talking to Ben who was all charm and smiles.

"Excuse me." Laura almost barged past them and sat down. The two women made a hasty exit. "You don't half attract attention to yourself."

"I only smiled at them when they smiled at me." He was so innocent in the ways of women that she just raised her eyebrows and handed him a menu.

"What do you fancy?" She scanned the many delicious dishes, herself opting for rump steak and chips.

"The mixed grill sounds wonderful." His eyes were wide in wonder. "All that meat for one meal though, it's gluttony."

"Not here it's not." And she headed back to the bar to order before he could change his mind.

"So do you think this could be permanent?" He asked a few minutes after she'd sat back down.

"I hope so." She placed a hand on his over the table. "Then we can actually get married; although there's still the question of a birth certificate and proof of residence."

"Well, I have my birth certificate and my ration book has my address on it." She couldn't help but giggle.

"Oh Ben." She squeezed his hand. "How can we use your real birth certificate, you're 106 in this century."

"Then let's get married in my century." He smiled and then just as suddenly he frowned. "But then with your birth certificate you're not even born and then you're not Catholic either." They both sat there rather downcast for a few minutes before Laura had a brain wave.

"We could just have a blessing." Ben looked at her as if she was speaking another language. "A friend of mine who was Catholic couldn't get married in church as the man she was marrying was divorced so they got married at the registry office and had a blessing in the church afterwards."

"But we wouldn't be married." Ben watched as the waitress walked over to them with an enormous plate. It was so large his chips were in a separate bowl.

"I know that and you know that." Laura thanked the waitress. "But everyone else would think we were already married. We could say we got married abroad or something like that. No one would ever know."

"I'd know." He looked solemn.

"It's only the legal bit where we wouldn't be married." She tried to reassure him. "The ceremony would be exactly the same, we can even exchange rings if we want to. It's just that there's no signing of the register and we wouldn't have a marriage certificate."

"So you wouldn't be Mrs. Matthews?" He questioned, spearing a piece of chicken, steak and sausage on to his fork.

"Not officially but I could always change my name by deed poll; and who calls people Mrs. Matthews anyway?" She watched him savour every morsel of food. "Everyone calls me Laura: they're not going to ever know that we weren't really married."

"We'd have the ceremony just as normal?" She could see he was starting to warm to the idea.

"Just as normal." She dipped a chip into her ketchup. "But it would have to be here. I don't think many people got married abroad and had blessings in your time." A sudden pain in her side made her wince.

"Are you okay?" He face was full of concern.

"I'm fine." She rubbed her side. "Probably just ate too fast." It subsided a little and she decided against anything else to eat, instead she watched Ben devour an ice cream sundae before they walked back home.

The pain in her side was getting worse. It came in waves from a dull ache to absolute agony and they were halfway home when she almost collapsed and had to tell Ben how bad it was. Without any hesitation he lifted her up and carried her as if she was as light as a feather. He stopped momentarily at the gate before a moan from Laura forced him through and into the house. He laid her gently on the sofa.

"I need to call the doctor." He picked up her mobile phone. "How do you switch it on?" He tapped the screen but nothing happened.

"My thumb print." He gave her the phone and watched as she pressed her thumb to the little button and the phone sprang to life. She pulled up the keyboard, dialled 999 and then handed the phone to him.

"999?" He vaguely remembered reading something about that. "But that only works in London for the police and fire brigade I think. How is that the doctor?"

"Which service do you require?" The calm female voice spoke over the speaker.

"I don't know." Ben panicked and looked at Laura.

"Ambulance," she croaked as another wave of pain made her double over.

"Ambulance," Ben repeated. He had no idea what was happening and felt so helpless.

"Putting you through." The lady's voice was replaced by a man within seconds.

"What's the emergency?" Ben tried to explain as best as he could, answering his questions about Laura with a little prompting. He was told to wait with the patient until the ambulance arrived.

It seemed to take forever and all he could do was pace up and down.

"Go and grab me a few things will you." Laura asked in between pains and gave him a short list of toiletries, underwear, and pyjamas to shove in the rucksack in her wardrobe. He didn't want to leave her but she insisted that she would need them, she had a feeling she'd be in hospital at least overnight.

"I'm going to see if I can still get out." He placed the rucksack by the front door and walked out, breathing a huge sigh of relief when he realised he could still get past the gate. A siren wailing and blue lights flashing alerted him to the approaching ambulance and he stood dumbfounded as it approached, parked up and two paramedics jumped out.

"Is she inside mate?" one asked, a rather heavy looking bag on his back.

"Yes … she's in the living room." They dashed inside and Ben was momentarily paralysed by the amazing piece of machinery he could see before him. How many lives would have been saved if they'd had equipment like this in the war and such a speedy response? You sometimes had to wait hours for the doctor in the forties.

The paramedic was soon back and this brought Ben back to the real world.

"We're going to have to take her in, I'm afraid." The second paramedic had opened the back of the ambulance and was wheeling a bed out and up the path. "Looks like an appendicitis."

The next hour was a whirlwind. Ben sat in the back with Laura as the ambulance dashed its way to the hospital. He'd never driven so fast and felt sick as it dodged vehicles and traffic lights. Laura was a little quieter now as they'd given her something for the pain and before they knew it the ambulance was backing up and the doors opened and Laura was wheeled out.

Ben couldn't hear what anyone was saying, he just walked behind them with Laura's bag, in awe of his surroundings. The hospital was like a maze, corridor after corridor, people everywhere, nurses, doctors, patients, and visitors. They were put in a cubicle with a blue curtain and almost instantly a nurse was taking bloods and offering words of comfort to Laura and Ben. He just nodded and smiled. Everything felt hazy as if he was in a daze and it was only when the doctor came with her results that he actually shook himself out of it.

"I'm sorry." Laura had drifted into a drug infused sleep and Ben hadn't really been listening. "What did you just say?"

"I understand that you'll be worried, Mr. Reynolds." They had assumed them to be married. "But if we don't operate soon the appendix could burst."

"Yes, yes, I heard that bit." Ben stood up and started pacing again. "You said something about the risks … to the …"

"Baby," the doctor finished the sentence for him. "Well there are significant risks to the baby but unfortunately we have no choice. If we don't operate then your wife will die and the baby too."

"Baby." Ben sat back down. "Baby." He repeated this over and over to himself and so shocked was he that he didn't even notice that they'd come to take Laura to theatre.

Chapter 27

Laura awoke late the next morning feeling groggy and in pain. She touched her side to find a white surgical plaster and then winced when she realised she'd pulled at the drip in her arm. She was in her own room and there was an orange button lying on her stomach. She pressed it and a few minutes later a nurse appeared.

"Good morning Laura." She went straight to the blood pressure machine and wound the cuff round Laura's arm, attaching the SATs reader to her finger once the cuff had started to inflate. "How are we feeling?"

"Okay I think," was about all she could say. "Could I have a drink please?" The nurse smiled and nodded, poured her a glass of water and then helped her to sit up. Her side burned as she moved.

"You'll feel some discomfort for a few days I'm afraid, but it will soon heal." The nurse wrote down some figures on the chart at the bottom of her bed. "No driving or lifting for three weeks either."

"Three weeks?" How was she going to get the Christmas shopping done? She couldn't send Ben; it would probably take him a week to get round the supermarket and then he couldn't drive her car. *Could he even drive?* She'd never even asked him that.

"We wanted to phone your husband, but we didn't have his mobile number I'm afraid." The nurse was tidying away the blood pressure machine and checking her drip.

"Husband?" Laura knew she was feeling out of it but was pretty sure she'd have remembered getting married. "I'm not married."

"Oh, I'm sorry." The nurse apologised. "I was told your husband had come with you in the ambulance last night."

"That's Ben, my fiancé," Laura corrected her. "We're getting married soon." It felt lovely to say those words. "Where is he?"

"He would have been sent home when you went into theatre." Laura felt sick with fear. *How would he have got home? Would he have known to get a taxi? Would he know to come in again today?*

"Is my phone here?" The nurse found it in her jeans pocket. "Thank you."

"I'll be back in a few minutes and get rid of that drip, you won't need it now you're awake." She headed to the door. "Would you like some toast or cereal? Or lunch will be coming in an hour."

"I'll wait for lunch if that's okay?" The nurse nodded and headed out of the room. The thought of food made Laura heave, but she knew she'd have to eat something. Her phone was almost dead, and she didn't know what to do about Ben. "Beth!" The idea came to her like a flash of lightning. Beth could go round the house and tell him what was happening if he was there. Please let him be there she begged, not even wanting to think what could've have happened to him.

"Look who I've found." The nurse was back again. "He's been in one of the family rooms all night waiting for you. My colleague just told me, so I went and got him for you." A rather tired and dishevelled Ben appeared behind her. He had huge dark circles under his eyes, his usually immaculate hair was sticking up in various places and his shirt was creased and crumpled.

"Thank God." He dashed past the nurse and started kissing Laura's face all over. Her eyes, her cheeks, and finally her lips. "I thought I'd lost you." He finally sat down on the bed beside her and took her hands in his. "I didn't know what to do or where to go." He kissed her again. "The nurse downstairs must have taken pity on me, and she said if I was quiet I could sit in one of the rooms and she'd find out how you were and which ward you were going to after the operation. I was so relieved when she told me you were okay. I must have fallen asleep after that because she woke me after her shift had finished and said I could go up to the ward as long as I didn't make a nuisance of myself."

"I've only just woken up." She stared at him, wanting to hold the memory of his face and words in her mind forever. "I was so worried when the nurse told me you would have gone home. I didn't know how you'd get there or if you'd even know where you were."

"They told me I had to go home but I refused." He shook his head. "I didn't want to leave you, but I was in such a daze with everything that was going on and then when they said about the baby I was just in total shock. I didn't even realise you'd gone to theatre till they came to clean the cubicle, which was when the nurse saw how much of a state I was in."

"Baby?" Laura hadn't heard anything he'd said after that. "What do you mean, baby?"

"You didn't know either?" He had wondered why she hadn't told him. "We're having a baby." He smiled such a joyous smile that Laura felt herself crying.

"A baby?" She wiped away the tears. "We're having a baby?" She kept asking the question over and over hoping it would sink in. "Is it okay? I mean I've just had an operation."

"I've spoken to the nurse and everything's fine." He saw the relief wash over her.

How didn't I know? Laura asked herself. "I've not been feeling sick and I'm sure I had my last period ... Oh ... how could I have been so stupid." She hit her hand on her forehead. "We've been so busy with the house and my new job that I haven't even thought, but now I think about it I haven't had a period for weeks and weeks."

"Well, I don't know anything about that." Ben didn't want to talk about periods and things like that. That was what women talked about.

"I can't believe it Ben; we're having a baby." She reached out to hug him, forgetting all about the stitches in her side. "Ow!"

"Shall I get the nurse?" Ben's face was full of concern.

"I just pulled the stitches when I moved, that's all." She smiled at him to reassure him. "I keep forgetting they're there." The nurse came back in, and Ben moved off the bed to allow her to remove the drip from Laura's hand. "Do you think I could have a shower and put my own pyjamas on?" She was desperate to wash and get out of the hospital gown.

"I don't see why not." The nurse smiled as she pulled the tube out of her vein and placed a plaster over the tiny wound. "Do you want me to help, or will your lovely fiancé here give you a hand?"

"I'll do it." Ben didn't wait for Laura to answer.

"Just remember that she'll be very wobbly to start with." The nurse warned. "No stretching and if the plaster comes off don't worry it needs to come off sooner rather than later anyway." She disappeared and Ben took Laura's bag from the cabinet and pulled out her towel and clean pyjamas.

"I need the shower gel and shampoo as well, please." Ben delved back in the bag.

"What's this shower gel stuff anyway?" He unscrewed the cap and took a sniff. "Smells like lavender."

"It's liquid soap." She watched him raise his eyebrows.

"Fancy stuff if you ask me." He screwed the lid back on. "You can't beat a good block of carbolic and a loofah." He took the things into the bathroom. "Any idea how this thing works?" He'd only just worked out the shower in the bathroom at home so Laura guessed he would be struggling with the one in the hospital but then she heard the water running and knew he'd worked it out. "It's okay, I've sorted it." He came out of the bathroom, dripping wet and she couldn't help laughing, wincing again as she did.

"What are you going to wear now?" He had already taken his shirt off and was beginning to unbutton his trousers when the nurse came back in.

"Oh, I'm so sorry." She covered her eyes with her hand. "I came to see if you had everything."

"It's okay." Ben did his trousers back up. "I had a fight with the shower and the shower won I'm afraid."

"I'll get you a gown to put on while they dry." She hurried away and Laura didn't know who was more embarrassed: the nurse or Ben.

The bell rang to signal the end of evening visiting and Ben reluctantly kissed Laura good night, and with strict instructions to catch a taxi, he headed off into 2016 all on his own. She hoped he would do what she said and not wander off; he knew the city in his own time, but it was so different now she was worried he would get lost.

The doctor had been to speak to her earlier and was hopeful that she would be discharged the following day. He couldn't tell her much about the baby only that it was safe and well and going by the date of her last period she was approximately ten weeks pregnant and that the baby was due in the middle of July.

Laura was still getting used to the idea of being pregnant and had no idea how she would tell her parents. They didn't even know that she was effectively living with Ben now so there would be quite a few things to tell them over Christmas dinner. She still hadn't worked out how on earth Christmas dinner was even going to happen. Hopefully she'd be able to hobble around the shops with Ben's help.

One of the support workers popped in with a cup of tea and some cheese and crackers for supper which Laura demolished in seconds. She flicked through the channels on the television, settling on the *Strictly Come Dancing* final. She never saw who won though as she had soon fallen asleep.

She awoke with a crick in her neck from falling asleep sitting up. It was only three in the morning, so she turned the TV off and inched herself carefully down the bed. It was then as she lay awake that reality began to hit her. Once again, all the things she knew about Ben's future whirled around and around in her head. How his wife died after their daughter was born. How nothing existed to indicate that Laura was part of his future in any way. That Lauren grew up without knowing her mother. She touched her stomach gently.

"I won't leave you little one," she whispered to her tummy. "I'll find a way to stay with you, even if it means I have to change the past, after all it's still in the future so it hasn't been written yet." This cheered her a little and she was soon asleep again, but her dreams were filled with sadness.

Chapter 28

It was finally Christmas morning and Laura awoke to the smell of bacon frying and freshly brewed coffee. She came down the stairs one at a time as her wound wasn't quite healed and found Ben already up and dressed in the jeans and shirt she had bought him from Next as an early present. He looked slightly stiff in them but was chatting away and serving a full fry up to her mum and dad.

"Merry Christmas sweetheart." Her parents spoke in unison and Ben turned, leaving the frying pan for a second to come over and give her a kiss.

"Merry Christmas," he whispered in her ear and patted her stomach tenderly with his back to Janice and Steve so they couldn't see.

"Happy Christmas everyone." She gave her mum and dad a peck on the cheek. "Why didn't you wake me up?"

"You need your rest after what you went through last weekend." Her mum turned her attention to Ben for her next sentence. "You really should have phoned us Ben," she scolded.

"I know I should have, Janice, and I really can't apologise enough." Laura knew he was in full charm offensive. "We just didn't want to worry you unnecessarily and have you rushing up here in the middle of the night." He placed two plates in front of them piled high with bacon, sausage, scrambled eggs, fried bread, and mushrooms.

"We know you were only sparing us the worry, son, don't think about it anymore." Laura raised her eyebrows at her dad's use of the word *son* and watched him tucking into his breakfast with relish. Before she knew it there was an identical plate waiting for her and one for Ben too.

"We do have a bit of news for you, actually." Laura and Ben had decided to tell her parents about the wedding first and then the baby a bit later on or maybe even in a few weeks' time; after all they were still getting used to the idea themselves.

"If you're about to tell us you're engaged you needn't bother." Her dad spoke without taking his eyes from his plate. "Your mum clocked that ring on your finger as soon as she saw you last night."

"We were just wondering how long it would take you to tell us." Her mum smiled. "We couldn't be happier, our little girl finally getting married."

"Less of the 'finally', Mum, you make me sound like an old spinster." She put her knife and fork down in mock protest.

"If the cap fits …" her dad teased. "No, seriously, congratulations to you both, we're sure you'll be very happy together."

"Any date set yet?" Laura could see her mum was eager to get involved but as much as it hurt this was the last thing that could happen.

"No, not yet." Laura wanted nothing more than to discuss wedding plans with her mum. "We might go abroad and just have a blessing here afterwards."

"You can't get married abroad!" Her mum was insistent. "How will all your family get to see you? Your Nan will never get on a plane, you know that."

"It's just I'm a Catholic you see, Janice." Ben tried to soothe the situation. "So we thought it would be easier if we got married just the two of us and then had the blessing and the party back home with everyone. We wouldn't even class ourselves as married till we'd shared the blessing with all the family. And it would be just like a real wedding with bridesmaids and Steve walking Laura down the aisle."

"And what do your parents have to say about it?" Janice wasn't convinced.

"I'm afraid I've lost my mother and father." A sudden motherly look crossed Janice's face and she got up and hugged Ben tightly.

"My dear, dear boy, I'm so very sorry." Laura didn't think she would ever let him go. "Then you can get married wherever you like, whatever helps you not miss them so much." Laura was in shock at this sudden change in her mum. She'd thought her mum was going to fight much harder for an actual wedding at home but she hadn't banked on Ben's charismatic voice and smile.

"How did they die?" Steve asked without thinking.

"Dad!" Laura was shocked.

"It's okay, Laura." Ben nodded reassuringly at her. "I lost my mother a few months ago to cancer I'm afraid. And sadly I never really knew my father, he died in the war when I was very small."

"Which war was that?" Steve had finished his breakfast and was now sipping coffee.

"The Fir …" Ben started to speak but Laura quickly answered for him.

"Falklands War wasn't it Ben?" It was the only British war she could think of.

"How sad," her mum sniffed. "I'd have liked to have met them."

"And I'm sure they would have loved to have met you." Ben wasn't sure of this at all. He couldn't speak for his father but he knew his mother would never have got on with Laura's parents, they were far too modern and modern had always scared his mother.

"So shall we wash up or open our presents first?" Laura changed the subject.

"I'll wash up." Ben was already by the sink running hot water. "You go through to the living room and I'll be there in a few minutes."

"Let me give you a hand." Steve had stood up and started to scrape the plates clean. "It will get done much quicker with the two of us. Let the ladies go and sit down."

"Well thank you Steve." Ben took the plates from him and placed them gently into the hot soapy water. "It's very kind of you."

"Come on, Mum." Laura linked an arm through her mum's. "Let's leave them to it."

The presents had been opened, dinner eaten and tidied away, and they were now sitting round the table playing Monopoly. Laura and her parents had always done this on Christmas Day night and were pleased to find that playing games had been a tradition of Ben's as well although Monopoly was a relatively new game in his time. Despite being full from dinner they all jumped at Laura's offer of cheese and crackers and she headed out into the kitchen after her turn knowing she had a good five minutes while Ben and her dad decided whether to buy houses or not on each of their goes.

"Well I can't believe she hasn't told you?" Laura heard her mum's voice as she headed back into the room. "We've never worked out why they left the house to her in the first place. We never knew Walter Matthews or his daughter and to write that note as if he was intimate with her when she'd only just been born ..." At this point Janice audibly shivered. "I find it a little spooky if I'm honest with you, Ben, and if it wasn't for the fact that he's obviously long dead I wouldn't have let Laura live here in a thousand years." Laura groaned inwardly, how on earth would Ben react to this? —and that was the first she'd heard her mum mention about her not living here, she'd been so enthusiastic at the beginning.

"It's all very intriguing I have to say." Ben showed no signs of the turmoil he must be in. "And this Jack chap sounds a real cad." Oh dear lord, she'd told him about Jack as well. Laura hadn't realised her mum could tell a story so quickly, she'd only been gone five minutes.

"Oh Mum, you haven't been boring Ben with all the nonsense about the house have you?" She thought this was the best way to play it, try and be nonchalant about it.

"On the contrary Laura." Ben stood up and helped her with the tray she was carrying. "I find it fascinating." He turned back to Laura's mum. "Do tell me everything, Janice." And that was it. Monopoly was forgotten as the whole story about Walter Matthews, everything they'd found out about him came tumbling out, quickly followed by Jack, and even about the old man on prom night. Laura sat down, helpless to stop the torrent of information flowing from Janice's mouth and just agreeing and nodding in the appropriate places. She watched Ben's face for any flicker of emotion but he just sat there taking it all in.

"Go fetch your prom photo and show Ben how beautiful you looked." Her mum seemed to have finally come to the end.

"I've already seen it, Janice." Laura looked at him. "I have a little confession I'm afraid." He caught Laura's gaze. "I took it out of her album a while ago. I was going to get it framed for her you see. Seems such a shame to have it stuck in an album; but I haven't found the right frame for it yet."

"Well, you'll have lots of wedding photos about the place soon." Janice hadn't noticed the tension that had suddenly formed a cloud above the table but her dad had. "Whose turn is it?"

"Is that the time?" Steve looked at his watch. "*EastEnders* is on in a minute, Janice."

"Why didn't you say so?" She shot up out of her chair and dashed into the living room where seconds later Laura could hear the familiar theme tune belting out. They sat in silence for a few moments.

"Please say something," Laura begged.

"What is there to say?" he said simply. "I know why you didn't tell me; you've always said you didn't want me to know my future and now I see why." He put his head in his hands and ran them through his hair. "Why does my daughter leave the house to you? Are we not together anymore?"

"I don't know, Ben." He looked at her as if he didn't believe her. "I really don't know." She was speaking the truth. "All the things you've been told are your future but they're in the past, but my future, well I don't know what my future is. Maybe you gave the house to your daughter to then leave it to me because that was the only way it could be in my name."

"But why do I move away and let it get so run down?" These were all questions Laura wished she knew the answer too.

"Perhaps we both move away," she said to him. "After all, I don't exist in the past do I? There's no record of me there because I haven't been born." She could see him thinking things through. "All I know is that we're here, together, and we love each other. That's all that matters."

"I suppose you're right." Laura knew he would continue to go over and over these facts time and time again but for now he seemed content to let it rest. "Like you said, it's in the past but also in the future and who knows what the future will bring."

"Exactly." She reached over and kissed him. "This time travel stuff is a complicated business."

"Speaking of time travel, have we missed *Doctor Who*?" Laura laughed, he had become obsessed with the *Doctor Who* series and Laura had brought him all the latest box sets as a Christmas present.

"We'll watch it on demand later." He had become accustomed to all the modern technology now and the Sky box was full of programmes he had recorded to watch at a later date.

"I can't believe we still have years to wait till we get television properly." He shook his head. "And even longer for colour pictures."

"Then consider yourself the lucky one that you don't have to wait." They had both stood up now.

"Oh I do." He took her hand and Laura knew he wasn't talking about TV anymore.

Chapter 29
January 2017

"So you're telling me that we actually see the baby?" Ben and Laura were sitting in the Maternity Department of the hospital waiting for an ultrasound. They had had to come in a taxi as Laura still wasn't allowed to drive and although Ben was more than happy to take the wheel they couldn't risk it as he wasn't insured and she didn't fancy the idea of explaining how a man of a hundred and six looked a third of his age, if they were to have an accident.

Although she knew he'd travelled the route to the hospital a few times, it was the first time with Laura conscious, as Beth had brought her home from the hospital after her operation, and his questions were endless. She answered them all as best she could, not really knowing when buildings had been built or what type of car went past. In fact, Ben sometimes told her things she'd never known. But the one question that he asked over and over again was about the ultrasound.

"Yes Ben." Laura was getting exasperated by now. She knew that it was all exciting to him, and it was exciting to her as well: but when you've been asked the same question, time and time again for the seven days since the letter arrived informing them of the scan date it did become a little monotonous.

"I think it's absolutely amazing." He placed a hand tenderly over her stomach. "Absolutely amazing." Laura was finding this to be his favourite phrase at the moment.

"Miss Reynolds." A nurse called her name from down the corridor and Laura stood up, Ben beside her. They walked towards the nurse and into the room. "Just hop on the bed and we'll get started." Laura eased herself up on to the bed and Ben sat down in the chair next to her.

The sonographer came into the room and dimmed the lights.

"It's a bit dark in here." Ben said looking around. "How will we see the baby if it's dark?"

"We can see the baby on the screen much better if the room is darker." The nurse explained this to Ben as she tucked large pieces of tissue paper over Laura's jeans and tucked her top up out of the way, exposing her stomach.

"On the screen?" Ben was confused. "I thought we were looking at the baby through Laura's tummy?" Laura groaned inwardly; she obviously hadn't explained the process to him properly.

"We are looking at the baby in the womb." The sonographer explained. "This will be a little bit cold." She said to Laura as she squirted gel on to her stomach. "Then we use this probe to send sound waves which produce an image of your baby on the screen." As she was explaining this she had begun to move the probe over Laura, tapping at the keyboard with her other hand now and again.

Neither Laura nor Ben could see the screen to start with and for a full five minutes Ben sat as still as he could. Then suddenly he stood up and moved behind the sonographer so he could see the screen.

"Could you sit back down please, Sir?" The sonographer asked and the nurse ushered him back in his seat. "I have to take a few measurements first to make sure everything is okay and then I will turn the screen around and show you both."

"I'm sorry," Laura said to them while giving Ben a withering look. "He's just very excited."

"I understand." She nodded to Laura. "We find some of the fathers very enthusiastic." She tapped away for a few more minutes. "There, everything seems fine Miss Reynolds. Baby is as it should be." She turned the screen around. "Here's baby's head. Baby's body and heartbeat. There's one of baby's arms and the legs are there." She placed a finger on the screen as she explained to them what they were seeing.

At first Laura couldn't see anything, just a mass of black and a few circles. She had the same trouble when Beth had sent her a picture of her first scan photo. But then as she looked closer she could make out what the sonographer was telling her. The baby had a huge head in comparison to its body and the heart looked tiny, but there it was, beating away.

"Why can't I feel it moving?" Laura couldn't believe that all this was going on inside her but she couldn't feel a thing.

"Baby is too small at the moment." She explained. "About the size of a sprout. As this is your first pregnancy you'll probably start to feel movements around nineteen weeks but it's different with everyone and you may feel them sooner or later than that."

"That's our baby?" Ben asked so quietly that they hardly heard him.

"That's your baby," the sonographer replied smiling. "Would you like a photo to take home?"

"Yes please." Laura looked at Ben. He was staring at the screen, a daft smile on his face and tears in his eyes.

"That's our baby," he said to Laura. "Our baby." The sonographer turned off the screen and cleaned Laura's stomach and the nurse handed them a small photograph of the scan.

"So, all being well you'll have another scan at twenty weeks and then the next time you see your baby will be when it's born." The nurse turned the lights back up and Laura got off the bed and walked to the door.

"Are you coming, Ben?" she asked as he was still staring at the screen as if waiting for the image to come back.

"That's our baby," he said once again, walking over to the door and out into the hallway in a daze.

"Thank you," Laura said, before following him out and taking his hand to lead him back through the maze of corridors to the taxi rank.

"I just can't believe it." Ben was starting to look a little more alert but his eyes were still glazed over. It wasn't until they were halfway home that he returned to normal and gave a little laugh. "Do you know what I thought would happen?"

"What do you mean?" Laura had just been sending Beth a picture of the scan on her phone.

"When you said we'd see the baby in your tummy." Ben laughed again. "I thought you meant we'd actually see the baby in your tummy." Laura looked at him confused. "You know, like somehow we'd see through your skin."

"Blimey." Now it was Laura's turn to laugh. "We're not that advanced."

"Well, how was I to know?" He was still laughing when they pulled up outside the house and got out of the taxi, then walked hand in hand up the path.

"Now isn't this cosy." A familiar voice chilled Laura to the spot and she turned round to find Jack standing by the gate. "Here's me, all ready to forgive you for dumping me like that, not a word for ages, blocking my calls and even moving house. But then I find you shacked up with some other bloke. Didn't take you long, did it?"

"Can we help you with something?" Ben's laughing had stopped now and he'd turned round to face Jack, taking a protective step in front of Laura as he did.

"It's okay, mate." Jack was tall, but Ben was taller and with years of hard work under his belt was far bigger. "I'm not here to cause trouble. Just that Laura and I have unfinished business that's all."

"Well from what I hear that's not really true is it?" Laura could feel the tightness in Ben as he held himself back.

"Can't she speak for herself?" Jack scoffed. "She's got you well trained." Ben stiffened even more.

"Just go, Jack." Laura took Ben's hand. "You're not wanted here."

"Clearly not." He turned away from the gate. "Always thought you were easy, coming on to me the way you did, hopping into bed after a few glasses of …" But he didn't get to finish his sentence. Ben flew down the path in a second and launched himself at him, knocking them both to the ground with a thud.

Laura ran into the street to see fists flying from both men although Jack's seemed to be hitting the air more times than they hit Ben. Laura was helpless to do anything and she just kept screaming at them to stop. Agnes had heard the kafuffle and was heading over the road for a better look.

"Mr. Matthews!" Ben's head shot up at the sound of his name spoken in shock and Jack, seeing his advantage, managed to punch him right in the face. Blood spattered from his nose and he grabbed it in agony. With a smirk on his face, Jack got up, brushed himself down and headed off down the street.

"You're welcome to her, mate." Ben made to go after him but Laura was by his side.

"He's not worth it Ben." She pulled a tissue from her coat pocket and held it to his nose.

"What on earth was all that about?" Agnes handed her more tissues as the bleeding was quite fast. "I thought better of you, Mr. Matthews, brawling like some thug in the street." The use of his full name instead of Ben was scathing enough without the matronly tone she was using as well.

"I don't know what came over me, Agnes." He stood up, his clothes covered in dust and blood. "I'm sorry Laura. I just saw red." He sounded like he had a cold and when he touched his nose he winced. "I think I've broken it."

"Serves you right." And with that Agnes headed home, shaking her head all the way.

"Looks like we're heading back to the hospital." Laura phoned for a cab and wasn't surprised when the one they'd just got out of pulled up. "University Hospital," she told the driver, helping Ben into the back. "Again."

After a three hour wait, two x-rays, five cups of tea and coffee, crisps, chocolate and sandwiches, numerous doctors and nurses unable to fathom out why they couldn't find any record of Ben Matthews, they were finally allowed home with the prognosis that the nose wasn't broken but would be extremely sore for a few days.

The taxi ride home this time was much quieter and Laura felt exhausted. When finally she sat down on the sofa it was almost eight o'clock. Ben headed straight upstairs to have a shower and change his clothes. When he came back down Laura was fast asleep. He gently removed her shoes and eased her legs onto the sofa, so she was lying down. He covered her with the blanket she used as a throw then with a soft kiss on her lips he headed back to his own time.

Chapter 30
April 2017

"Can I ask again why we have left it so late?" Beth said, parking the car and turning off the engine. "It's only six weeks till the wedding and you leave it till now to go dress shopping." They both got out and wearily shut the doors. It had been a long day, driving round to various shops and trying on what felt like hundreds of dresses.

It had been immense fun to start with. They'd found the perfect dress for Beth. It was in blush satin, A-line with tiny cap sleeves, and the lady said she would make a Bo Beep style dress for Jessica in ivory with the same blush satin made into a sash.

"Because I didn't know how big I was going to be." In hindsight Laura wished she'd started months ago. She was almost six months now and hardly showing at all. She had a neat bump which while the spring weather was still cool hid nicely under baggy jumpers and shirts. It was now the Easter holidays and the wedding was set for the twenty-seventh of May.

They had struggled to find anyone willing to perform the ceremony under such strange conditions but luckily a new and very young priest had recently arrived at All Souls Church and he was more than happy to *'unite two people in God's love'* in any circumstances.

"I was twice your size at this stage." Beth had been a wealth of knowledge over pregnancy issues. "If I didn't know otherwise I'd have sworn you were having a boy." Laura had told Beth everything, even her concerns over the fate of the future Mrs. Matthews. But as Laura also kept telling herself, Beth just said, *"But you aren't ever going to be Mrs. Matthews, not really,"* and that was enough to quieten the fears until the next time they arose.

"I didn't realise it would be this small." Laura's heart sank as she looked at the tiny shop front of The Bridal Gallery. "If I couldn't find a dress in the big shops with all that stock, how on earth will I find one in here?"

"Well, we've driven all the way across town and it's the last one in the whole city so we're going in." She took her hand and almost pulled her inside.

The shop was bright and larger than they had expected with a long row of wedding dresses to the left and bridesmaid dresses to the right. A blonde woman came out to meet them and introduced herself as Sarah. Beth filled her in on the day's events and how late they'd left it and why, but this didn't seem to faze Sarah and she turned to Laura with a huge smile.

"I've had far worse than six weeks' notice Hun, don't you worry." And she started rifling through the dresses on the rack. "Now, what was it you were looking for? White? Ivory?"

"Definitely ivory." Laura and Beth were both now looking through the dresses.

"I can see you're not showing very much at the moment." Sarah pulled out a dress. "But in my experience that can change by the day let alone the week so might I suggest an empire line. Low cut at the bust, and who doesn't have a great bust when they're pregnant?" She gave a little wink. "Then the dress flows from underneath so it will hide whatever size of bump you have and you won't feel restricted or uncomfortable. So very important on your wedding day. I can't stand seeing brides hitching up off the shoulder dresses all the time because they don't fit properly."

She unzipped the bag to reveal an ivory satin dress. It had small, puffed sleeves and tiny embroidered flowers on the bodice in the same blush colour that Beth's dress was made of. Both of them squealed in delight. Sarah turned the dress around to reveal tiny satin covered buttons down the back and a small train.

"It looks perfect," Laura exclaimed.

"Then let's try it on." Sarah led Laura to the back of the shop and pulled a long cream curtain across. In just a few minutes the dress was on and it fitted to perfection. The curtain was pulled back and she stepped out.

"Oh my God Laura." Beth put her hands over her mouth. "That's the one. You look wonderful." Sarah took Laura over to the full-length mirror and she couldn't believe what she was seeing.

"I can't believe it." She swished around from one side to the other, looking at herself from every angle. "Why didn't we just come here in the first place?"

"Some brides find their dress straight away; others take their time." Sarah was tucking a tiara and veil onto Laura's head. "But sooner or later fate lends a hand." Laura looked at herself again now that the ensemble was complete. Beth was so emotional she couldn't speak and Laura was choked with tears. "Now, that's the reaction I was hoping for."

"Laura, you look incredible." Beth had finally found her voice again. "Ben's jaw will hit the floor when he sees you in it."

"I just can't get over how we just walked in here and you knew exactly what I was looking for." Laura couldn't stop staring at her reflection.

"Years of experience." She started faffing with the veil. "Now I don't know if you want a veil or not, lots of brides like them for the ceremony and photos but take them off after that. And were you looking for a tiara or having something else in your hair?"

"I hadn't even thought about my hair." She'd been so busy with all the other preparations, trying to get a nursery sorted for the new arrival and still working, that her hair had been the last thing on her mind.

"I am a fully trained hairdresser and beautician as well." Sarah handed them each a leaflet. "What date is the wedding? I can see if I'm free and if you want me I can do hair and makeup and help you dress on the day as well."

"It's the twenty-seventh of May at four." Laura felt that fate had certainly lent her a hand when they decided to come here.

"You're in luck." Sarah had flicked through her phone. "I've got a smallish wedding on the morning but I'll be finished there by eleven. Now how many bridesmaids are there? And will mother of the bride and groom want anything?"

"Just me and my little girl as bridesmaids," Beth answered. "And she hasn't got much hair yet so just me and Laura."

"Ben's mum died a few months ago so it's just my mum but I'm sure she said she'd booked in with her hairdresser the day before so she might just need a little tweaking so to speak."

"Then you're all booked in." She flicked back through her phone. "When did you want a trial run?"

They spent the next half an hour with Sarah discussing various styles. The dress and tiara were ordered, Laura had decided against a veil, and feeling very pleased with themselves they headed back into the car and drove to the local Harvester after they both realised they were famished.

"I really need to talk to you about something." They had demolished two bowls of salad and were waiting on the mains when Laura turned serious.

"Sounds ominous." Beth took a sip of coke. "You're not having second thoughts are you?"

"No, not at all." Laura couldn't wait to 'marry' Ben. "It's just if something does happen to me …"

"Don't talk like that." Beth shook her head. "You're going to be fine. How many women do you know that have died in childbirth in this day and age?"

"I know that Beth, but something keeps niggling me and I can't shake it." Laura needed her to understand. "If something …"

"I'm not listening to this." Beth put her hands over her ears.

"Just hear me out." Laura pulled Beth's hands away. "Please."

"Okay." Beth put her hands on the table. "But I think you're being daft."

"I know you do." The waitress came with their food. "I'll feel a lot better though if you just promise me something." Laura waited for the waitress to leave before she continued talking. "Say I get stuck in Ben's time for example, there isn't the care in the 1940s that there is now and I just need you to promise me that you'll try and explain to my parents. I'd hate them to never know what happened to me if that was to happen."

"You're not going to get stuck in Ben's time." Beth was tucking into a rump steak and didn't seem to be taking the matter very seriously. "You've been coming and going through it for months now."

"That's the problem." Laura took a small bite of a chip. "I've been thinking that maybe it was the baby that enabled us to move around in each other's time."

"How do you mean?" Beth looked perplexed.

"Well, we couldn't leave the house in each other's time before but then when I was pregnant we discovered that Ben could move around in our time, and it works for me as well although I haven't made it past the end of the street yet." She took another bite of chip. "Maybe the baby is the key, because it's half Ben's time and half mine."

"Hark at you." Beth was impressed. "I hadn't even thought about it for a while. Ben spends so much time in this century I forget he's from the last one."

"So I'm worried that when the baby's born the link will break." This was the first time she shared this fear out loud and it scared her.

"But the link was there before you were pregnant." Beth dunked an onion ring into some ketchup. "It might not work fully again afterwards but then if it is the baby creating the link then maybe the baby will keep the link going."

"There's just too many variables." Laura put down her knife and fork and looked seriously at Beth. "Just promise me that if something happens, that if one day I just disappear, then you'll tell my parents for me."

"Laura, you really are being silly." Beth took one look at Laura's face. "I promise Hun, I promise to do whatever I can."

"Thank you." Laura started eating again. "Now that's over, what have you got planned for my hen night next week?"

The following Saturday found Laura and Beth down in London back at Laura's old haunts with her university friends and old teaching colleagues. Beth had bedecked her with a pink sash emblazoned with 'Bride to be' and L plates along with a novelty tiara made entirely of blown-up condoms and sparkly gems. Laura's bump had grown suddenly and try as she might she couldn't hide it anymore. The day had been hot and sticky and the thought of wearing a jumper in a crowded night club gave Laura a hot flush.

Instead she had opted for a tight-fitting white top, black jeans and killer heels which she knew she would live to regret later on. Beth was dressed almost identically and she wore a sash with 'Maid of Honour' written on it.

They had downed a few drinks in the pub next to the hotel while they waited for everyone to arrive, Laura was on orange juice but she had vowed to have just one drink before the end of the night.

"Surprise." A tap on Laura's shoulder made her turn round.

"Lucy!" She screamed and hugged her childhood friend. "It's been years."

"Too long." Lucy hugged her back, then hugged Beth with equal gusto. "You've been busy I see." She nodded to the bump.

"What about you?" Laura had kept in touch with Lucy via Facebook and she'd had four children in six years including a set of twins.

"Rob wants another three at least." She smiled, pulling out her phone and showing them both a recent photo.

"The twins are the spitting image of you." Beth pulled out her phone and showed Lucy a photo of Jessica.

"I can't believe how much she's grown." Lucy and Beth proceeded to swap baby stories and as Laura didn't have any to tell yet she made her excuses and headed off to the toilet.

The toilets were down the stairs at the back of the pub and because of this they felt much cooler than the stuffy bar full of people. As per normal she was bursting and it always amazed her how weak her bladder had become since the baby had grown. It felt like she was constantly going to the loo. After washing her hands and checking her hair, she straightened her sash and stepped out into the corridor.

"Well, well, well." Laura looked towards the voice. "Fancy seeing you here."

Chapter 31

Jack was leaning lazily up against the wall opposite the ladies' toilet. His arms were folded tightly across his chest with one hand on the other arm, his fingers tapping restlessly.

"Not again, Jack." Laura wasn't in the mood for a fight. She didn't even know why he was here; this wasn't his side of the city.

"Not again?" He uncrossed his arms but stayed leaning on the wall as if barring the way. "You disappear on me for no reason, can't contact you, and couldn't even find you when I came to look for you, and when I do, what do I find?" He paused before answering his own question. "Shacked up with another bloke."

"No reason?" Laura didn't want to get in an argument with him but she wasn't about to let him talk to her like that. "I saw you Jack, in the shop, playing happy families." She thought that would knock the superior look off his face but if anything it made it worse.

"Just because I'm married doesn't mean I can't see other people." Laura's mouth dropped open in shock.

"What?" Had she heard him right? "You mean you cheat on your wife? On a regular basis?"

"Well of course." Jack was standing in front of her now. "One woman can't have all this to herself; that wouldn't be fair." And with that he kissed his scrawny biceps one after the other.

"You are so up yourself," Laura laughed. "I can't believe I fell for you."

"Like you're so prim and proper." He was scowling now. "All that nonsense about inheriting a house from the strange Matthews' family when all along you were seeing him anyway. What was it, some kind of insurance scam?" Laura just stared at him so he continued. "Had me for a proper mug the pair of you, and now I find out you're getting married." Jack's voice was raised in anger now.

"It wasn't like that, Jack." Laura couldn't believe she was having to defend herself. "Ben isn't anything to do with the Matthews," she lied.

"Oh pull the other one, it's got bells on it." His London accent was becoming more noticeable as his voice got higher. "I heard that old woman calling him Mr. Matthews so don't be telling me he's nothing to do with it. All that pretending not to know who they were and that obviously fake letter: all for my benefit was it?"

"You don't know what you're talking about, Jack." Laura tried to get past him but he stood in her way. "Let me get by," she told him as calmly as she could.

"But we're not finished yet." He side-stepped in front of her every time she made a move to get past. "There's just the small matter of a very expensive antique cameo that you owe me."

"You gave me that as a present." Laura was hoping he wasn't serious.

"I did." He smiled coldly. "But that was before I knew you were a conniving little bitch." He didn't see the slap coming until he felt it across his cheek. "Truth hurts does it?" Laura went to slap him again but this time he was ready and he caught her by the wrist.

"Let me go, Jack." She squirmed in his grasp, managing to wrench her arm free. "You're not having it back."

"I'll give you a couple of weeks to think about it." He made a step back away from her. "After all you're so busy with your fake wedding." The look of horror on her face made him laugh. "Didn't take much to find out you weren't even getting married. A little more digging around and I wonder what else I might discover?" And with that he made a mock bow and walked up the stairs.

Laura went back into the bathroom and splashed cold water on her face, it made her feel a little better but still she was trembling from Jack's words. She jumped a little when the door opened but it was just Beth.

"Was that Jack I just passed on the stairs?" Laura nodded. "What the hell was he doing here?" She looked at Laura's face. "Are you okay?" She took her hands. "You're bloody shaking."

"He wants the cameo back." Laura leaned back against the sink.

"Shit!" Beth hugged her tightly. "What are you going to do?"

"No idea." A few tears trickled down her cheeks. "I can't give it back to him. I mean, I know the mirror worked for Ben without it on my side but only for a few hours a night. We can't go back to living like that, not with the baby on the way."

"He can't make you give it back." Beth pulled a tissue out of her bag. "He gave you that as a present, he can't just take it back because you're not together anymore." She dabbed Laura's cheeks then under her eyes. "Now, let's forget all about Jack bloody Williams and get back outside. Everyone's ready to move onto the club."

"You go on ahead. I just want to fix my makeup." Beth gave her best *I don't believe you* look but she knew when her friend needed a few moments.

"I'll go tell the others to drink up then." With a reassuring squeeze of her hand she opened the door and was gone.

Laura stared at herself in the mirror. Her mascara had run a little and she wiped it off before reapplying a little foundation and powder. She topped up her lipstick and after a quick fluff of her hair she looked as she had at the start of the night. Pushing all thoughts of Jack away she opened the door only to find him standing there once again.

"I've had a little think and I've decided that you can pay me for the cameo instead if you like." He had his arms above his head, his hands on top of the door frame, keeping the door open with his foot.

"How much do you want?" She pulled her purse out of her bag.

"I didn't mean in money." At first Laura didn't understand but then as she watched the sleazy smile drift across his face as he looked her up and down she realised.

"You're unbelievable!" She shoved her purse back in her bag.

"You know you want to." He started walking towards her, Laura backing away as he did. "I'm not asking for anything you haven't done in the past." She could see he was serious and she was starting to panic. "You've slept with me while sleeping with him before so what's the difference?"

"For the last time Jack, I did not cheat on you." She'd run out of room now and her back was up against the cold tiles. Instinctively she tucked her bag in front of her tummy.

"So you say." He was right in front of her now. "But the evidence speaks for itself I'm afraid." He placed his hands against the wall on either side of her waist pinning her in his grasp. "Don't be hiding yourself away from me now."

He pushed the bag aside and then gasped as he noticed her swelling stomach. Laura prayed this would put him off but it only seemed to increase his desire. His eyes narrowed and he licked his lips.

"Please Jack." The way he was looking at her made her feel violated. "I'm pregnant."

"I knew you still wanted me." He had purposefully mistaken her 'please'. "Nothing more beautiful than a woman carrying a child." His face had suddenly turned almost tender.

"But it's not your child." As soon as she said those words she knew it was a mistake. His face changed instantly.

He brought his head down to kiss her and just at the moment the door burst open as three giggling women stormed in. Jack's head shot round to look at them and seizing the opportunity Laura kneed him straight in the crotch. He doubled over in pain and she ran past him, past the three now silently shocked women and straight up the stairs.

"What on earth?" She almost fell into Lucy's arms. "Laura, what's happened?"

"Jack's just nearly attacked me in the toilet." She was shaking uncontrollably now and Lucy led her over to sit at a quiet table in the corner of the pub, catching Beth's eye as she did.

"Ex-boyfriend Jack?" Lucy could remember a few Facebook conversations.

"What's the matter?" Beth had reached them now, a look of concern on her face.

"Jack tried to attack her in the bathroom." Beth didn't wait to hear any more and she flew off towards the back of the pub only to appear a few moments later.

"Bastard's gone." She was furious. "I knew I shouldn't have left you alone."

"It's not your fault Beth." Laura was starting to settle a little now she knew he'd gone and she was no longer on her own.

"You need to call the police." Beth was always the sensible one. "They'll have it all on CCTV."

"But he didn't actually touch me." Laura didn't want to think about it anymore. "It was more threatening than physical."

"It doesn't matter." Lucy explained. "It was obviously enough to upset you as much as it did and what if he tries it again?"

"I think he was just trying to scare me." Laura knew she was making excuses for him and she really didn't know why.

"I'm calling the police." Beth went to walk outside so she could hear on the phone but Laura stopped her.

"I'll do it." Laura stood up. "I just need to tell everyone I'm heading back to the hotel; I'm not ruining their night as well."

"Let me tell them." Lucy gave her a quick hug. "I'll just say you're not feeling well, pregnancy related probably." She turned to Beth. "We'll ring the police from the hotel, she'll be calmer then."

"Thanks Lucy." Laura smiled at her and she walked off. A few of the girls came to say goodbye and after kisses and hugs it was time for Laura, Lucy and Beth to flag down a taxi.

"Feels like old times," Beth said as they drove to the hotel.

"I'm glad you're both here." Laura was sitting in the middle of the other two on the back seat of the black cab. "I'll ring the police now." The others nodded their agreement and she rang the local station. "They're sending a constable out to the hotel to take a statement." Laura put her phone back in her bag just as they pulled up at the hotel.

It was the next afternoon when the constable rang Laura back with some information. She was on the train home with Beth and still a little shaken up. She hadn't really slept, even with the comfort of Beth and Lucy next to her, and they'd spent most of the night recalling their old school days.

"Well, that was a waste of time." Laura slammed the phone down, waking Beth with a jolt after she'd nodded off, her head resting on her folded arms on the table.

"What?" Beth stuttered, rubbing her eyes.

"The police." Laura shoved her phone away as if it was to blame. "They can't find him."

"What do you mean, they can't find him?" Beth was still groggy after her nap. "You told them where he lived and about the shop."

"The shop is all boarded up. The constable said they asked in the bar opposite and they said it closed a few months ago and as for the address he gave me well that was obviously fake because there's an old couple living there who have lived there since they got married in 1964."

"And that's it." Beth couldn't believe it. "They just stop looking for him?"

"Well they don't have a lot to go on." Laura sighed. "Most of the things he told me about himself weren't true. The police couldn't find any record of him so looks like he made everything up. Who is to say he's even called Jack Williams?"

"What are you going to tell Ben?" Beth had asked her this question over and over again and she'd always got the same answer.

"I'm not," was Laura's simple reply. "What good would it do? He'll only get upset and angry and there's nothing him, me or anyone else can do so I've just got to try and forget about it and hope that he never shows his face again." But even as she said those last words she had a sinking feeling that it wouldn't be the last time that she would see him.

Chapter 32
May 2017

"You really need to tell me what's wrong." She could tell Ben was worrying about her. It had been over two weeks since Beth had dropped a very pale and fatigued Laura back at the house with some made up excuse about not feeling well due to the pregnancy. Ben had been so concerned that he hadn't asked any questions initially but he was starting to fear the worst now.

"I'm okay, really I am." She knew he didn't believe her. She wasn't eating properly; she hardly talked and sudden noises made her jump. They'd even noticed the change at work and the Head had taken her to one side yesterday and asked what was going on. It had all come pouring out and Laura had felt much better for it but the thought of telling Ben filled her with dread.

"I'm taking you to my favourite café." He stood up and held out his hand. "And I'm not taking no for an answer." She looked up at his face and knew she wasn't being fair to him. He had a right to know what had happened so she took his hand and followed him up the stairs and through the mirror.

It was still such a novelty to go through the mirror and into another time, she hardly did it. Ben liked to be in 2017 and she preferred it that way. They'd even started picking up old money from antique shops in her time and off eBay for Ben to use in his but he was hardly there so it was piling up quite nicely in the bank, he said. Ben was fascinated by the antique shops especially when he came across something that to him was relatively new.

It was a perfect Saturday afternoon for Laura but here in 1943 it was a Thursday and Ben luckily had a day off as he'd finished work on his current contract and the next one wasn't due to start till the following Monday.

"Why have you never bought a car?" Laura asked as they walked to the bus stop at the end of the street. This was the furthest she'd been so far and the new surroundings were making her forget her troubles.

"Never really needed to." He shrugged his shoulders, glad that they were talking even if it wasn't about what he wanted to know. "Mother didn't want me to have one, called them 'nasty, smelly things' so I suppose I never thought about it. And now with petrol rationed, what would be the point? I just get the bus to work or into town."

"What do you do when you want to go on holiday?" Laura understood all about buses coming from London, in fact a car was hardly any use in the busy streets there but she couldn't imagine it being a problem here. So far she hadn't seen a car drive past or even one that was parked outside a house.

"Mother and I always took the train to Blackpool." He spoke with a nostalgic tone. "I loved it, I used to get so excited that I couldn't sleep the night before so invariably we were at the station a good hour before the train was due." He smiled suddenly. "It was probably the times she was at her happiest, like she'd forget for a few days about losing my father. We took donkey rides on the beach and ate chips as we walked along the prom."

"I went to Blackpool once for a hen weekend and my friend was sick on The Big One." Laura laughed at this but stopped when she looked at Ben.

"What's The Big One?" But Laura didn't have time to answer as the bus came into view and Ben held his arm out so it would stop. It was a red and cream double decker bus just like the one Laura had seen in the transport museum. It had *City Centre* written on the display at the front and the lights had covers on them.

"What are those for?" She whispered to Ben.

"They're to cover the lights at night in case of air raids." He had walked to the back of the bus and Laura followed him confused until she remembered that you always got on buses at the back in these days not at the front like modern times.

"Where to, my lovelies?" A lady dressed smartly in a black jacket and skirt asked as they stepped on. Laura had forgotten all about bus conductors and watched fascinated as she pocketed the money Ben had given her into her money bag and spun two tickets from the ticket machine that hung around her neck. She then pressed the bell and the bus began to move.

Laura lurched forward and Ben steadied her before they went up the spiral staircase to the top deck. Laura felt like she was actually walking through history, which in a way she was, she told herself.

Towards the back of the bus were three soldiers, all in full uniform with bulging kit bags and Laura wondered if they were heading back to the front after being on leave or if they had just joined up. They looked young and fresh faced so she presumed that the latter was true and wondered if any of them knew what they were actually heading into. All three were smoking as were the two middle aged ladies seated at the front of the bus, so Laura headed back down the stairs, not used to sitting in a smoky atmosphere and not wanting to put her baby at risk of passive smoking.

"Why can't we sit up top?" Ben had followed her down and they were now sitting on some very uncomfortable seats in the empty downstairs.

"I'm not sitting up there breathing in all those toxins." Ben looked at her gobsmacked.

"What are you talking about?" And Laura found herself having to explain once again about nicotine and the dangers of smoking and how it was banned in public places because of how dangerous it was to even breathe in other people's smoke.

"I told you about it before Christmas when we were in the pub." She was positive they'd had that conversation.

"You told me about the law but not how poisonous smoking was." Ben was silent for a while so Laura looked out the window.

She couldn't believe that this was the same city. The streets were the same yet everything seemed so different. The bus was rickety and noisy as it trundled along the roads stopping now and again to let someone on or off. Laura was shocked by the devastation she saw as they drove towards the town centre. Sometimes they drove past a street that had been completely destroyed by the German air raids, a few of the streets were perfectly intact one end and non-existent the other and one particular road they drove down was absolutely pristine except for one house in the middle of a terrace row that had no front walls. You could see right through to the kitchen.

But what amazed Laura the most was the people. Everyone they passed seemed happy. There were no sad faces or looks of depression. She saw housewives nattering over garden fences, babies sitting in prams while their mothers hung out the washing. Children playing chase in the streets or with no fear for their safety, running in and out of bomb sites. She watched as two children around the age of five raced down a grassy hill in a homemade go kart without an adult in sight.

Even with the possible threat of air raids and the ongoing rationing these were innocent times. Kids were kids. There was no television, no games consoles, children made their own fun and played outside till their mothers called them in for tea. Everyone knew everyone else who lived in the street: not like nowadays when most people didn't even know the names of their neighbours who lived next door.

"It's very different isn't it?" Ben asked, interrupting her thoughts. "You look so enthralled by it all."

"I am." She couldn't take her eyes off the view and now she knew why Ben was so interested in everything new he saw in her time, doubly so for him because Laura had at least seen photographs of old Coventry but Ben would never have seen anything of the future world he had found himself in.

The bus stopped in Broad Street and they stepped off. The town was busy with all kinds of people going about their business but no one was in a hurry, none of this dashing about everywhere that Laura was used to. The people were mostly women and children, Ben had to remind her that most of the men were off at war. They passed a few shops with people waiting patiently in queues for their weekly rations, and it was only then that Laura noticed the looks they were getting.

"Is it what I'm wearing?" she asked Ben, realising that jeans and a flowery pink top were not your usual 1940s attire.

"It's me they're looking at." Ben took her hand and steered her down a side street as he saw a group of women up ahead with white feathers. "They think I'm a coward for not fighting for my King and Country," he explained. "It's nowhere near as bad as in the last war, but unfortunately it still happens."

"Well that's just bloody ridiculous." Laura turned round. "I'll go tell them you're in a reserved occupation and you're needed here." Ben grabbed her hand and pulled her back.

"So are many other men, but still they go and fight." She could see the turmoil he felt inside. "I want to do my bit, I want to fight the Nazis, but how can I leave you and the baby?" Laura had no answer for this so they just carried on walking in silence.

When they reached the end of the little alleyway Laura was unprepared for the sight before her. There in all its war-torn glory was Coventry Cathedral. It stood proudly against the skyline, its whole roof gone but its walls and tower standing as if in defiance of the bombs that had threatened to destroy it completely.

"I've never seen it look so beautiful." She had tears in her eyes. "And so strange to see it without the new cathedral right next to it."

"I'm not fond of that new one," Ben said matter-of-factly. "It's far too modern." Laura laughed at this and followed him as they turned right and headed back into the city centre. The women had moved away but not wanting to risk a confrontation, Ben hurried her along and into a small café simply entitled *Betsy's*.

The café was full and the noise of chatter welcoming. Ben noticed a couple at the back were just leaving so he weaved his way through the tables and asked politely if they could have their seats. The man was dressed in an RAF uniform and the lady in a WAAF uniform and Laura felt the sudden urge to sign up herself to help with the war effort.

"It's Bill isn't it?" Ben was looking hard at the man's face. "Bill Preston?"

"Ben? Ben Matthews?" The two men shook hands enthusiastically. "I haven't seen you since school. How's tricks?"

"Can't complain." Ben turned to Laura. "This is my wife Laura." He said the word 'wife' without any hesitation. "Laura this is Bill, an old school chum."

"Pleasure to meet you." He shook Laura's hand then introduced his girlfriend Marcie.

"Will you join us for another cuppa?" Ben asked as he pulled the chair out for Laura to sit down. "It'd be great to catch up."

"Another time, Ben," Bill said. straightening his cap. "We've got to get back to the air base and the bus leaves in five minutes." He shook Ben's hand again. "Great to see you again buddy. You take care of that wife and baby now." He gave a cheeky wink to Laura before heading out of the café and taking Marcie's hand, they ran out of sight.

"I can't believe it." Ben was smiling happily. "Bill Preston!" He shook his head in disbelief. "In the RAF. He always loved planes when we were kids though. He used to live in the next street."

"Hello Ben, haven't seen you for a few months." A plump lady with a crisp white apron approached them. "What can I get you and your lovely lady?" Laura felt her eyes hover over her pregnancy stomach.

"Betsy, this is my wife Laura." More shaking of hands and an obvious sigh of relief from Betsy that they were married. "Two teas and some of your fabulous sponge cake."

"Coming right up." Betsy hurried off but was back no more than five minutes later with two mugs of tea and two huge slices of Victoria Sponge cake with strawberry jam oozing out of the sides.

"I don't know how she does it on the rations." Ben had immediately tucked into the cake. "Now, are you going to tell me what's wrong?"

And there, in 1943, Laura found herself able to tell him all about the encounter with Jack. Being in the different surroundings made it easier as if she was just telling a story rather than an actual event, after all, in this time it hadn't even happened yet. Ben sat listening without comment and at the end of the tale he just nodded his head, took her hand and raised it to his lips.

"He won't bother you again," he said simply.

"But how do you know?" She finally felt able to eat and took a huge bite of the delicious cake.

"Because I'm there to protect you now." He called Betsy over for a refill of tea. "And I'm never letting you go."

Chapter 33

May the twenty-seventh dawned bright and clear. Laura woke early to find an empty bed and a single red rose where Ben had been. Her dad was still snoring away in one of the spare rooms and she found her mum sitting in the garden enjoying a cup of tea in the morning sunshine.

"Morning Mum." She leaned over and kissed her on the cheek before sitting down next to her and pouring herself a cup of tea.

"And how's the bride to be, this morning?" Laura didn't think she'd ever seen her mum looking so happy. "You couldn't have asked for a more perfect day."

"I was so worried it would rain." Laura lifted her face up to the sun.

"Not on my baby's wedding day." Janice patted her arm. "It wouldn't dare."

They sat there for almost an hour before Steve finally joined them and made a fresh pot of tea. Janice made toast for everyone and then the three of them sat there for another half an hour in almost silence just relishing the peace and each other's company. A knock on the door heralded the arrival of Beth and Jessica, and Janice suddenly became a mother hen clucking over her chicks.

"Where's Ben gone then?" Beth asked as she watched Janice and Steve cooing over Jessica.

"He left this morning for the hotel." Laura laughed as her dad made funny faces. "He should have been there all night but he just sneaked out early this morning instead." A little kick from the baby made Laura wince. "You are fidgety today," she said stroking her ever increasing stomach.

"That's a good sign," Beth reassured her. "Nothing worse than not feeling them, then you just panic that there's something wrong."

"Look at my parents." Her dad was now playing peek a boo behind his hands.

"I bet they can't wait to be grandparents." Beth had already seen the pile of baby clothes that Janice had brought.

"I think they're more excited than Ben and I are." Laura pushed away the thought that they may never actually meet the baby, that she would be born in 1943 not 2017; today was a happy day, not one for dwelling on events that hadn't even happened yet.

"First granddaughter, you see." Beth realised she had spoken louder than she meant to but luckily Janice and Steve hadn't heard. "Why haven't you told them?"

"We gave them the option and they said they didn't want to know." Jessica started crying and rubbing her eyes so Beth went to pick her up.

"Nap time I think." She started rocking her gently to soothe her a little before tucking her into her pushchair where she fell instantly asleep. "And you'd best get in the shower, Sarah will be here soon." Laura looked at her watch, she hadn't realised it was that time.

"Bloody hell." She dashed off upstairs just as Sarah knocked on the door.

A few hours later and everyone was ready and waiting for the cars to arrive. Sarah had done a marvellous job with Laura and Beth's hair and makeup and an even better job at calming everyone's nerves. Even though they weren't actually getting married Laura and Ben had made it feel as if they were.

Her mum had cried when she'd walked down the stairs in her dress and her dad had just beamed with joy. The whole day so far had been perfect, even Jessica was behaving herself and looked a picture in her little dress even if she did keep pulling her flowery head band off. The bouquet matched the colour on the dresses to perfection and once again Laura was glad of the loose-fitting dress. Even though it was halfway through the afternoon it was hot and sticky outside, the weatherman had predicted a little heatwave, but she felt cool and elegant in her flowing dress.

Two vintage Bentleys pulled up outside and Laura and Beth screamed with delight, it was finally time to go. Janice, Beth, and Jessica climbed into the first car with Laura and her dad in the second one. A few of the neighbours had come out to see her off, and Agnes was standing by her gate wiping away a tear. She and Wilf had been invited but she had refused saying Wilf didn't like to go out but maybe she would come along later, although Laura was sure that she wouldn't.

It was only a twenty minute drive to All Souls Church but to Laura it dragged. She couldn't wait to see Ben in his wedding suit. Beth's husband Mark had been roped in as Best Man and with a complete lack of guests on Ben's side everyone had been told to sit wherever they liked in the church and not just on the bride's side.

The two cars came to a smooth standstill outside the church and each chauffeur got out to open the doors. Janice gave Laura a quick kiss before heading in to take her place in the front pew. Beth and Jessica went first with Laura and her dad behind. They were just about to go through the wooden door when Laura heard a noise behind her.

"Psst!" She turned round to find Jack standing a few metres away. Laura felt suddenly sick with fear and grabbed onto her dad's arm for dear life. "I'm not here to cause trouble." He walked towards them his hands held up in surrender.

"Jack!" Steve was surprised. "What the devil are you doing here? Laura's getting married today." Trust her dad to speak the obvious.

"I know sir." He was in front of them now. "I just wanted to apologise for my terrible behaviour to Laura. I have been an absolute asshole and caused her so much pain and sorrow and for that I am truly sorry." She looked at Jack and knew he wasn't talking about how their relationship had ended but about his failed attack in the club, but her dad didn't know that.

"Quite right too." Steve kept hold of Laura's arm.

"Will you forgive me, Laura, for my despicable treatment of you?" His face was full of remorse and Laura couldn't help but nod, not trusting her voice to speak, hoping that this would get rid of him once and for all. "Then I shall leave you a happy man and wish you all the best for the future." And with that he was gone.

"I always knew he was a decent chap deep down." Laura didn't think this was the appropriate time to correct her dad so she pushed all thoughts of Jack to one side and walked into the church.

They had decided against the wedding march and instead an instrumental version of Christina Perri's *A Thousand Years* was played as the bridal procession began. Laura had played hundreds of songs to Ben but this one had been an instant favourite and they had also chosen it for their first dance.

As she walked down the aisle all thoughts of everything vanished, the only thing she could see was Ben standing before her. At a little nudge from the priest, he turned to look behind him and the look he gave her, turned Laura's stomach to jelly and her heart to mush. He was looking at her with such adoration and love that she felt as if she could conquer the world. He took her hand as she reached the altar and squeezed it gently. The priest stepped forward and began to speak.

"After you, Mrs. Matthews." Ben opened the door to their hotel room.

"Well thank you, Mr. Matthews." She giggled as she swept past him.

It had been a wonderful wedding, one of Laura's favourite parts had been where they had snuck off to watch the sunset together away from everyone else. It had been their first moment alone and they had stood looking out into the hotel garden as the sun streaked the sky with red and orange.

The whole day had gone smoothly and although they weren't officially married Laura had already changed her name to Matthews by deed poll. All the guests had said what a lovely time they'd had and a few were still in the late bar enjoying drinks before heading to their own rooms.

Laura kicked off her shoes and Ben came up behind her and placed his arms around her now non-existent waist.

"You look beautiful." He reached round to kiss her cheek. "Just how I pictured you would." He ran a trail of kisses down her neck.

"Say that again." Laura had heard those words before.

"Say what again?" Ben was kissing along the top of her dress.

"What you just said?" She had to be sure. "Exactly how you said it before."

"You look beautiful." He had stopped kissing her and was now looking at her a little oddly. "Just how I pictured you would."

"Oh god!" Luckily the bed was to the side of her and she collapsed onto it. "It was you."

"What was me?" He sat down in front of her, one leg crossed under him the other dangling down the side.

"On my prom night." She looked into his eyes. "In the house, it was you." She took his hands. "You said those exact words to me that night." She shook her head. "How didn't I see it before? Why didn't I recognise your voice?"

"I don't understand." Ben was confused. "Are you saying the old man you met in the house that night all those years ago was me?" She nodded. "But why would I do that?"

"I don't know, Ben." She shook her head and then suddenly burst into tears. "I left you there. I ran away and left you and you died all on your own."

"Hey, stop that." He took her in his arms and tried to soothe her. "You were sixteen, and had every right to run away, you didn't know me." He kissed her eyelids. "Like you've said to me before, it's in your past but it's my future and I can change it." She stopped crying at this. "And I've got nearly sixty years to work out how." She threw her arms around his neck and kissed him.

"I love you, Ben Matthews," she said simply, knowing that whatever the future held for them they would face it together. He smiled and began to unbutton her dress. A ringing noise pulled them apart.

"Is that your phone?" Laura reached into her bag. "On our wedding night?"

"It's Agnes." She looked at the screen. "I'd better answer it." Ben flung himself back on the bed. "Hello Agnes, everything okay? What?" Ben sat up at the sound of shock in her voice. "We'll be right there." She put the phone in her bag and looked over at Ben. "We need to get home straight away."

"What's happened?" Ben could tell by the look on her face that it was something serious.

"There's two policemen at the house." She was busy putting her shoes back on and grabbing their things. "Someone's broken in."

They arrived back at the house in half an hour. Laura hadn't been drinking due to the baby and Mark had dropped Laura's car to the hotel earlier for them to bring home in the morning so they had just jumped in and driven home. A police car stood outside; one officer was taking notes from Agnes on the doorstep and they assumed that the other was inside.

As they walked up the path Agnes turned to look at them.

"Here they are now, Officer." Agnes smiled reassuringly at them. "What a thing to happen, on their wedding night as well." The officer took in Laura's dress and Ben's suit with a sweeping glance.

"I'm so sorry, Mr. and Mrs. Matthews." He tucked his notepad away in his top pocket. "Mrs. Rogers here heard a disturbance and called us straight away."

"I said to my Wilf, it sounds like glass breaking so I looked out and saw a tallish man going in the front door. I didn't get a good luck at him but he looked familiar." Agnes loved a good tale. "Well, I knew you weren't in so I called the police straight away and then these two lovely officers arrived." The other policeman had joined them.

"There's no one here now." The second officer said. "Looks like they've smashed the front door to get in and gone straight to your bedroom. Pulled a few drawers out and strewn your jewellery everywhere."

"You'll need to go and see if anything has been taken." The first officer was speaking again. "I've called forensics to take some fingerprints but he was probably wearing gloves so we'll be unlikely to find anything but you never know."

Agnes took herself off home as the two officers accompanied Laura and Ben upstairs. None of the other rooms had been touched and the police seemed to think the thief knew exactly what he was looking for. Laura couldn't think of anything even remotely valuable that would be of any interest to a burglar and after a quick inspection she found that nothing was missing.

After a visit from forensics and photographs taken of the scene, the glass on the front door was boarded up for safety, the policemen left. Laura and Ben started to tidy up the room, slotting the drawers back into place and folding up clothes.

"Well that's a mystery?" Laura had finished putting the last of her jewellery back in its case.

"Isn't it just," Ben agreed. "Who breaks into a house and doesn't steal anything? What could he have been after?"

"Search me." She stood in front of the mirror to take out her tiara. "The cameo!" She caught sight of it in its usual place. "I bet it was Jack." This thought made her want to kill him even more than she did already. "He came to the church to apologise but it was obviously just a ploy to make sure we were out of the house."

"So why didn't he take it then?" Ben couldn't work it out.

"Because he wouldn't know it was in the mirror would he?" It was now so obvious. "To him it's just a necklace and where do people keep necklaces?"

"In drawers and jewellery boxes."

Laura nodded. "Exactly." She smiled. "He wouldn't have thought to look on the mirror."

"What if he had found it though?" Laura's smile faded. "What if he'd taken it and I'd been dragged back to 1943 in front of everyone?

"What if he comes back?" Laura was worried now.

"That's it. I'm moving here." Ben was adamant.

"What do you mean moving here?" Laura looked at him slightly confused. "You already live here."

"Permanently I mean." He sat on the bed. "I've been thinking about it for a while now and it just seems stupid to keep going backwards and forwards so I'm going to quit my job, board up the house, and live in your time permanently."

"I can't ask you to do that." Laura knew that as much as he loved her and loved her time he loved his own world just as much.

"Well I'm not leaving you on your own ever again." He took off his tie and started undoing his shirt. "And if that fucking bastard ever shows his face again he'll get what's coming to him." Laura looked at him in surprise at his use of modern swear words. "Don't you worry about my language; I've learnt a lot more from this century than swear words."

"You'd do that for me?" Laura couldn't believe it. "You'd give up your whole life for me?"

"But Laura, you are my life."

Chapter 34
July 2017

"**Y**our blood pressure is a little high." The midwife pulled the Velcro cuff off Laura's arm and took the stethoscope out of her ears. "How have you been feeling?"

It was three weeks to when the baby was due and Laura had just finished work the previous week to start her maternity leave. She had found the last week at work tough. If she sat down for too long the baby pressed on her bladder and if she stood up too long she pressed on her back. She was finding it difficult to sleep especially as the nights were so muggy and had taken to sleeping on the sofa downstairs with a pillow tucked under her bump for comfort.

"I'm just tired." She was lying on the bed in the midwife's room, her bump exposed.

"Any extreme tiredness? Headaches? Swollen ankles?" Laura shook her head. "Well let's see what this little monkey is up to, shall we?" They had never officially found out the sex of the baby, what was the point? So it was only Laura, Ben, and Beth who knew it was actually a girl.

"I've not been sleeping well." Laura thought she'd best mention it as the midwife felt the baby's position and listened to the heartbeat. It was always such a reassuring sound to hear. Even though she felt her moving around all the time, that echoing thud thud from the sonic aid was the most beautiful sound Laura had ever heard. It was the sound of her baby, alive and well.

"Well, baby feels fine and heartbeat is good." She covered Laura's belly back up and helped her to sit up on the bed. "But I'm still not happy with your blood pressure."

"What can I do?" Laura was positive the drive to the doctor's surgery in hot weather and morning rush hour wouldn't have helped.

"Plenty of rest," the midwife prescribed. "And any signs of swollen ankles or problems with your vision then phone me straight away." She gave Laura's book of notes back to her. "I'm putting you onto weekly appointments now." She tapped on the computer. "Next Monday at half past ten?"

"That's fine." Laura nodded. "I'll miss the school traffic then."

"And have you done your birth plan yet?" The midwife looked at Laura knowing full well from her notes that she hadn't.

"I'll do it today." Laura had been putting it off, she didn't really know what she wanted.

"It's just a guideline for us, we don't need a detailed account of how you want your birth to go because trust me, they rarely go as planned." She reached into her drawer and pulled out a leaflet. "It's just things like, do you want pain relief? Does Dad want to cut the cord? Do you want the baby cleaned before you see it? Just little things like that."

"I promise I'll do it this afternoon sitting in the garden with my feet up." Laura headed to the door.

"Now that sounds like a good plan to me." The midwife smiled. "See you next week."

"Will you please stop fussing?" Laura wished she hadn't told Ben what the midwife had said. He hadn't stopped worrying for the past four days since her last appointment. She had found it quite sweet to start with but now the constant asking if she was okay was wearing thin.

"I'm only trying to look after you." He was slightly hurt by her harsh tone.

"I know you are, I'm sorry," she apologised immediately. "I'm just so fed up. I can't sit still; I can't lie down. If I stand up my back hurts; I just can't get comfy."

"Shall we go for a walk?" Ben suggested.

"Not in this heat." She fanned herself with a newspaper. "You go home for a bit, there's still loads to do." Laura was hoping he would take her up on her suggestion. She could do with a little time on her own and there was so much that needed doing back in 1943 if Ben was to live in 2017 for good.

"Are you sure?" Ben didn't want to leave her alone but he had a to-do list as long as his arm.

"Honestly, I'll be fine." She reached for her book from the table. "I've got my new book and a big bottle of water." She looked for the water. "Damn, must have left it in the kitchen." She stood up quickly then sat back down straight away. "We need to phone the midwife."

"What's the matter?" Ben was all concern.

"It's like someone has put blinkers on me." Laura felt strange, like she was staring down a tunnel. "Can you ring her please?" Ben now had his own phone. It only had a few numbers in it but he just loved the novelty of it. Laura had set it all up for him but it didn't go on the internet, she was still afraid of things he might discover and until he was here permanently or until she knew she wasn't going to die in childbirth she wasn't taking any chances.

"We have to go straight to the hospital." Ben said in a panic. "I'll ring a taxi and grab your bag."

"Did she say why?" Laura was trying to stay calm.

"She said something but I don't remember what it was." He was already on the phone to the taxi company. "I just heard, *'she needs to be checked at the hospital straight away'*."

"I'm sure it's nothing serious." Laura wasn't sure at all but needed to calm Ben down, he'd be no use in this state. "It's going now anyway." And it was. Her vision was returning to normal but she still felt strange.

"Well you're getting checked out either way." He ran off up the stairs to grab her already-packed hospital bag then helped her up to wait for the taxi outside.

"Can I please go home?" Laura had been in the hospital now for over a week. The baby was fine but the doctors and midwives were worried that she may be suffering from pre-eclampsia and when her ankles swelled to the size of elephant feet after her third night there they weren't taking any chances.

"If your blood pressure stays down we'll do some more blood tests and we'll allow you to go home." The doctor didn't really want to let her go. "But it will be on strict instructions of bed rest."

"I understand, Doctor." Laura prayed her blood pressure would behave. All she had thought about in hospital was how Ben was unprepared if something was to happen to her. She needed to put everything in place so that he would know what to do in the future if the worst was to happen. The midwives tried to reassure her that in most cases pre-eclampsia caused no complications but sometimes the baby had to be delivered early.

"Good news, Mrs. Matthews." The doctor was smiling at her. "Your blood pressure is still within normal range so we'll get those bloods taken and I'll arrange for your discharge. Now you'll need to visit your midwife every day and you'll have to come here at weekends."

"Whatever you say, Doctor." Laura would have agreed to anything if it meant she could get out of the hospital and back home.

An hour later and she opened the door to find a surprised but relieved Ben dusting the living room. He took her bag from her and helped her to the sofa before racing into the kitchen and coming back a few minutes later with tea and chocolate biscuits.

"Are you sure you should be home?" He sat on the sofa next to her. He'd picked some leaflets up from the maternity department and had read them over and over again.

"They wouldn't let me out if I wasn't," she reassured him. "Lots of rest and daily checks." She rolled her eyes. She felt fine apart from her swollen ankles but even those had gone down a little since she'd been off her feet.

"You'll be going to those checks you know." He could tell from her attitude that she was planning not to. "Even if I have to drag you there myself."

"I know, I know." And she did know that she had to, for her health and the baby's. She had to do everything possible to keep them both safe and sound. She didn't want anything to go wrong.

They spent the afternoon and evening finally having the Harry Potter marathon that Laura had wanted months ago. Ben was an instant fan after they'd watched the first film and by ten o'clock they had reached the end of *The Order of the Phoenix*. Ben wanted to watch another but Laura was tired and longed for bed.

She headed upstairs to bed while Ben washed up. She took the opportunity of being alone to dig out a pad and paper and placed it under the bed with her notebook all about Walter Matthews and his family. She feigned sleep when Ben came to bed and smiled as he crept in trying not to wake her.

He was instantly asleep as always, so she grabbed the pads and sneaked through the mirror. She sat on his bed for a while just staring into space. His room was almost empty now that most of his clothes and things were in her time. She didn't have a clue how to start the letter, a letter she knew she had to write but hoped would never be read.

It took over two hours, fifteen tissues and three re-starts, and once she'd finished she didn't have a clue where to put it. It needed to be somewhere hidden but not so hidden that he would never find it. She looked round the room, then remembered his keep safe box. Luckily it was still in his bedside drawer.

She opened it and was surprised to see the photograph from her prom night on top of everything else. Perhaps he had been looking at it after he'd discovered that he was the stranger she had met that night. Maybe he had sat here staring at it wondering why in sixty years' time he would feel the need to meet her in this very room.

Tears welled up in her eyes again and she placed the letter in the box before an idea struck her. She took the pen and with a shaky hand wrote the words *'It will all make sense in the end'* on the back of the photo before tucking it inside the letter. She placed the box back in the drawer.

A sudden pain in her head accompanied with flashing lights made her sit back down. In a panic she called out for Ben, but of course he couldn't hear her, he was seventy years away on the other side of the mirror.

She got up slowly and walked back through the mirror. Ben was fast asleep still so she woke him gently.

He was his normal panicked self as he called for an ambulance. Laura was feeling worse and worse with every minute that passed. Ben paced and paced while they waited. He sat in the back of the ambulance with her as the paramedic kept her eye on Laura's SATs. Her blood pressure had rocketed and she was complaining of severe pains in her head.

They were rushed into A & E and yet again Ben felt out of his depth, this time it wasn't caused by the hospital surroundings but by his feeling of helplessness. The doctor was with them in seconds and before he knew what was going on Laura was being rushed off.

"What's happening?" Ben grabbed one of the nurse's arms. "What's the matter?"

"Your wife is very ill I'm afraid, Mr. Matthews." His face drained of colour as he watched them race away with Laura. "And if we don't get the baby out soon I'm afraid your wife might die." Ben collapsed back on to the chair as if his whole world had just come crashing down.

Chapter 35
August 2017

"Good morning sleepy head." Ben's face was smiling over her as she stretched lazily in the bed.

"What time is it?" She felt a little dazed, like she'd missed something really important.

"It's half past ten." He was still smiling.

"Half past ten!" She shot up in bed, wincing as she remembered the half-healed scar across her stomach. "The baby needs feeding. Why didn't you wake me?"

"Relax." He placed his hands gently on her shoulders and pushed her back on the bed. "Our little princess has had her morning bottle and a little play with Daddy and now she's fast asleep again with Chester on guard."

Laura looked to the side of the room and sure enough their new daughter was fast asleep in her crib with Chester fast asleep underneath. He had reacted so strongly to the new arrival and was always by her side.

"We really are going to have to think of a name for her you know?" Laura already knew what they would call her and found it so hard not to say it or even suggest it, she wanted Ben to name her.

"I've been thinking about that and I'd like to call her Elizabeth." He sat down beside her.

"Really?" Laura was in total shock. "Elizabeth?"

"After the King's eldest daughter and our future Queen." Laura was stunned.

"Elizabeth it is then." Perhaps the future wasn't mapped out for them after all. A huge weight lifted from her shoulders at this thought. "You really have to get the house sorted back in 1943 you know." Ben hadn't been back to his own time since Laura had been rushed into hospital.

The doctors had performed an emergency caesarean and although it had been a little touch and go for a while, not long after baby Elizabeth had been born, Laura's blood pressure started returning to normal and the headache subsided.

It had now been three weeks since the birth. Janice and Steve had spent the first week with them, Beth had also been a regular visitor, and all the children in her old class had sent handmade cards and pictures.

She still wasn't back to full strength and tired easily. Ben had been amazing. He doted on his new daughter and loved playing the attentive husband and father. He had taken to modern fatherhood like a duck to water, changing nappies and making bottles.

"Your mum was on the phone earlier." Ben helped her sit up so as not to pull at the scar.

"Same old conversation?" Ben nodded. Janice had phoned every morning and every evening since they had returned to London and quite often Face Timed during the day as well. Ben was intrigued by Face Time. He would chat to Janice for hours on Laura's phone just for the sake of it.

"Do you fancy a trip to the park today?" Laura hadn't been out yet since the birth. "The midwife said you should start taking gentle exercise."

"We can give it a go." She got out of bed. "I'll have a quick shower and a bit of toast then when Elizabeth wakes up, she can have her bottle and we'll head off." It felt strange to call her Elizabeth when for the past few months she'd been calling her Lauren, even if it was only in her head.

"I'll pop the kettle on then." He kissed her and bounded off the bed and down the stairs.

"Well then little Elizabeth Matthews." Laura walked over to the crib and stared at her daughter stroking her strawberry blonde hair gently. "Looks like we really are re-writing the past doesn't it."

Later that day and the house was in turmoil. Elizabeth wouldn't stop screaming, Laura's head was banging, and she was shattered after their walk around the park. It had been lovely to get out and enjoy the sunshine, so many people had stopped to talk to them and admire the baby that they were out for nearly three hours and Elizabeth was ready for another feed but was refusing to drink it.

"I'll take her upstairs." Ben could see that Laura was suffering, so he took the screaming Elizabeth and her bottle upstairs. This didn't make any difference and Laura could still hear her in the living room. After another five minutes of screams there was sudden silence and Laura sighed, relieved that she had eventually taken her bottle.

There was a knock on the door and with a huge amount of effort Laura heaved herself off the sofa and walked into the hallway. She couldn't tell who it was from behind the frosted glass so was shocked when she found Jack standing there. She went to shut the door straight away but he jammed his foot in the way and barged past her.

"Thought you'd like to know that your little message worked." She could tell he was angry and she was scared although she tried not to show it. At least Ben would be down any second after hearing Jack's raised voice in the house.

"What message?" Where was Ben? "I don't know what you're on about Jack." She almost shouted these words so Ben could hear.

"Your Facebook message to my wife." Laura looked bemused for a while until recollection dawned on her.

"I sent that over a year ago!" Where was Ben?

"Well she's just decided to tell me about it now." Jack almost spat the words in her face. "Seems she didn't believe it when you first sent it but apparently other things have slotted into place over the past year or so and she's decided to leave me and taken my kids with her."

"And how is that my fault?" Laura was starting to think Ben was deliberately avoiding the situation. "You cheating on your wife is entirely your doing." She started edging towards the stairs to make a dash to Ben.

"But she wouldn't have known if you hadn't have told her." He had moved down the hallway and was outside the kitchen so she made a break for it and shot up the stairs.

Jack was hot on her heels and before she had time to shut the bedroom door on him he was inside with her. She was no match for him in her current state. She scanned the room quickly. Ben was nowhere to be seen and Elizabeth wasn't in her crib. Where had he gone? Surely if he was upstairs he would have come and helped her by now.

As she neared the mirror it started to ripple and she realised then that Ben had taken the baby to 1943 so Laura could get some peace. She had to get through it somehow. She had to let Ben know what was happening.

"What did I ever do to you?" Jack was standing in front of the doorway.

"You lied to me." She didn't know what else to say. The mirror was right behind her back now, could she just fall into it?

"I never did." He took a step towards her and another. "I didn't tell you I wasn't married."

"And you never told me you were either." If she could just step backwards into the frame she'd be gone.

"You never asked." He was in front of her now. "What the hell is that?" He was pointing at the mirror. "Why's it doing that?" But Laura had no need to answer as Chester came flying out of the mirror with a hiss and lunged at Jack's face. He screamed and tried to pull the massive ball of fluff off but Chester just dug his claws in deeper the more he struggled. Jack weaved around and Laura jumped out of the way as he tripped and fell forward into the mirror.

The mirror was immediately solid again at Jack's presence but still Chester clawed and scratched and still Jack swayed this way and that way. Laura didn't know what to do, she tried to wrench Chester off but he was having none of it and Jack tripped once again.

Laura watched in slow motion as he fell forward, his arms splayed out in front of him as he toppled onto the mirror. A scream of pure pain and horror stuck in Laura's throat as she watched the mirror fall to the ground. The frame splintered and the glass smashed into a million tiny pieces.

"What have you done?" Laura sank to her knees. "My god, what have you done?" Chester had finally let go of Jack's face and was busy washing his paws.

"What have I done?" Jack couldn't understand why she was suddenly so upset. "That bloody cat nearly had my eyes out."

"I've lost them." Laura couldn't control the heart wrenching sobs that threatened to engulf her. "I've lost them forever."

"What are you talking about?" Jack was even more confused now, why was she so upset? He'd broken the mirror, not her. He glanced on the floor to see if it was fixable but quite clearly it wasn't. The frame was cracked and chipped and the mirror just a mass of glass on the floor. It was then that he found the piece from the top of the frame with the cameo in and handed it to her.

"Well it's no bloody good now is it?" She threw it against the wall. "It needs the mirror to work." She stopped crying suddenly. "Can you get me another one?"

"What?" He looked at her as if she'd gone mad.

"You said you'd seen similar ones but none as good as this one." Hope restored, Laura went to retrieve the cameo, luckily it was still intact.

"I lied." The look she gave him was pure hatred. "I just said it to impress you. I know nothing about antiques, it was Pete's business not mine: I was just the dogsbody."

"Get out!" She screamed and threw a pillow at him and when he didn't move she threw another one. "GET OUT!" Jack didn't need telling twice, he scarpered as fast as he could, not understanding anything that he had just seen or heard and not wanting to either. She was welcome to the cameo; it was only worth a few hundred quid anyway.

Laura stared at the mess of wood and glass in despair. There was no way she could fix it and no way of telling Ben what had happened. She sank onto the floor not caring if the shards of glass cut her legs. A crunching sound under her knee made her look and she found what appeared to be a tiny glass bottle, now smashed, with a cork stopper and a wrapped-up piece of paper tied in a bow.

She unwrapped the paper to find it was actually a photograph. Staring serenely at the camera were the faces of Iris and George Matthews, a young Ben sat on his mother's lap, a tiny ginger kitten in his arms. So was this how Ben's father had made the mirror work? Had this been some kind of spell?

Chester nuzzled her hand and she picked him up on her lap.

"I know you were only trying to help." She could hardly speak between the tears that had started to fall again. Her heart had broken into as many pieces as the mirror and she just sat there as the sun set and the moon rose, casting shadows into the room.

She heard a car pull up outside and a male and female voice exchanging words. It sounded like someone had come home in a taxi. She heard the car drive off and the sound of heels clicking on the pavement. A gate squeaked open—wait, wasn't that her gate? More clicking of heels and then a quiet tap on the door.

Laura wiped her eyes but didn't move. She wasn't up to visitors. But the tap came again and again, more insistent with each knock. With Chester still in her arms she came down the stairs, turning the lights on as she went. She flicked the outside light on before opening the door. Reassuring herself that it wasn't a returning Jack, she opened it.

A tall woman with auburn hair and bright blue eyes stood in front of her. She was elegantly dressed in a light green suit and Laura thought she looked around seventy years old. She was carrying a large cardboard box in her hands and stood there staring for quite a while.

"Can I help you?" Laura couldn't shake off a feeling of recognition. Was she a neighbour or something?

"I might have known you'd be here, Chester." She was well spoken as she stroked Chester in his favourite spot behind his ear.

"Can I help you?" Laura repeated again. The woman lifted her eyes to look at Laura. Tears were streaming down her cheeks and she simply said,

"Hello, Mum."

Chapter 36
Fifth of July, 2002

"But why, Dad?" Ben watched his daughter stick out her bottom lip and turn puppy dog eyes on him.

"For the last time, Lauren, teenage strops didn't work before and they certainly won't work now." He was busy filling a cardboard box with numerous amounts of A4 envelopes all labelled with different years from 1943 to 2002. "You're sixty next year, not sixteen."

"I want to meet her." She had to stop herself from stamping her foot as she used to do when she didn't get her own way as a child, but that had never worked on her dad either.

"Where's the one from 1986?" Lauren watched as her dad started searching frantically. He would be ninety-two on his next birthday but he still had all his hair even if it was completely white. He had seemed to age years in just the past few months, like he was starting to give up. He'd always been so strong, bringing her up all on his own all these years.

"Are you sure it's not there?" She came over to help him look. He had become unsteady on his feet lately as well and had taken to using a walking stick. Lauren searched through the envelopes and found 1986 stuck to the back of 1985. "It's here, Dad."

"Thank goodness for that." He looked through the box once again to make sure they were all there. "1986 is an important one, it's when she was born."

"Why did you get me to fill in the documents for the house?" Lauren had always pondered over this.

"Because I couldn't have her knowing about me from the start." Ben put the lid on the box.

"Tell me about her." Lauren sat down on the bed. They were in her house but this was her dad's room. He'd lived with her and her family since Christmas 1986. He had phoned Lauren in tears one day after he'd bumped into Laura's parents and a baby Laura in her pram and it had broken him. He could no longer stay in the area watching her grow up, walking past the house on her way to school, knowing that she had no idea who he was and knowing he could never tell her.

"It was always your favourite story." He stroked her auburn hair. "Did you know we named you Elizabeth to start with?" Lauren had never known this and she shook her head. "When I realised the portal had broken I changed your name to Lauren. It seemed the perfect name for you, half of your mum's and half of mine."

"Will you at least tell me where you're going?" She had asked him this question time and time again but always received the same answer.

"You know I can't." He kissed her gently on the cheek. "I've got one more letter to write then I'll be leaving this in your hands." He tapped the box. "Now you will remember to keep sending your mum a card at Christmas and on her birthday?" Lauren nodded. "And write her a letter now and again with some photos." This last sentence wasn't a question.

"You sound like you're not coming back?" Lauren had found her dad's behaviour the past few weeks strange to say the least. He had been compiling this box of memories for Laura since the day they'd been separated, ready for Lauren to take to her in the future. Each year he would put birthday cards and Christmas cards, letters, photos and drawings that Lauren had done at school. He had even put in her first tooth and a curl of her baby hair.

"You could pop some photos of the wedding in." He was deliberately avoiding the question because he knew he wasn't coming back. He knew that today was his last day on earth and that sometime later on tonight he would die back in his childhood home. He smiled at this knowing that it finally meant he would see her again. A day he'd been waiting nearly sixty years for.

"I will, Dad." She kissed him, hoping it wasn't the last time she would see him. "I love you Dad." And she flung her arms round him, hugging him tightly.

"And I love you too, my little princess." He kissed her on top of her head. "Now you remember what to do with the cameo?" Lauren nodded through tears as he handed her the cameo he had taken from the mirror almost twenty years ago.

"Why has it got today's date and the words *please remember me* engraved on the back?" Lauren wiped her eyes, determined to try and stay strong. "It was never there before."

"It's a message to your mother." He checked the box full of envelopes once again. "So that when HE gives her the cameo for her thirtieth birthday she'll remember the first time that we met, which is tonight."

"Have I really got to wait another fourteen years till I can see her?" Lauren asked again.

"I'm afraid so sweetheart." He tapped the lid on the box, finally satisfied that everything was in place. "If you met her now it could completely change the past, I mean the future and you may never even be born." Lauren nodded at this. "Now let me get this last letter done and I'll come down and join you for a cup of tea before I go."

He went over to his desk and pulled out his writing pad and pen and started to write. He had written this letter so many times in his head that he knew it word for word.

My dearest Laura, my wife, my love, my world

The day I have been waiting for has finally come, the day when I will see you for the very last time. When you read this letter it will only have been a few hours since we were parted but to me it has been a lifetime. I don't know how the portal got broken and I suppose now I never will, but know this my dearest heart, not a day went by that I did not think of you or miss you.

I took our baby girl through the mirror so that you could enjoy some much-needed rest but I found your notepad and while she slept after her bottle I couldn't help but read it. I only realised the portal had stopped working almost an hour later. It was a few weeks before I found the letter you had written to me explaining everything.

It all made sense then except for the part about the cameo. I had no clue how that ever found its way to you until a few weeks ago when our beloved daughter remarried and became Mrs. Carmichael.

Speaking of our daughter, I hope you don't mind but I changed her name to Lauren. I don't know why we didn't think of it in the first place, both our names merged into one. But I know now that you already knew her name would be Lauren, it must have made you wonder when I suggested Elizabeth instead.

When you read this letter, Lauren will finally be with you. I wish I could have sent her to you earlier but as you used to tell me all the time, we can't risk anything changing. That's why I had to erase the warning I sent you about Jack with the house deeds.

I have sent Lauren with a box of memories for you so you can see her growing up. There's even a few home videos which I hope you will still be able to watch. I know it isn't the same but I hope it will help ease some of the pain you must be feeling.

Alas, I must leave you now. It's getting late and I have an hour's journey to get back to the house. As I haven't been there for quite some time I dread to think what state it will be in although if I remember rightly you told me it was quite run down so hopefully it will not be too much of a shock. I have got the prom photo that you left for me to bring with the message you wrote to yourself, I just hope that you turn it over.

Please remember my love that although I may die tonight, our love has conquered time.

Until we meet again.

Your Ben xxx

He folded the paper into an envelope, wrote *Laura* neatly on the front then taped it to the top of the box so it would be the first thing she opened on that August night in 2017. This was accompanied by a letter to Lauren explaining where he had gone, what he was doing, and how she was not to inform anyone of his disappearance. He wiped tears from his eyes as he walked out of the room and down the stairs for the last time. But he couldn't think of that now, he had things to do, he had to start the ball rolling, he had to go and see his wife for the last time even though to her it was the first time she would ever lay eyes on him.

Although he knew the house had been neglected he hadn't expected it to be quite this bad. He'd remembered about the garden being overgrown and had brought a strimmer to cut a path through the brambles and weeds. This was harder than he thought it would be. At his age, everything was ten times as hard as it used to be but he persevered and after almost an hour and numerous breaks it was done.

He reached the front door to find the house sign lying on the floor and a couple of the windows smashed. He still had the key and it still worked although it certainly wasn't anywhere near as sturdy as it used to be and it wobbled loosely on its hinges.

Checking his watch he realised he had a few hours till Laura and her friends arrived just after midnight.

"That's why." He spoke out loud as he had the answer to something that had bugged him for years finally came into his head. "The reason the portal only worked at twelve twenty-two was because that's the time we first meet." He thought some more. "I still can't work out why it used to send me back just before three o clock though."

He had a last look around his old home. Childhood memories merged with memories of Laura and then memories of Lauren growing up. A familiar meowing met him in the kitchen.

"Hello Chester." He picked the fat ginger cat up carefully.

With Chester in his arms he headed upstairs to the front bedroom. It was just how he had left it. The mirror was inside the alcove where the wardrobe used to be. He had put it there for safe keeping when he had left back in 1986. After putting Chester down, he dragged it back to its normal position by the window. It was just an ordinary mirror at the moment. He had years to contemplate its magic but had never come up with an answer and still clung to the fact that his father must have instilled something inside it when he had carved it all those years ago for his mother.

After covering it with the white sheet he had left there as well he sat down and waited. He must have dozed off because it was the door crashing a few hours later that startled him awake. He got to his feet with the help of his stick and stood and waited. His heart was pounding in his chest and his stomach was doing flips. She was finally here; he could finally see her again.

And then he heard her voice. It was slightly different to how he remembered but then she was only sixteen not thirty as she had been when he knew her. He held his breath as the door opened and she stepped into the room. She looked so beautiful in the moonlight that for a moment he couldn't speak. She had reached the mirror now and taken off the sheet.

"You always loved that mirror." He saw her look of horror in the reflection of the mirror and tried to reassure her with the photo and message she had sent for herself. "You look so beautiful. Just how I pictured you would." He watched as she took the photo from his hand and stepped away from him.

He hadn't even begun to imagine that she would be this frightened of him and it filled him with sadness.

"That's me." Her voice was squeaky. "But how …"

"I knew you'd be here tonight, Laura." He wanted to explain, he wanted her to look at him as she used to but she just turned and ran, dropping the photo so it fell through a gap in the floorboards. He had no chance of catching her so instead he watched her leave from the window. "Goodbye my love, you'll see me soon." And he blew her a kiss as she linked arms with Beth and Lucy and walked away down the street.

He stepped back towards the mirror to re-cover it with the sheet. Sensing his presence it began to ripple, it hadn't done that when he'd moved it and although he was sorely tempted to step through he had no idea where it would lead so he threw the sheet over it and sat down leaning up against the wall, just staring at it.

Chester came back into the room and curled up on his lap. Ben sat there for a while, he knew he should get up but he was just so tired all of a sudden, maybe he'd just have a little nap. With a deep sigh he closed his eyes, stroking Chester as they both fell asleep.

At two minutes to three Chester opened his eyes. Realising that he wasn't being stroked anymore he nuzzled Ben's hand, but it didn't move. He looked up into Ben's face with his big yellow eyes and with a sorrowful *meow* and a lick on his nose he jumped off his lap and headed back through the mirror.

The End

First published in 2017, Please Remember Me was originally titled Reflected Destines. Written in the Spring of 2016, it was my escape from a time of great sadness. My beloved father had been taken into care due to his worsening dementia. He never knew that I was a published author, but I know that he would be immensely proud of me. He died in May 2019 and not a day goes by that I do not miss him.

Please Remember Me has been released on what would have been his 77th birthday.

About the Author

Florence Keeling adopted for her penname her Great Grandmother's name, chosen because of the shared birthday of April Fool's Day. She is married with two almost grown-up children. Born and raised in Coventry, England she now lives just outside, in Nuneaton.

Florence Keeling also writes for children as Lily Mae Walters.

Twitter - @KeelingFlorence
Twitter - @LilyMaeWalters1

~o~

Other books by Florence Keeling
A Little in Love (Simon & Schuster 2021)
The Word is Love (Parcel & Page 2023)

Books by Lily Mae Walters
Josie James and The Teardrops of Summer (2020)
Josie James and The Velvet Knight (2022/3)
Brittle's Academy (2022/3)
Five Minutes Alfie (2022/3)

Printed in Great Britain
by Amazon